Miss Nucleus

JASON LEVINE

DEDICATION

I dedicate this book to everyone I met in the psychiatric hospitals. We may
never get better, but we'll always have each other.

ACKNOWLEDGMENTS

Always to my parents. Thank you.

1

"Please. Drop the gun, put the money on the counter, apologize to the baristas, and leave. Again, please. You're wearing a ski mask. No one knows who you are. I don't want to punch you. For my sake, not yours. Your blood will get on my clothes, and I don't want to go back to my apartment to change shirts."

This is what happens to superheroes when they quit. When I quit. Crime continues forever, and it makes a point to find you. Over and over again. Forever.

"Girl, sit down and shut up."

"Look, I really like this t-shirt. So drop the gun. Put the money on the counter. How are you doing? You doing okay? If life is so bad that you need to rob a few hundred dollars from a mom-and-pop coffee shop, we can hang out and talk today. I'll skip work for you. We'll see a movie. I'll buy you ice cream – two scoops maximum. Yeah? Sound good? And apologize to the baristas. Really apologize too, like sincerely with promises that you'll send them Christmas cards each year with you wearing sweaters of cartoon reindeer and explaining how you turned your life around. You do that and nothing bad happens to you. Or to my shirt. Please, I beg you – I need this shirt in my life."

"Sit down. Shut up."

"Okay, you convinced me. I'll buy you three scoops. You'll have a mountain of ice cream and a shoulder to cry on. How's that sound? Awesome, right?"

"Sit down. But you continue with this? I will shoot you. I will."

Armed robbery gets criminals five to ten years. The stakes are high. So why rob a coffee shop? This isn't even one of those fancy chain coffee shops. What's a drink here, two bucks? How much money could there possibly be in the register or safe or tip jar or back office? The only snacks they sell are potato chips and pretzels. And generic too, nothing organic or sea salt or whatever basil is. But too late for him to back down, I guess. He's committed.

Of course, he isn't scared of me. I'm not physically intimidating, and the criminals tend to brush off my threats as false bravado. I get it. That's why most superheroes hit the gym five days a week and wear outfits that show off every well-defined crease of their well-defined abs. Looking buff and scary prevents fights and saves lives. But I never had that kind of build even back in my costumed days. I barely crack five feet tall. I'm eighteen years old looking like I just graduated from the tenth grade.

"Okay," I respond. "I'm a superhero. Was a superhero. Do you remember Miss Nucleus? That was me. Remember a few years ago when I saved that cruise ship? A whole cruise ship, man. Have you ever saved an entire boat? Even like a tugboat or Jet Ski? If you have, I'll apologize. You still probably have a good few minutes before the cops arrive, so get out of here and save us both a bunch of trouble."

He shakes his head.

"Forgive me if I don't believe the superhero story. You're wearing gym shorts and a Hoobastank t-shirt. Last chance before I murder you."

"First off, I do forgive you. Second, Hoobastank rocks—"

He cocks his pistol. I shut up. I'm trying to be nice. I really am. Honestly, if he runs with the cash, I don't even think I can stop him. I have little legs and I'm far too hungover. But no, he wants to be the tough guy and stare down the tiny girl in front of him.

How many people are in this coffee shop? Maybe ten or

eleven? The baristas already ducked behind the counter, and the other customers haven't moved or spoken since this moron brandished his gun. But that's not uncommon — by the time every citizen in this city reaches adulthood, he or she has witnessed a superhero fighting crime at an uncomfortably close distance at least once. Hopefully as long as this dude concentrates on me, they won't spook him into doing anything rash. I continue to negotiate, but I'm not terribly optimistic anymore.

"Put the gun down. Give me the money. Go away. No? Okay, forget it, I'll stop pleading. How about some fortune telling instead? Because I can see into your future. If you shoot that gun, here's what's going to happen: the bullet will bounce off my forehead, I'll break your face, and the police will add twenty years to your prison sentence for attempted murder. So please, do what I ask because I don't want to give a police report or go down to the station or listen to your painful yelps while I pretend I didn't enjoy seeing all that blood pour down from your broken nose or your broken jaw or your broken ears or whatever body part I hit. My hand-eye coordination hasn't been great lately. I don't want to hurt you, but I don't dislike punching either. Does that make sense? I like the adrenaline spike. I just want to drink my coffee before it gets gross and cold and then pick up some Lunchables at the grocery store. The pizza ones. Can we both agree the pizza Lunchables are the best? Now we have something in common — that makes us friends. You wouldn't shoot a friend, would you? Right? We're good?"

We're not.

The robber pulls the trigger, and just like I frustratingly prophesized, the bullet bounces off my bulletproof face and lodges into the ceiling. My jab catches him on the bridge of his nose and he stumbles to the ground. His broken nose splatters blood across my shirt. I kick him in the head. Again. On the third try, he goes unconscious. Victory goes to me. I check his bag — was the amount he stole worth attempted murder? Eighty-six dollars. That's it. That's like sixty Lunchables or six Hoobastank shirts at best.

This is why I shouldn't leave the apartment.

My prescription pills stopped working a few weeks ago. I don't even like coffee, but my therapist says it'll keep my mind off my other vices, since apparently society frowns on catching a buzz at ten in the morning. Coffee is at least the same color as whiskey, I tell myself.

I can hear the police sirens approaching. I won't have time to switch out my ruined t-shirt before they arrive. And now this guy earned himself decades in prison, and way worse, cost me two hours of police questioning and signing forms.

I should have just slept in this morning, but I say that every morning.

———

I hate paperwork. Citizens assume superheroes zoom off into the sunset with smiles on our faces from the self-satisfaction of a job well done, but the lawyers caught up to us.

Three years ago, a new superhero named Tornado stopped a mugging outside the Salsamatic Dance Club, using some sort of wind device to blow the gun out of a mugger's hand and saved the life of a drunk clubber. Cheers and applause all around. Except the sudden blast of wind triggered the mugger's asthma. In the confusion — or justice — the mugger died. He couldn't get to his inhaler in time and no one helped him. The mugger's family sued Tornado after the police found a set of fingerprints our poor heroine left behind. They traced Tornado's identity to Rita Fernandez, a twenty-three year-old college grad working for the Three Smith Chemical Company. Further investigation found Rita was the victim of loose safety regulations that soaked her in experimental chemicals. Her mind could transform the atmosphere around her into gale force winds. So taking advantage of the situation, she built some type of gun to channel that power into a weapon she could aim. But the jury found Rita guilty of manslaughter and the Three Smith Chemical Company guilty of negligence, and in the civil trial immediately afterwards, awarded the mugger's family millions in restitution. Her lawyer eventually got the manslaughter charges reduced to probation due to Good Samaritan Laws, but the cash settlement still had to be paid. The Three Smith Chemical Company simply cut a check to the mugger's family before marching out their public relations army, but Rita lived in a rundown loft with two roommates and made twenty-eight thousand dollars a year. So how does Tornado, with a major chip on her shoulder, pay her settlement? She turns to crime, of course, eventually being apprehended by the superhero Metroplexer a few weeks later and thrown into Horace Penitentiary, where she's currently serving a ten-year sentence.

So now the police make sure every superhero-thwarted crime gets written up in enough paperwork to protect the good-intentioned superhero from being sued. Which means I'm signing pages after pages of everything from what coffee I ordered to how the barista's face looked after the initial threat to exactly what sound the robber's cheekbones made when I frustratingly struck him with my sneaker.

After signing the chunk of paperwork – I barely skim the pages anymore – the police captain motions toward me. Captain Albert Hanson, the eternally exhausted man put in charge of superhero-related cases and events alongside managing his own underfunded precinct.

"Liza, come into the office. Take a seat. You know the drill."

The Burlington Police Department decided after the Tornado situation that if they couldn't stop the superheroes from whatever good they validated by wearing tight costumes and punching bad guys, then a working relationship must be established between the two very different types of justice. For mainly legal reasons. The police department gets to go on record discouraging the superhero – no matter how many lives he or she saved – and the police get to use this incident as extra ammo when they go up against the city council in determining their next year's budget. After all, a citizen instead of the police had to step up and use her invulnerability to protect all those innocent people in that coffee shop. Crime is no doubt on the rise and more money for police protection is needed. A lot more money. Like all of it the city can spare.

"Liza, come inside and sit down."

His mustache tickles his upper lip at the mention of my name. I've always wondered if men with bushy mustaches have trouble eating without food getting caught in their facial hair. I mean, I found two Cheerios in my hair the other day, and my hair rarely even gets near my mouth.

"Liza," he repeats. "Come in here and sit down."

He turns on his digital recorder, I take a seat across from his desk, and he begins the legally required speech he must make to save the police department and myself from any legal action. With each word he enunciates, I can smell the cigarettes on his breath. Everyone possesses some imperfect vice, and I feel a slight comfort when I discover other's flaws. Misery and company and whatnot.

"Liza Lewis, the superhero known as Miss Nucleus, knows the official Burlington Police Department stance on the use of citizens' actions in defending others from criminal behavior. She knows she should have waited for police intervention. She knows that what she did could have possibly endangered lives. She knows that her actions could have had disastrous consequences by not following proper police protocol. But with zero citizen injuries, only minor property damage, and Miss Lewis' breaking of the criminal's nose serving only to prevent the criminal from discharging his firearm further, the police department agrees that Miss Lewis' actions were not executed with reckless behavior or malicious intent."

And now comes the part I hate the most.

"With Miss Lewis' past misdemeanors, which include several counts of underage drinking, we can conclusively proclaim that she was indeed sober at the time of the incident. Do you agree to everything that has just been said?"

"Yes sir," I respond, though a bit more aggressively than I should have. The police captain turns off the recording.

"Are you staying sober, Liza?"

"How do you define sober?"

"Have you had any alcohol in the past week?"

"I didn't drink on Tuesday, if that helps."

"It doesn't. Have you been going to your therapist?"

"How do you define a therapist? Because I've drawn a smiley face on my whiskey bottle, if that helps."

He shuffles in his seat. How many times has he repeated this argument? For the tenth or twentieth or thirtieth time, he just wants me to know that he cares about me! He wants to see me get better! Think of my potential! But, sir, have I not accomplished enough? I was a superhero for five years, my entire identity revolved around facing danger for those who can't defend themselves from gun-wielding idiots in coffee shops. And even when I stopped being Miss Nucleus, I'm still stuck fighting crime. But he does care about me. But he does want to see me get better. Fine. Okay, fine.

"I'm sorry," I respond. My guilt quickly catches up to me. "I am going to my therapist. Thank you for caring about me and whatever else I'm supposed to say. You're a good person, and I always treat you worse than you deserve. You're my favorite police officer; please don't tell the other cops. I'm sorry again, sir. But I need to leave. Not to drink. I have work in an hour, and I have to go home first to change my clothes."

"But you'll drink after that."

"I'm not an alcoholic."

"But you're going to drink after work, aren't you?"

"I, okay, look, I'm leaving. I'm well aware of my problem. But it's not alcohol and it never has been. I have that illness. Mentally. You know that. The alcohol, at least for the hour or two, lets me forget for just a while. I know it's bad for me, it's illegal at my age, and I'm only prolonging whatever treatment you think I need. I'm sorry. I know it's not a solution. But I'm leaving. I can't go to work with blood on my t-shirt, especially when the boss wrote me up yesterday for showing up in my Eeyore slippers."

I stand up, scratching the chair against the floor as I walk toward the door. No other superhero gets asked about their substance abuse. I sometimes wish I had super strength, so I could make a dramatic exit from his office. Rip the door off its hinges.

"Goodbye, sir. I'll stop drinking when you stop smoking."

On my way out, I knock some of my signed papers off the receptionist's desk. A small act of defiance I'll regret the moment I walk out the police station. She didn't do anything to deserve that. I march quickly to the elevator, my eyes locked on the floor to avoid conversations.

———

Fifteen years ago, a man calling himself Freedom held up a makeshift bomb in the South Burlington Mall, threatening to ignite it and reduce the area around him into a smoldering ruin of former commerce. As the police negotiator sullenly agreed to meet his demands (several million dollars, I believe), a red blur streaked across the mall food court, sweeping both Freedom and his bomb away. And just as quickly as Freedom's plan failed, his unconscious body and the disarmed bomb appeared in front of the confused Burlington Police Department.

Thus, the city witnessed its first glance at their new majestic savior. A man hovered in the sky with his chiseled physique and stunning confidence, sucking in all the adoration from his newly adoring public. Welcome to Burlington, Metroplexer. As the criminals found out quickly over the next year, Metroplexer was faster, tougher, and stronger than any superhero before him. The man could juggle tanker trucks. Explosions just annoyed him. He could fly. And my goodness, his smile – *People* magazine named him Sexiest Man Alive twice in the next five years. The population of Burlington increased 50% over the next decade with just the simple reassurance that this god-like man would protect them from whatever evils attempted to ruin their lives, regardless that the experts crunching numbers didn't find proof that crime actually decreased.

And today, I clock in to my job a few minutes late as security for the same South Burlington Mall. My coworker awaits me, saying nothing but definitely judging me. Kid Metroplexer, our savior's son. Same super powers as his dad. Same super good looks. Same frustrating perfection. His costume couldn't be any tighter. Women and men stare at this beautiful human canvas.

I'm wearing a t-shirt and sweatpants.

Seven years ago, at the tender age of twelve, Kid Metroplexer and his twin sister Lady Metroplexer made their dramatic entrance into the world of crime fighting. Sure, maybe two dozen superheroes wandered Burlington's streets at that time, but none of them came close to Metroplexer's superpowers. And Metroplexer can only punch so many criminals at one time. So seven years ago, Bricklayer – a man made out of bricks, I swear I'm not lying – had his opponents on the ropes. As Bricklayer was about to kill the superhero Screwdriver, two children burst onto the scene by bursting Bricklayer. Screwdriver, then thirty-seven years old, was saved by sixth graders who each stood a proud four foot eight. Their father acquiesced their superhero ambitions, trained them the best he could, and they happily joined the crime fighting scene.

During the afternoons and evenings a few times a week, the mall hires superheroes to stand watch beside the food court. This way, the citizens feel safe from whatever criminal threat would dare attack them. And the mall pays us well.

"I don't like it when you're late, Liza. We're a team. You make us look bad," Kid Metroplexer announces.

"Sorry. Busy saving lives this morning."

He rolls his eyes. Yeah, sure. Whatever. No one can blame him for his condescension. How else could he possibly act? This is a teenager who grew up impossibly gorgeous. With unbeatable superpowers. A celebrity father. He doesn't even have a pimple or mole or ingrown hair. And as proof for his justifiably high self-esteem, every five or ten minutes, people come up to us and ask for a picture. Kid Metroplexer drapes his arm around their shoulders. They grin and gasp. I agree to take the picture for them.

He continues to chide me, but I'm used to his disdain.

"I keep telling you that you should wear a costume, and let people know you're here to protect them. You must have your old costume lying around somewhere. Security guards carry guns or Tasers; these tools assure the people that they're safe. Our costumes have that same purpose."

"My costume was a hoodie, dude. You remember it, right? I painted my symbol on the front and the back – you know, those crisscrossing circles with a smaller circle in the middle. That atomic symbol thing."

"Liza, you didn't even wear a mask—"

Before Kid Metroplexer could finish, a family walks up to us eager for a photo. His perfectly-aligned, sparkling white teeth complement his perfect smile. But on the plus side, I've become very skilled with cell phone cameras.

Our presence serves to prevent anything exciting from happening, and in its effectiveness, there's not much to do except stand around for eight hours.

Well, no, that's not entirely true. In the past, Kid Metroplexer has stopped some shoplifters. Twice a robbery. A couple of domestic abuses. And once a lady who tried to stab a cashier when he wouldn't accept her expired coupon. But I once complained to mall administration that the Chinese restaurant at the food court overcharged for sesame chicken, and they lowered the price by thirty cents. So I think we're both equally important employees.

"Why are you even working here, Grant? What does the Kid Metroplexer need a paycheck for?"

"My dad says my sister and I need jobs to build up our work ethic. I think he's going to make us start paying for our own college next year. Plus, getting three hundred bucks a day to lean against a pillar and take a few pictures with fans is far better than a fast food place or movie theater or wherever other teenagers work. And don't call me Grant. Secret identity, okay?"

"You called me Liza ten minutes ago."

"Yes, but you quit. I'm still in the field daily. I'm doing my best to save the world. I need my identity to be secret, okay?"

Five months ago, his family stopped the North Korean dictator's launched nuclear arsenal, seizing a half-dozen suitcase-sized nukes from being dropped on their neighbor to the south. Metroplexer and his kids stopped World War 3. I can't even argue with him – Kid Metroplexer *did* save the world.

"Liza—"

"Miss Nucleus. The same rules apply to both of us. We're a team, after all. An equal team of equal importance and equal worth who both get paid the same equal amount of money."

I give credit for Kid Metroplexer holding his tongue. In the holy presence of one of the revered Metroplexers, he and I both know that I'm wildly unnecessary. Sure, I'm invulnerable, but so is he. Also, he's super strong, can fly, and I'm sure two or three more powers that I don't know about. So he scoffs when I mention the same three hundred dollars each of us takes home every day. But he was also the one who recommended me for this job – to which I'm very much grateful. Though I suspect his motive was less altruistic and more of a guaranteed method for him to always be in contact with me when I stopped answering his texts six months ago.

"Liza, there's a party tonight at War Soul and Spiromaniac's condo. A bunch of superheroes will be there. I think most of the Child Soldiers—"

"You know the best part of quitting the superhero business? I don't have to tell people I'm in the Child Soldiers anymore. The Internet hasn't given them enough crap over that name? I kept telling them that we should change the team name to the Infantry. It's military with a type of child already in the name. Infant-tree. Infantry. We'd feel exactly as dumb as Child Soldiers but without the unnervingly outraged messages I get in my e-mail from Internet strangers."

He won't agree or disagree with me. If Kid Metroplexer has any weakness, he possesses a terrible desire to be liked by everyone for everything. Even when he tells me to cut my hair or go to the gym, it's his attempt at advice rather than criticism. He just wants to be helpful. I'm not angry; he's almost always right. I do need to get a haircut and go to the gym.

"Well, you're still sort of a member of the Child Soldiers. No one kicked you out. War Soul and Spiromaniac are hosting the party tonight. It'll be fun. My sister asked me to invite you. She misses you. And, well, we figured you could use your connection to bring, you know, some alcohol. We're all too young, and I know so are you, but you always seem to find some, right? Can you get wine? My sister wants wine. I think this party will be good for you. I know Bamboo asked about you. If you bring some alcohol, I think it'd help the others to warm up to you again, you know what I mean?"

"You want me to bring alcohol to the party?"

"Yeah, but mainly because we would all like to see you. Bamboo asked about you. My sister wants you to go. But if you could also bring alcohol, that'd be great."

Unfortunately for Kid Metroplexer and Lady Metroplexer, they have a public reputation to maintain. Their dad would rather the two of them accidentally blow up the moon than be caught smuggling alcohol or cigarettes or condoms or even fly past a liquor store where someone with a rogue camera might take a picture of them with the unwholesome retailer in the background. But my reputation isn't as golden. And six months ago, I drunkenly made out with Bamboo. That was my mistake.

"Okay, I'll see if I can stop by. Also, Spiromaniac sent me an invite this morning."

"Thanks, because my sister says she hasn't seen you in a few months and she wants to catch up. You've only hung out with Spiromaniac since you quit. And you told me several times you think War Soul's cute. But, also, if you're going to the party—"

"Bring some alcohol."

"Yeah, do that. But mainly because my sister—"

I stop listening to him. It's no secret in the superhero community that I can get alcohol. A year ago, I stopped a robbery at a local liquor store. The owner, in his relief and excitement and an uncomfortably long hug, gifted me a few of the rarer bottles. Without checking my ID. Now, I never hid my secret identity or wore a mask, succumbing to my own low self-esteem theory that no one really cared who I was, but it's not as if I handed out a business card or left a phone number for him to call. By the second time I visited, the owner realized his mistake. And I blackmailed him. At that time, it wasn't uncommon for a few of the more morally superior superheroes to report stores for selling alcohol or cigarettes to underage kids – I know War Soul set up stings a few years back when the more dangerous crimes dipped in number. So in return for the store selling liquor to me underage, I won't report the store for selling liquor to me underage. It's an empty threat that they haven't called my bluff on. No one gets hurt and my therapist has extra ammunition to blame for my lack of improvement. And tonight, War Soul – age nineteen – will drink the alcohol I buy without hesitation or any moral justification.

"You should definitely shower, Liza. War Soul won't want to hook up with you if you don't shower, and you probably should put on maybe like a cocktail dress. Nothing too fancy. Like if a t-shirt is a one and a wedding dress would be a ten, you should aim for like a four. War Soul's recently single. This is your chance."

"I'm not hooking up with War Soul."

Unfortunately, the teen superheroes of Burlington tend to get incestuous when it comes to superhero romance, mostly because there are only twenty of us. And thirteen of us are girls. If I wanted to date War Soul, that dull sack of hypocritical garbage, then I'd suck face with the same man who dated at least four or five of my fellow superheroes. And War Soul doesn't even have superpowers.

Kid Metroplexer nudges me with his elbow.

"When was your last boyfriend, Liza? You're into civilians, right? You'd date a civilian, right?"

"I haven't had a boyfriend in a long time."

"What happened to the last one?"

"We took an Internet test to see what type of croissants we were. I got custard. He got raisin. Our relationship couldn't survive that."

"You can tell a lot about a person by their spirit pastry."

"Totally agree," I laugh. "I'm in my kitchen yelling, 'Well, make up your damn mind! Am I more buttery or flaky? Tell me!'"

He raises an eyebrow.

"Wait. Did you and your last boyfriend really break up because of a croissant argument?"

"It certainly didn't help. Hey, seriously, I know that you want me to be happy," I sigh. "Thank you. But I don't want to date yet."

I lie to Kid Metroplexer. To Grant, a man who has dated enough teen superheroes and civilians to fill a full-sized school bus. He'd date the rest of the Child Soldiers too, but I'm me, one of those is his sister, and the last two prefer each other. And Belial, because she's fourteen.

It'd be nice to date though. I want that emotional satisfaction of being loved by someone who doesn't have to love me. My parents love me, but they have to. They're my parents. But a stranger? He *chooses* to love me. I want that. I need that. But I have to be deserving of love, right? And Kid Metroplexer isn't wrong; I haven't showered in a couple days. I don't smell horrific, but I can't imagine I'm emanating anything pleasant. To have a stranger love me, I'd have to bathe every day. Clean my apartment. Probably sober up. Be witty and flirty and brush my hair. So sure, I'll go to this party tonight, and I'll make myself pretty. And War Soul will corner me, taking long, deliberate sips of his light beer. He won't break eye contact, and he'll make up an excuse to twirl my hair. We'll make small talk for a few minutes, talk about my coffee shop incident today or whatever he accomplished recently ("I'm just glad that I took down Wizardman before he could hurt those poor children at the museum. They call us heroes, but the children who stayed strong during this traumatic experience are the real heroes," to which I smile and don't reply with, "Wizardman is a senile old man and I want to strangle you.") before he does whatever understated territory-marking sexual move he thought of to alert the other men to stay away from me. And while I thoroughly dislike him as a person and a superhero and everything about a man I find unappealing, I badly want that interaction. Just enough flirting to prove that someone finds me attractive. My therapist tells me this attitude is unhealthy, but he's paid to say that.

After a few beers though, I'll probably just hang around Spiromaniac all night. I think she – real name Stella Martinez – may be my only real friend right now, in the aftermath of my whole high school graduation and my superhero quitting and my self-destructive past couple months.

I mean, I had a few friends at school, but no one close – it's hard to build deep friendships when I had to bail on plans every other time for whatever heroic emergency popped up. I realized soon that in my chosen profession, my best chance at friends would be my coworkers. But even then, I was desperate for validation and attention and I wasn't going to meet any of my future bridesmaids if the only thing we ever talked about was how weird supervillains' broken arms looked when we dropped them off at the police station. But I didn't have the social skills to broach other subjects my coworkers and I may have had in common. I'd try, but after three or four times of, "Are you watching any TV shows? No? You don't own a TV?" and so on, I resorted to a safer approach where the rejection was more minor. Twice a month or so, I'd mass text everyone a comment I'd thought of. A joke. No one would reply except Stella. Without fail. Usually just a simple "LOL" or "Gross!" or "I'll look for that!" Nothing lengthy nor engaging nor rarely did she ever ask any follow up questions – but she'd always reply. Soon I stopped texting everyone but her. I'd text her once a week. Then twice a week. Then daily. Then we would go out to eat after school every day. Then we would stay at each other's houses after night patrol. I devoured her kindness and optimism while she claimed that I was opinionated and strange in a way she found fascinating. Her mom and step-dad even once invited me to go to New York with the family. It was delightful.

As I fell deeper into my alcohol-numbing depression once I stopped superhero-ing – a depression until then I'd been able to decently hide since my initial diagnosis in middle school – we stopped talking and meeting up as often as we once did. My fault. But once a week, we'll still get a meal. And that meal still gets marred in my own constant, relentless worry I'm slowly pushing her away with my unavoidable aura of unquenchable misery. This party could be a good chance to repair the small cracks in our friendship. And I'll just make out with War Soul a little.

———

Around ten, I leave my apartment. I stash four bottles of wine in my backpack and carry two six-packs of beer in my hands. That'll be enough. Too bad if the Child Soldiers want something else.

As I turn the corner of my apartment complex, I see a flurry of sirens down the street. Of course. Crime rises at night because our adult superhero team, the boringly named Burlington Safety Organization – a mouthful we shorten to the BSO – goes to bed early. So what are the police in front of? Someone must be robbing the bank. Didn't the bank close five hours ago? The police wouldn't have that many cars parked there unless the bad guys are still inside. Isn't all money digital nowadays? The bank can't possibly be holding that much cash, plus there's almost certainly a state-of-the-art security system. The thief must be a supervillain. Someone who enjoys the confrontation. The supervillain Boulder used to rob banks a few years ago, but he would have already clapped his superpowered hands, opened the earth's surface, and watched with glee as the police cars tumbled underground.

If I keep my head down and stick to the alley, maybe I can avoid becoming a part of this. I have a party to go to. My therapist says being social helps with my mood. The cops have this under control.

I hear a deep voice come from the direction of the bank.

"Liza! Miss Nucleus! Liza!"

No. No no no no no no.

"Liza Lewis! Get over here! Miss Nucleus!"

Captain Hanson. Why does he like so much to lead crime scenes? Isn't that micromanaging? How many cigarettes does the captain smoke per day? Maybe in the next few seconds, he'll have a stroke and lose his ability to verbalize. He can't call me over in sign language if I don't look at him.

"Liza, we need you! Come here! Don't take another step!"

"I quit being Miss Nucleus! Sorry!" I yell back.

"I don't care!"

"I'm busy! I can't fight crime tonight."

"There are hostages!"

I stop. Fine. Fine! No escape now. No party. No fun.

I walk to the semi-circle of cop cars. I see news reporters a block down the road. I put down my beer and place my backpack on the ground. I'm the wrong person for this. The captain, slightly red in the face from his short jog over to me, tightly grabs my shoulder. I hate when he touches me.

Maybe I can still worm out of this.

"Hostages aren't really my specialty, sir," I tell him. "I'm not a great improviser and I don't negotiate very well. Let me text Kid Metroplexer."

"We need you. You're our best option."

"Why?"

"Desperado. She explicitly asked for you and you haven't answered your phone. We went to your apartment, but apparently you lied about your address in your file."

"Oh. Oops."

I check my phone. Ten missed calls. I really need to just leave my phone on vibrate. And more importantly, I have stuff in my apartment I shouldn't have.

"She explicitly asked for me?"

"Yes."

Desperado's real name is Bonnie Wang, a twenty or twenty

five or thirty year old (I'm not really sure) former Taekwondo Olympic gold medalist. Two years after she won the medal, the government deported her and her parents. I think they were here illegally. Rumors spread that their green card forms were counterfeit. Who knows? But when her parents stepped off the flight at the Shanghai Pudong International Airport, Bonnie was nowhere to be found. Every few months after that, her name would be linked to a terrorist threat somewhere followed by a video of her ranting about American injustice or whatever. I never watched the videos. During one of her broadcasts, the Child Soldiers were able to track her down. The world watched Bonnie declare, "When you think you're safe—" followed by a fist knocking her out of her chair. Specifically, my fist. That video amassed tens of millions of views, and in Desperado's embarrassment she dropped her political agenda, now consistently breaking out of prison to steal and vandalize and whatever else will make her either rich or a nuisance. And she loathes me. For many reasons.

Bonnie spent fifteen years mastering Taekwondo and plenty of other martial arts. That woman spent every morning, afternoon, and evening practicing these techniques. No one would disagree that Desperado is almost certainly one of the finest fighters on the planet today. I've beaten her twice. It was luck both times.

I don't know how to fight. I never bothered to learn. Being invincible meant I never needed to learn any skills to protect myself. Or end a fight quickly. Or even do any strength training. And all this drives Desperado crazy. That woman has struck me with swords, shot me, and lobbed a grenade at my feet. She even poisoned my food once. But nothing harms me. I was born with my powers. I did nothing to deserve them. So I assume Bonnie hates me out of jealousy or principle, and how could anyone blame her?

"Liza, is that beer next to your feet?"

I change the subject.

"How many hostages?"

"Three. Desperado attacked right as the bank closed for the

night. She has two tellers and the manager. She refuses to negotiate with us."

"I still don't know if I'm the best choice to go in there. Bonnie isn't fond of me."

Captain Hanson sighs to himself, barely audible. He's just as unhappy about me going inside the bank as I am.

"We rarely manage to get ahold of Metroplexer at night, and his kids are already back at the station finishing their paperwork for a warehouse fire they contained an hour ago. Liza, if we storm the bank, we'll lose officers. Probably the hostages. Desperado tends to be—" He pauses as he thinks of the right word. "Unpredictable. But she asked for you and maybe you can talk some sense into her. See if she has any demands."

I don't have a choice now. I list my own demands.

"Okay, I'll do it. In return, you let me leave with my backpack and my beer. And I don't have to go down to the station afterwards."

"No to both."

"Then I'm leaving."

"No, you're not."

The captain instructs a fellow police officer to collect my alcohol, depositing it in the back of one of the squad cars. He releases his hold on my shoulder.

"Liza, you're underage. Because you're helping us, I won't write you a ticket for possession. But we're confiscating your alcohol. All of it. And the procedure for after a successful superhero rescue includes paperwork and audio recordings back at the station. Despite all that, you'll still go into the bank and attempt to free the hostages. Because you're Miss Nucleus. Because you're a good person and that's what a good person would do."

I look away to hide my flush of shame.

"Okay. You're right."

If I have no choice, I can do this – I can psyche myself up. I'll rescue the hostages. I'll defeat the bad guy. You'll rock this, Liza. This won't be like six months ago. No one is going to die.

I march forward and open the front doors of the bank.

———

Everything is dark. Desperado must have cut the power. I hear the muffled cries of the hostages deep within the bank, but I can't figure out where Desperado stashed them.

What's her tactic here? A fistfight would probably be her best option. I don't have super balance – I fall over just as easily as any other civilian. If Desperado planted an explosive on a pillar or a wall or the ceiling, she can attempt to trap me. It won't hurt me, but I'm not strong enough to push concrete or stucco or whatever else off of me. I'd be stuck there for hours. The only reason I won against her the first couple times we battled was because she underestimated my durability. She won't do that again. But any explosions will almost certainly be followed by a dozen cops, and the chances are high that Desperado will be killed in the firefight. No, she'll want to talk. And I annoy her. That'll be my only advantage.

"Hey! Bonnie! You hear me? Botched a bank robbery, huh? Happens to the best of us. Since both our nights are already ruined, how about you give up and release the hostages before the police throw in a bunch of tear gas?"

From the darkness, a female voice yells back.

"Screw you!"

Off to a great start.

"Screw me? You're not really my type, Bonnie. But if you let the hostages go, I'll let you hold my hand as we walk out of the bank. Maybe I'll bring a decent rosé to visit you in prison and we'll see what happens."

Desperado stays quiet. How long until my eyes adjust? I walk forward and almost trip on a chair. As I let out a surprised cry, she finally shouts back.

"I'm not your type? Because I'm a woman? Because I'm Chinese?"

This is why I tell talented athletes and aspiring superheroes not to spend eighteen hours a day at the gym. Desperado spent years of her life learning how to master punches and kicks, and zero amount of time developing her charm or personality or anything that makes her remotely interesting. We can't banter if she immediately jumps to accusations, and bantering is my favorite part of superhero-ing. I mean, tied with saving lives.

"What? No. Bon. Can I call you Bon? No, I'm a bit weird and I just find it hard to be attracted to anyone once he or she's punched me. Or attacked me with a sword. Or Taser. Or ninja star. But I told you, I'm weird."

"Last time, I fed you cyanide."

"Great conversation, Bonnie. What's it going to take for you to release the hostages?"

Silence. My eyes have adjusted well enough to avoid furniture, but I can't tell where anybody may be hiding. I hear shuffling on my left. The hostages, almost certainly. Bonnie wouldn't give away her position. If this woman won't speak, then I will.

"Look, we're both having bad days. I empathize with you. You've once again failed your misguided agenda for political and immigration change because the world now sees you less as a revolutionary and more as a below average burglar. You've already messed up tonight and you'll be punished with an additional ten years on your prison sentence. And me? A few minutes ago the police took away all my beer and wine. So we're both not doing well. Do you want to chat about your feelings? I know I'm not a great listener, but I'll do my best to pretend."

She doesn't respond. I hear a crash on my left – glass breaking. Did someone knock over a lamp? I can hear muffled shouts. C'mon, Bonnie. Respond. I pause for another few seconds. Nothing. I shuffle slowly toward the hostages, careful not to bump into any more furniture. My cell phone has a flashlight app, I think.

"Miss Nucleus!"

"What?"

I'm interrupted as the power returns to the bank, the fluorescent lights blinding me instantly.

A swift kick from behind knocks me to the ground. Bonnie pins my chest. I can hear her hurried breathing. I struggle to throw her off – in vain – and as she comes into focus, she shoves her forearm against my neck. We lock eyes, our faces inches from each other. Under her jumpsuit, I can see the outline of Kevlar. She prepared for tonight. And Bonnie cut her hair short. That's a good look for her.

"Miss Nucleus, do you see the pistol I have aimed at the bank employees? Do you see it?"

"Yes."

"Do you see the gun? I'll shoot them."

"I already said yes."

Desperado fires off a shot. I see one of the tellers fall to the ground. Where did she shoot the teller? Is the teller dead? Bonnie shoots to kill. Definitely dead. No! No, I can't lose my composure yet.

"What the hell, Bonnie?"

Bonnie smiles. Using my knees as leverage, I push her back just enough for the two of us to roll over and switch places. Before I can pin her down, she elbows me in the face, following that with a surprisingly hard upward shove. I tumble over an office chair. She waits patiently as I pick myself up. Okay, let's do this, Bonnie. I'll avenge that teller.

Desperado sidesteps my first punch. She ducks under my second punch. Before I can swing at her again, she kicks me in the stomach. I stumble back into the same office chair – breaking it this time – and Desperado again waits patiently until I stand up.

"You're a terrible fighter, Liza. No skill. No discipline. You're sluggish and sloppy. Do you really think you could take me down in hand-to-hand combat? I asked the police for you, but I can't believe they actually agreed. Why didn't the police send Metroplexer or one of his brat kids?"

On the desk to my right, I grab the stapler and chuck it at her. She effortlessly swats it away. Fine. Let her have her kung fu. I reach down, grabbing a broken chair leg. I make a broad swing in her direction. Bonnie leans back, dodging the attack. She counters with a strike on my chin, knocking me down for a third time. Desperado rolls her eyes.

"Stay down or I'll shoot the other hostages. Miss Nucleus, we've wasted enough time, don't you think? To be honest, I didn't break out of jail this time. I have no demands to make or money to steal. The Chinese government bought me from the Americans. I'm boarding a private plane in a few hours so I can spend the rest of my life as China's James Bond, and the Americans no longer have to be embarrassed by my escapes. I disappear, and everyone wins. Communism has plenty of enemies that need killing, and I'll be happy to oblige. But before that, I have a message from Freedom."

"Couldn't he have just e-mailed me? He must know my e-mail."

She shakes her head.

"No. I killed that teller. She's dead. That's your fault – you failed and a woman died because of you. How drunk will you be before you can forgive yourself? What about when you apologize to that woman's family?"

"I don't talk to victims' families."

"Freedom wanted someone to make a scene, and I wanted to properly say goodbye to you. I happily volunteered to be the lucky one."

She pulls a slip of paper from her pocket.

"Liza," she reads. "You need to go to Harold Industries tomorrow. Find a way to get your hands on a new drug called Liberate. You'll hand it over to Freedom tomorrow night. Don't search him out. Don't say a word to any Metroplexers or other superheroes. Freedom will tell you where to go. Unless you want a much larger repeat of six months ago, you'll do as he says. Goodbye."

"That's all? Anything else?"

"You're ugly and everyone hates you."

Desperado walks toward the side entrance. Her triumphant smirk grows wider with each step she takes. When she opens the door, I hear gunfire exchanged, but the noise becomes more distant as the firefight moves down the street. With that armor she was wearing, I'm sure she escaped. Soon I can only hear the hostages' inconsolable weeping. The police barge in. A team of EMTs follow. I'm taken in a squad car back to the police station.

I arrive back at my apartment at one thirty in the morning. I drink until I pass out on the couch.

2

Audio Transcript for September 8th, 11:00 AM

Licensed Therapist: Dr. Mel Johnson

Patient: Liza Lewis

JOHNSON: How are you feeling today?

LEWIS: Not (bleep)-ing great.

JOHNSON: Let's avoid the harsh language today.

LEWIS: Sometimes to articulate or emphasize how I'm feeling, I need words like (bleep) and (bleep).

JOHNSON: You know that's not true. You use those words because you know I dislike them. Let's be better than that today.

LEWIS: Okay. Yeah.

JOHNSON: Good, thank you. I heard about the events of last night. I am sorry; it must be very hard for you today. Would you like to talk about the bank incident?

LEWIS: No, not really. Many people have died because of me before.

JOHNSON: That woman didn't die because of you. She died because of Desperado. You also saved two people last night.

LEWIS: No, it is my fault. Any other superpowered hero would have taken out Desperado before she had a chance to pull out the gun. And even non-powered superheroes like War Soul would have probably rappelled down from the ceiling and used his thighs to suffocate Bonnie's stupid (bleep)-ing head until she passed out.

JOHNSON: Language.

LEWIS: Sorry. I don't want to talk about last night. I'm not reading

25

any of the newspapers or watching any news on TV. I turned off that little device in my phone that alerts me anytime my name appears on the Internet.

JOHNSON: I won't force you talk about it. We can talk it when you're ready. Remember though, part of the healing process for any potentially emotional incident includes discussion.

LEWIS: Not today. It's way too fresh.

JOHNSON: If that's what you would prefer. Let's move on then. Last session, you brought up your parents for the first time. In the short time you've been going to me, I'm happy you finally trust me enough to open yourself up more to me.

LEWIS: I know I've been fighting back on therapy pretty hard this whole time. But I also realized that if I'm paying for our sessions — and it's a crapload of money — I might as well get the most out of our time.

JOHNSON: Hmm. Do you get along with your parents?

LEWIS: Yes.

JOHNSON: But you're angry with them.

LEWIS: Yes.

JOHNSON: Will you tell me why?

LEWIS: That's not right. I'm not angry with my parents. But, okay, I was born with my powers. My parents are both scientists. Very important, very busy scientists. Both of them geniuses.

JOHNSON: Did they spend a lot of time with you as a child?

LEWIS: Yes. Hold on, I'm getting to my point. You should know this. So many years ago, they were both working in one of Harold Industries' experimental research labs. The pharmaceutical company Harold Industries. I don't know what the project was called or what it was about. Something bizarre, I'm sure. One late night — one *very* late night — they order a pizza. So they're in the lab eating pizza. My dad snuck in a bottle of white wine. They were tipsy, so you can imagine what happened. I wish they never told me this story. But nine months later, I pop out. And because two of the world's smartest people were just drunk enough not to notice a leak in one of their machines before they dropped their inhibitions long enough to make disgusting love on the floor of their research lab – I emerge from the womb. They now have an invulnerable baby. I've never bled. Never bruised. I can't even drown.

JOHNSON: You were exposed to radiation?

LEWIS: What? No, oh, the Miss Nucleus name. No, I don't even think Harold Industries has anything that's related to something atomic or radioactive. I started fighting crime right as I hit puberty. I was a stupid kid and stupid kids pick stupid names. By the time I wised up, I was too well-known to change my name. Okay, but now because of my parents, I have these superpowers. But it's also because of my parents that I have to take prescription drugs or see a therapist or try to make it through my day without crying.

JOHNSON: Because of your depression.

LEWIS: Yes, the broken brain type of depression. My brain spends most of the day against my will trying to sink deeper in that swamp of medical, incurable depression. All the pills and all this therapy are to attempt to bring my mood back to normal, but that hasn't been working terribly well. But back to my parents and the question you asked originally, my parents didn't know about the leaking machine on the night of my conception. I forgive them for that. But they both take meds and they both see therapists and they've known about their own messed up brains since they were teenagers.

JOHNSON: You blame them for your depression because they knew about their conditions and still decided to risk passing that on to you.

LEWIS: Something like that. And isn't that messed up? Not them. Me. That I blame them for my suffering. They wanted a daughter, and while they passed on their terrible emotionally-based genetics knowingly – or maybe not, I could be overthinking this – they did do their very best as parents. Lots of love. They care about me and they love me. I love them. They're great parents. Yet I still furiously point my finger at them, wondering what could possibly come over them that they wanted to risk passing these awful genetics and force their kid to go through all this emotional (bleep). Why that instead of just adopting some abandoned baby somewhere nearby? I shouldn't blame my parents. I'm sorry, I feel like I'm being ungrateful. Am I ungrateful?

JOHNSON: I wouldn't say that.

LEWIS: Out loud.

JOHNSON: Ever. While the healing process can take a long time, maybe years, I hope today you're feeling a bit more cathartic than our previous sessions. You're a good woman, Liza. You're an inspiration to thousands of teenagers going through the same thing as you.

LEWIS: Except they don't have superpowers.

JOHNSON: That's irrelevant and you know that.

LEWIS: I don't feel any better.

JOHNSON: You must be patient.

(A long silence)

LEWIS: Do you know anything about this new drug called Liberate?

JOHNSON: Hmm?

LEWIS: Harold Industries makes it.

JOHNSON: There was a small blurb in a science journal I read recently. Liberate is a nickname. The drug is still in the trial stage. I believe Liberate acts as some sort of pain killer. Like a stronger Tylenol. I'm not a pharmacist, so don't take my word on that.

LEWIS: What? I don't understand.

JOHNSON: It's an experimental pain killer. It targets pain neurons in a different way than traditional medicines do. That's all I know, unfortunately.

LEWIS: Our time's just about up, right? I can leave a few minutes early?

JOHNSON: We have plenty of time. Quite a bit of time left. Leaving early isn't advisable, but I can't stop you.

LEWIS: Can't stop me? Seriously? There's no one alive that you can't stop. I can't believe you just said that.

JOHNSON: That's enough, Liza. Are you getting along with my son at work? Is he behaving himself?

LEWIS: Yes. Grant is doing fine. He's always doing fine. I'll see you next week, Metroplexer.

JOHNSON: We don't use codenames in my office, Liza. My civilian life and my costumed life are separate, as should yours. And I want you to stay away from alcohol this week, okay? Do your best. Alcohol isn't going to solve any of your problems.

LEWIS: Yes, sir. I'll do my best.

———

I arrive at Harold Industries around four o'clock. I'm drunk. You can judge me. Therapy messes me up. Look, I know therapy has helped millions of people. I'm sure it's helping me, but when I'm asked to speak about upsetting events or my attitude toward myself or anything related to my mood – it's not cathartic as Metroplexer claims. I don't heal myself by being honest. Instead, the pain sits at the forefront of my brain for the rest of the day. I cry on the bus ride home. I cry when I get home. I cry that evening. And maybe I'm supposed to. Maybe dealing with my depression is like those action movies where the hero has to get a bullet removed from his body. Sure, it hurts the guy when the attractive doctor or the attractive nurse digs around for the bullet, but he'll ultimately be better off once the bullet is removed. Hopefully. I'm drunk and I'm rambling and I apologize. To push my pain back inside, even maybe unfortunately undo whatever Dr. Johnson helped me with, I crack open my liquor as soon as I walk back into my apartment. And before you judge me too harshly, the bus from my apartment takes an hour to get to Harold Industries, so by the time I walk through the company's doors, I'm now only strongly buzzed. I grab a handful of mints and shove them in my mouth to cover my breath from my parents.

Also, I want to say I'm not an alcoholic. An alcoholic needs alcohol to function as he or she lives his or her daily life – that's the definition I found on the Internet – and I didn't drink last Tuesday. So there you go.

Harold Industries has become far more impressive than when I last visited a few months ago. The building is like 90% glass now.

There's a plant at every corner. People walk around in fancy business clothing or lab coats. They have three receptionists at the front desk. How tall is this building? Thirty floors? I think five floors in the basement? I still have no idea how I'm going to get my hands on this Liberate. But first, I need a visitor pass. I pick the receptionist who looks the busiest. She hopefully won't have time to argue with me.

"Hello, good day. How are you? Everything going well? This place is a little cold, huh?"

The receptionist doesn't say anything back. I lean against the counter and place both palms on the glass. I wait for her to look up at me before I continue.

"Hello there. Hello. I'm Liza Lewis. I'm here to bring lunch to my parents. They forgot their lunch today. You know them, right? Doctor Lewis and Doctor Lewis? Is it Doctors Lewis? Doctor Lewises?"

We stare at each other. It's her turn to talk. That's how conversation works.

"Your name is Liza Lewis?" she finally says. "You're here to bring your parents lunch? Is that what you said?"

"Yes."

Another long pause.

"Ms. Lewis, it's four o'clock in the afternoon."

A longer pause. I can do this. I can bluff my way in.

"My parents forgot their lunches. They asked me to bring lunch to them, but this is the earliest I could arrive. I'm very busy. Too busy to bring them lunch earlier."

That was a good enough lie, right? I'm a little proud of myself. What floor are my parents on? Didn't they get moved recently?

"Ma'am. Ms. Lewis. Where is this lunch?"

"What?"

"This lunch you're bringing them. Where is it?"

Oh. Of course. Fantastic job, Liza.

"I meant, I'm bringing them money for lunch. A couple of

30

Lincolns, maybe a Jackson if they want to go big today."

No way she believes me. I attempt a smile, but I fear I sneered instead. I should have done this sober. But everything I do should be done sober.

"Okay," I attempt to fix this situation. "Receptionist lady. Carol, is it? That's what your nameplate says. Look, my parents are very important. They have a lot of work to do. They don't want to come down here and get me. The company doesn't want that. I know where they work; I'll quietly stop by. The two of them work on the sixteenth floor. Please? I'll go away if you say yes. If you tell me no, I'll argue with you. You'll have to call security. Look, I've had a tough day."

I think a good ten seconds passes before she looks down. I'm almost certain I'm sneering now. I should practice my smiles in the mirror. She sighs audibly, loud enough so that she knows I know she's sighing. Carol is going to be talking about me at her family dinner tonight.

"Go. Just go. Be quick. Please just go drop off the money to your parents and then leave. And leave quickly. We're a professional place of business and you don't belong."

"Carol, I'm wearing a clean, unstained t-shirt."

"I'm talking about your pajama pants."

I swiftly back up from her desk. I'll take this small victory. I eat another handful of mints and enter the crowded elevator. Everyone else has on a suit and tie.

———

When I was born, my parents discovered my powers pretty quickly. They sued Harold Industries, as one should do when faulty safety regulations breed a super baby. But as the Harold Industries lawyers negotiated with my parents, and when everyone soon figured out that my superpower was more a positive than a negative impact on my life, my parents settled for lifetime guaranteed jobs instead. And a decent pay raise every year. They are scientists, after all. They love science. They want to be around science. So instead of a small fortune from Harold Industries – and I can imagine in the aftermath that other pharmaceutical companies wouldn't be too enthused to hire them – they get to continue being scientists. Doing science. And trust me, they need something to pin their legacy on besides me. By the time I hit middle school, my parents sadly realized I hadn't inherited either their intelligence or work ethic.

My parents share a small lab. On the seventeenth floor, actually. It's just the two of them. In the morning, my mom and dad wake up in the same bed. Drive to work together in the same car. Spend all day together in the same lab. Drive back home together. Eat dinner together. Go to bed together. Repeat. They spend their every waking moment at each other's side, and they wouldn't have it any other way. Not to be a bummer, but I pray in the next thirty years that their lab explodes or a chemical fire takes both of them out at the same time because I can't imagine what either would do without the other. And you have to admire that quality in them. I don't even want to be around myself all day, much less another person.

Their lab holds all the science-like things one would expect. Test tubes, goggles, microscopes, colorful liquids. I think I spot forceps? Forceps look like tiny salad tongs, right? I spot a petri dish. A few syringes. They have that tool that lights things on fire. It looks like a metal candle. I don't recognize anything else. I didn't make great grades in school. Oh, and I smell a lingering whiff of pastrami. They must have gone to the deli for lunch. Not to brag, but I know my deli meats. While I can't tell you what a graduated cylinder looks like (a graduated cylinder is a cylinder that went to college?), I can write essays about the difference between corned beef and pastrami.

"Hello. It's your daughter. What's up?" I announce when I enter the doorway.

My parents stop their work. They test pills for side effects, I think. I don't ask as many questions as I should about their lives. The two of them sit on either side of their work table, and my dad loosens his tie when he looks up at me. My mom speaks first.

"What a surprise, Liza! How great to see you! I heard you had trouble last night. We saw it in the newspaper this morning. I'm sorry."

"You and everybody else."

"Do you need money, sweetheart?"

"No, that's not why I came."

Every conversation with my parents goes down the same winding path. Let me sum it up and save us all time:

"Yes, mom, I'm still taking my medicine. Yes, dad, I'm still seeing the therapist once a week. No, I'm not doing better. Yes, I know there are billions of people who have it worse. No, knowing that so many people are suffering worse than me only makes me hate myself more for being as miserable as I am. Yes, I want to know what's going on in your lives. Oh, your friend's daughter is only twenty years old and she's already been accepted into a top law school? Your other friend is saving up money because all three of her children are in happy, serious relationships that will soon become happy, expensive weddings? Awesome. Yes, mom, of course I would like to date, but first I have to master showering every day and not sobbing during the afternoons. I don't know how to be happy. Yes, I know that sounds melodramatic. Okay, I don't *need* money, but I'm not going to refuse it. No, I won't use the money to buy beer. Yes, I love you too. I know I don't do a great job of showing how much I love you, but I do. No, please don't hug me. No, I'm serious, please don't hug me. Please, I don't want to talk about this anymore. I know you care. I know you want me to be honest. But everyone has problems and I'm never going to be selfish enough to dump my miseries on someone else. That's not fair to anyone. Okay, I'm serious now. Please, I'm done talking about this. Please."

Once the cycle ends – a repeat of every conversation we have – I get to the real reason I'm here.

"By the way, what do you know about a drug called Liberate?"

"Are you going to sell it or snort it?"

"Seriously, mom? What do you think my vices are? I don't do drugs."

"Alcohol is a drug."

"I need Liberate for superhero stuff," I reply. "I can't give you details without compromising the safety of the proud, noble, and hard-working people in this great city."

"I thought you quit superhero stuff."

"I did too."

They glance at each other before my dad explains the situation. Yes, they were given a Liberate. A single pill. Sometimes labs send samples down to my parents for second opinions and additional tests.

"It's illegal for us to give this to you, Liza."

"I need it to save lives, I swear."

My parents look at each other again.

"Okay," my mom says. "You've never lied to us about superhero business. You can have it if it will save lives. But if we find out that you snorted it—"

I grab the pill from my mom's hand before she can finish.

"I love you, mom and dad."

As I grasp the door handle and open the door, my dad calls out to me.

"Liza, how's Stella doing? Are you still hanging out with her?"

"She's fine, I saw her last week and we ate pizza. She's the best part of my week. Love you both. Bye. Have fun science-ing."

Stella is always fine it seems. I spend the elevator ride down to the lobby thinking of awful things to say to the receptionist, but I lose my nerve when I enter the lobby. The loose pill bounces around in my pocket. Mission complete. My buzz begins to wear off as I get on the bus home. I should probably just buy a flask.

———

Around sunset, I receive a text message from an unknown number instructing me to head to an address in our warehouse district. I am to arrive no later than eleven o'clock. I didn't even know Burlington had a warehouse district.

If I'm to be a superhero tonight, then so be it. I search my closet for a hoodie with my Miss Nucleus symbol on it. Jogging shoes. The jeans that make my butt look decent. So for the first time in six months, I'm wearing my Miss Nucleus costume. I even brush my hair. If I'm to be threatened into delivering an untested drug to a dangerous supervillain, then I should look my best. At least then I have something to be proud of.

And trust me, Freedom isn't a supervillain anyone should cross. He's the original supervillain, the bad guy who propelled Metroplexer into savior status. Despite all these years, none of us know the full extent of his powers. He's bulletproof and I think he can float. We don't know much else. He'll usually hire or manipulate other supervillains to fight for him instead of fighting himself. But because he antagonizes Metroplexer and his offspring – the invincible god warriors – everyone in the city freaks out when Freedom breaks out of prison. Or tunnels out of prison. Or bribes his way out of prison. Or his army of lawyers gets him out of prison on a technicality. The guy escapes a lot. But when Freedom is loose in Burlington, only one thing is for certain: people are going to die. So when I receive word that Freedom will kill someone or many someones if I don't meet him in his spooky warehouse with the Liberate pill tucked safely deep in my pocket, I have zero doubts. I get off the bus a few blocks from the warehouse and walk the rest of the way through the alleys and loading areas until I reach the address.

I arrive a few minutes early. I stand under the warehouse's floodlight, making sure I'm as visible as possible. No crickets are chirping. No car engines rumble in the distance. All noise has ceased. It's like everything around me is holding its breath. Right as my phone's clock hits eleven, I hear a male voice shout from the roof.

"What the hell are you doing here?"

Oh. Oh no. I recognize that condescending voice. I see him scale down the side of the warehouse, the muscles in his skintight uniform pulsating with each move. His black boots make only the slightest of noise as he touches the ground and marches toward me. He wears a thick black helmet and goggles, but I don't need to see his face to know that he's livid. He towers over me, pulling the collar of my hoodie toward him. I can smell his sour breath on my face. Did he drink milk recently? Who drinks milk this late at night?

"Liza, get out of here. Leave."

"Let me go, War Soul."

He shoves me away and I barely maintain my balance. I've seen War Soul work before. I'm experiencing the persona he saves for interrogating bad guys. It's unpleasant and War Soul has no sense of humor. I've never seen him laugh or make a joke or say anything even accidentally funny.

"Liza, I have spent months alongside Hacker Plus gathering information, dismantling Freedom's criminal networks, and meticulously combing through terabytes of data to find out what he has planned. Everything I've done leads to this warehouse. I can't have you here. You need to leave. Do you understand?"

I pause.

"Do you understand?" he repeats.

"I don't know what meticulously means," I answer.

"Dammit, Liza! Get the hell out of here!"

"No."

Wrong answer. His fist smacks me in my jaw. I fall back. He actually hit me? Why would he hit me?

I see his knuckles shaking. His whole body is trembling as if he's desperately trying to hold himself back from full-on assaulting me.

"Listen to me," he finally responds. "Five months ago in the sky above North Korea, the Metroplexer family safely downed six planes carrying six suitcase containing nuclear weapons. They saved the world. But when the United Nations went into North Korea, they discovered the seventh suitcase from their nuclear arsenal had gone missing. Everything points to Freedom. North Korea sold a nuke to Freedom. A nuke! All my reconnaissance leads me to this warehouse."

I stand up, and brush off some of the dirt. Then why would Freedom want the pill? What's the point of Liberate when he has a nuclear weapon?

"You know what, Liza? I don't care why you're here. I don't care how you found out. You need to go."

"I'm supposed to be here."

Another wrong answer. War Soul strikes me again. As I hit the ground, his boot presses firmly on my cheek. I struggle to push his foot off my face, but I struggle in vain.

"You're not a superhero anymore. Six months ago, your mistakes killed twenty-three people. And how many more over the years? You stumble randomly from crime to crime, the only person you could ever guarantee safety for was yourself. You have no training. No respect. You're responsible for more death and destruction than half of the supervillains that we fight. And that's not even a guess. I calculated myself. I went through the records filed by the police department and on the Internet. Half. I was so happy when you quit. You destroy lives. You made the announcement and I was so relieved. I hoped the city would have thrown you in the mental hospital and kept you there. But no such luck. Here you are, dressed up and ready to kill again. Have you not seen enough destruction? Caused enough deaths? And because I didn't stop you sooner, you killed another person last night. Liza, go ahead. Make your stupid jokes. Do it. Refuse to take this seriously. Go ahead."

"Okay," I answer. "But this is the worst first date I've ever been on."

He releases his foot, and walks toward the warehouse. War Soul can't even form words, just harsh screams bellowing at a volume far too loud for the outside of a supervillain's lair.

His breathing slows, and I see him clench his hands and jaw. As he gathers his thoughts or his temper or whatever unhinged him, his eyes lock with mine.

"If I ever see you again, I'm going to kill you. I don't know how, but I'll find a way. I mean it. Now, I have a mission to accomplish. I have to stop Freedom and secure the nuke. Don't be here when I come back."

War Soul grips the ledge on the side of the warehouse and scales up, climbing inside through a small window near the roof. Within seconds, I hear shouts and gunfire. And I cry. I can't stop. War Soul didn't say anything that I disagree with. The same thoughts I have about myself even as my parents and therapist and Stella reassure me that I was wrong. And I know War Soul is an asshole. I know. But I cry.

The sounds of the battle inside cease after a few minutes. Congratulations, War Soul. Thank you for protecting our city once again. We're lucky to have you. It's time for me to leave. If War Soul was that pissed off at me before, beating a warehouse full of dudes with his fists isn't going to mellow him out. Time to wipe my tears away. Stay strong.

The doors to the warehouse's loading bay begin to open. Too late for me; I'm still here. But instead, three men in dark suits walk out. All of them are carrying machine guns slung over their shoulders. As they advance toward me, I recognize Freedom following behind them. A large man, easily six-and-a-half feet tall with a bodybuilder's physique, wearing a tight blue t-shirt, cargo shorts, and – hold on, wait till the light hits him – okay, definitely sandals. His hair is slicked back. And, oh. Yup. That's a soul patch. This is the terrifying arch-nemesis of the world's greatest superhero. He's drinking something. Wait, I know that can label. Beer.

"Hello! Sorry for the delay, Miss Nucleus. It's wonderful to meet you! We had to deal with your boyfriend first – I'm sorry about your lovers' spat."

"Everything you just said is wrong," I correct him.

"I don't care," he corrects me. "Thirteen men, all equipped with fancy, high-tech, expensive guns, are lying unconscious on our building's floor. All thirteen beaten by an unarmed, angry teenager. We watched War Soul yell at you. Thanks to a fantastic engineer we kidnapped, we planted hidden cameras all over the warehouse, undetectable by the naked eye or most modern technology. I'm a wanted fugitive, you know. So about your boyfriend, because honestly, I think you can do better than War Soul. What do you see in him? Men shouldn't treat women like that. Well, not without good reason anyway, and you warranted none of War Soul's abusive—"

"That's great," I interrupt him. "But I've just listened to a lengthy speech by another megalomaniac so if you could spare me a lecture, I'd really appreciate it."

Freedom grins. His men look back to him for any orders, but instead, he lowers his head slightly and motions me inside. He tosses aside his empty beer can as one of his henchman hands him another one.

"Do you want a beer, Miss Nucleus?" he asks.

I nod vigorously. He points at his henchman, then the beer, then me.

"I think she's a teenager, sir," he stutters. "Are you sure?"

Brave man. Or stupid. But only a flash of confusion splashes across Freedom's face.

"What's wrong with you, William? I pay you to never question me ever for any reason no matter what. Yes, I'm sure! I'm a mass murderer! If I get arrested again, I have multiple life sentences waiting for me, so who cares if I give booze to children? Give her two beers, just to spite you. You know I can crush your skull in my palm, right?"

William doesn't hesitate this time, scurrying to give me my beers. One for each hand. When we walk into the warehouse, Freedom places his arm around my shoulder and my stomach churns.

I see Freedom's men lying across boxes or hanging over rails or strewn along the ground. Regardless of my current feelings about the guy, War Soul can certainly fight.

At the back of the warehouse, computers line the wall. Piles of cords and wires encircle the area. A small man, dressed in a suit and wearing glasses far too big for his face, is typing at one of the computers. Freedom calls him over.

"Charles, examine the pill Miss Nucleus brought us. You did bring the Liberate, correct? Unlike certain employees I surround myself with, you seem capable of following basic directions."

"Yes," I say.

"Good! Charles, go make sure she brought the real thing. I do trust you, Miss Nucleus, and please know that involving you in my plan was entirely out of convenience. Out of all the superheroes or supervillains I could have picked, you can imagine my excitement when I found out your parents worked for Harold Industries. I was practically giddy! Maybe it's a power move or a fetish of mine or whatever, but I have a thing for making others do my bidding against their will. When they don't want to. Drink your beers while you wait. I don't like anything I buy to go to waste, even with my insane wealth."

"Not the only thing insane," I mutter.

He squeezes my shoulder.

"I've been nothing but polite to you, child, and I expect you to be the same. You're taking too long to drink. Chug the beer."

I do, but not because he made me. His arm still drapes over my body like the world's creepiest scarf.

The two of us stand in the middle of his row of computers while his three remaining guards lean back against the wall. In the corner – there he is. War Soul. He sits tied to one of the computer chairs. His uniform is soaked in blood. Like a lot of it. But he's breathing. They didn't kill him. Freedom points to him.

"Look, Miss Nucleus. I'm not a good man, but I am an honest man. I take pride in my honesty. You see, I didn't expect War Soul to find this warehouse. This was a surprise for me. I hate surprises. All surprises. Well, except for surprise birthday parties. And when my girlfriend surprises me with dinner. And when I was given box seats to the Burlington Eagles game last week. You know what? I take that back. I do like surprises. But if War Soul knows about us here, then the Metroplexers won't be more than an hour behind him.

I have to call an audible. You know what an audible is, right? It's a football term. Chug that other beer."

I say nothing, my gaze fixated on War Soul's bruised and bleeding face. Charles hands the pill back to Freedom, assuring him I brought the right drug.

"Thank you, Charles. Chug that other beer, Miss Nucleus."

Everyone pauses as I finish my second beer. Freedom appears satisfied. He continues talking – at this point less a conversation and more a monologue.

"Here, take your pill back. I needed Liberate for Metroplexer, but I fear I need to change my timeline. Do you like surprises? Tell me a surprise you like. Now would be good."

Oh my God. I'm dealing with a crazy person. I'm off my meds, sure, but this man clearly needs a truckload.

"Oh, okay. Let me think," I tell him. "How about those videos where returning soldiers surprise their kids at schools?"

He squeezes my shoulder again.

"I agree. Good answer. Well, I have a surprise for you! You and I are going to play a quick game. The game I was supposed to play with Metroplexer. Different people, but same premise. I said take your pill back. I'm going to give you two choices, and you must pick one."

He strolls over to War Soul, placing one of his gigantic hands on the top of War Soul's head. Freedom's smile disappears, leaving his face twisted into a frustrated scowl.

"Well, the cat's out of the bag. Your boyfriend War Soul told you that I have a nuclear weapon. Charles, tell her about the nuke. I want her to know all the details before she makes her choice."

The tiny man, dwarfed even further by the immense size of Freedom, scrambles over. He pushes his glasses up.

"It's a nuclear weapon able to fit inside a duffel bag. Impressive technology. Maybe even supernatural. The explosive only weighs fifty pounds but would detonate at a ten kiloton blast. Everything within a half-mile radius would be incinerated. Fatalities would almost be guaranteed for anyone unlucky enough to be standing with a mile of the explosion. Depending on the location detonated, fifty to a hundred thousand casualties are expected."

Freedom pats Charles on the cheek, sending him back to the computers. I wonder if Charles works willingly. I once heard a rumor that Freedom spends a large chunk of his massive wealth every year on lawyers, bribes, and other sorts of corruption. Charles seems nervous, but I've seen his henchmen's paystubs before and the guy pays really well. Freedom calls out my name.

"Look at me, not Charles. Keep your eyes on me. I'm sorry if eye contact is uncomfortable for you, but I need you to pay attention. The suitcase nuke isn't here, by the way. A stroke of luck."

He asks one of his guards for the time. The guard replies fifteen past eleven.

"We should speed this game along," Freedom sighs. "I'm guessing less than half an hour until Metroplexer arrives. Anyone want to take me on that bet? If you win, I'll give you $100,000. If I win, I make Charles leak your Internet search history to your loved ones. No? None of you are any fun. Back to our game, Miss Nucleus. Eyes on me. Here's your first choice. I kill War Soul. I'll break his neck. It'll be quick and painless. Then I'll tell you the location of the nuclear weapon before my men and I leave. You'll be a hero! You'll have saved the city! Yay, Miss Nucleus – the hero of Burlington! You'll probably get a parade. You like parades?"

He spots my skeptical gaze.

"I told you, this is the same game I'd have played with Metroplexer later this week. Instead of War Soul, I'd use his BSO buddies Screwdriver or Mermaid. He likes those two bores for some incomprehensible reason."

Freedom refuses to break eye contact with me, intent about our gazes meeting. Far more intensely than a normal person would stare. Do I have a booger on my face? Is this normal? Does Freedom ogle everybody like this?

"Miss Nucleus, I don't lie. My business success relies on

others trusting my words. Trusting my actions. I'm an honest man. Well, mostly. I do lie sometimes. My girlfriend thinks I'm currently meeting my company's stockholders, for example. But that's stupid – it's nighttime. She's a dumb girl. But I never lie during games or anything involving superheroes. Ever. Not once. Here's your second choice. I don't kill War Soul. He'll live to fight another day. I won't tell you the location of the nuclear weapon, and know that I still plan to detonate it very soon."

War Soul coughs, blood dripping off his chin. Freedom strokes him, like one would a pet.

"Make your decision, Miss Nucleus. Definitely save the city and War Soul dies, or lose the city and War Soul lives. A significant portion of the city, anyway. Don't you see the brilliance in this game? I'm quite proud of myself. Tell me how awesome I am. Do it."

My eyes well up again despite anything I can do to stop myself. I'm still feeling War Soul's cruel rant. My vision blurs as tears begin to roll down my cheek. Even if Freedom escapes, Metroplexer can still stop him from detonating the nuke. Hopefully. Maybe. Freedom's plans usually take days or weeks to complete. But if I apprehend the nuke, I could redeem myself for the tragedy of six months ago. Save fifty thousand people. Erase all the pain I caused. And War Soul isn't even awake right now. I don't know how hurt he is, but he looks bad. He could be beyond medical help at this point. And the way he treated me. Freedom tightens his grip on War Soul.

"First, tell me how awesome I am. Then make your decision. I won't wait any longer. Stop the tears and make your decision. No sudden movements."

War Soul was right to yell at me. Everything he said was true. I do get people killed. People die because of me. But not today. I'm not going to kill anyone today.

"I pick War Soul."

"Sure," he announces. "Live with the consequences. Because I like you, I'm going to give you a one-time pass and assume you silently think I'm awesome. One last thing. Swallow the Liberate. I still need to see if it works, and as you know, I don't have time to test it on Metroplexer. No more one-time passes. You can guess what will happen if I have to ask twice."

Yeah, I can guess. I toss the pill into my mouth, making sure Freedom sees me swallow it.

"Well, there you go," Freedom gloats. "No turning back."

He finishes his beer, throwing the empty can across the room. Charles and two of Freedom's guards start packing up the computer equipment and move it to a truck outside. To a third guard, Freedom instructs him to watch me. Anything hasty and War Soul eats a bullet. The henchmen begin to wake up, though none of them are in any condition to stand up, much less get in a vehicle. When Charles questions about the injured guards, Freedom shoots him a glare and Charles goes silent.

Within fifteen minutes, I hear Freedom's truck pull away, leaving me and War Soul alone in the warehouse with the remaining concussed and beaten guards. I wait a few minutes longer to make sure I'm not still being watched by Freedom. Figuring we're in the clear, I undo the ropes tying War Soul to the chair.

My phone vibrates. A text message pops up from the same unknown number as before, warning me that Freedom isn't done with me yet. What the hell is going on? He made an invincible woman swallow a pain killer. I'm the world's worst person to test this drug on.

As I'm debating whether to leave, War Soul wakes up. He spits blood and saliva onto the floor. The superhero looks around before his bewilderment focuses on me.

"Liza? What happened?"

So he's okay. As Freedom said, he'll live to fight another day. War Soul asks me again.

"We failed," I tell him.

3

I can't tell you too much about War Soul. Like, as a person. No one can. The only certain facts we know about him come from a single arrest record back in his early days of superhero-ing under a fake name and an origin story he changes small details of every time he tells us.

But no one can deny that War Soul's physically attractive. Like objectively. Less than an hour ago – despite his personality – if he asked me to a movie or mini golf or a boat ride or prom, I would have said yes. But now? Now he might as well be smeared in dog crap for how much I'm repulsed by him. And it's not that he yelled at me. My self-esteem is low enough that I can brush off verbal harassment. But War Soul hit me. With his fists. He hit me. It doesn't matter that I'm invulnerable. I may not be a desirable catch, but the moment someone strikes me, they might as well take that bag of dog crap and rub it deep in their pores. Use it to exfoliate. So yes, War Soul has the physique of the world's hottest gymnast. A perfectly symmetrical face. And now? Now he's a half-man, half-poop slime emerging from a dog's anus.

I help War Soul down the street and onto the bus. He's definitely unable to walk on his own. The other bus passengers stare, and I quickly blurt out how fun our costume party was. Everyone continues to stare. Probably because of all the bloodstains.

I group text the Child Soldiers the moment we start moving. I haven't used the group text in six months.

"Need all active superheroes tonight. War Soul is hurt, meet at my apartment ASAP, and Freedom has a nuke hidden in this city. Thanks XOXO!"

My phone immediately starts blowing up. Bamboo demands more details. Lady Metroplexer says she's flying back from Asia. Mentalmind needs my address. Missile asks why I'm using the group text if I'm no longer part of the team. Spiromaniac asks if Missile will shut up and mind her own business. Fisherwoman is pursuing pirates out of state and won't be able to make it. Firestarter sends a text asking for a ride. Spiromaniac tells Firestarter she can pick her up. Belial wants to know if she can bring her dog. I tell her to leave the dog at home. Missile asks if Spiromaniac can also pick her up. Bowhunter says he can pick up a few pizzas along the way if we all want. Spiromaniac tells Missile that she lives on the other side of town and can't pick her up. Belial says if she can't bring her dog then she's not coming. Kid Metroplexer requests Bowhunter get at least one pizza with black olives. Friendleader's parents are still awake and he can't sneak out. Hacker Plus can pick up Missile on her way to my apartment. The Amazing Punchfist asks why I'm with War Soul. I think those two recently broke up.

———

I don't know how Spiro does it. She somehow channels all this chaos and hormones and egos of the Child Soldiers into a structured, capable force of teenage superheroes.

Stella has led the team for five years, all dating back to a single night that's become distorted over time. But it's a great story.

The mayor of Burlington was re-elected in a landslide victory, except the guy was opulently corrupt, dining with supervillains, and spending millions of taxpayer money on lengthy hotel stays for his mistresses and business partners. He bought a yacht too, but he didn't have it for long before Fisherwoman sank it one vengeful night. No proof of a rigged mayoral election ever showed while potentially incriminating documents and witnesses disappeared.

In their righteous and justified anger, a mob of about

hundred people gathered at Central Burlington Park a few weeks after the election, intent to march down to Burlington City Hall and rip the man to pieces. The police set up numerous blockades, but without the police's time to prepare or the funds for previous training, the mob rolled over the cops. Two policemen died – one from trampling and the other from assault. A police dog was beaten to death. Tear gas dispersed them, only for the mob to reunite two blocks later. Nothing could stop this indignant force of nature.

With the mayor's office in sight, the unstoppable crowd marched down an empty, quiet street. And in the middle of the road – alone – stood a fourteen year-old girl wearing a mask and a t-shirt emblazoned with a spiral emblem, holding only a broken piece of wood that she pulled from a fence nearby.

"That's far enough," she yelled. "We will remove the mayor from office, but this is not the way! If you come any further, you must get past me!"

A few people charged her and she fought them off. More attacked and she held her ground. A third wave fought and retreated. The remainder of the mob, not willing to risk further embarrassment, withdrew. The mayor was saved to face the law instead of a lynching.

That's the story on Spiromaniac's Wikipedia page.

While most of this story is exaggerated, we do have one irrefutable fact: a photo taken by a cameraman surfaced the next day featuring a small, masked girl in a spiral t-shirt carrying a long slab of wood and staring down a ravenous mob. Ready to fight a swarm of adults to protect the mayor from the injustice he so often inflicts on others.

None of the other Child Soldiers had dared attempt anything as bold or public – Kid and Lady Metroplexer wouldn't join the team until a year later – and Spiro was overwhelmingly voted as leader at the next Child Soldier election. She easily won the next couple years and since then, no one's bothered to run against her. Plus, and maybe this helps more than her heroic stand, she's the only one of us that everyone agrees they universally like and admire.

———

Thirty minutes later, War and I hobble off the bus. As we approach my apartment building, I spot three superheroes crowded around my front door. They tell me six more are on the way. I really regret not cleaning my apartment.

By the time a few more show up, the injured War Soul is lying on my bed, his blood ruining my sheets. War Soul's real name is still unknown to most of us the police, so we'll have to do our best to take care of him here – we can't chance bringing him to a hospital. And that means mainly soap and Band-Aids. I play housekeeper for everyone else while answering their barrage of questions. No, I don't have any bottled water. Just use tap water. You can eat the chips in the pantry. I don't know how old they are. Yeah, you can use my bathroom, but you really shouldn't go in there. I know my apartment smells weird. You can open the window. Just wait till the others gets here and I'll tell the story. Don't you dare touch my beer.

Spiromaniac arrives soon after, flamboyantly bursting through the door. Marching straight at me, Stella wraps her arms around my torso and our embrace lingers until I briefly feel all my problems and worries fade away. She breaks off the hug and places both her hands on my cheeks.

"You fought Freedom? Liza! You fought Freedom!"

"Hell no, I didn't. I'll never fight that guy. If you stood on my shoulders and a clone of me stood on your shoulders and we each magically gained fifty pounds, only then would we be the same size as that gigantic, scary man."

"No kidding," she nods. "I only saw him in person once and he's, what? Six foot seven? Three hundred pounds? I'm so glad you're safe!"

"I'm always safe."

Missile drops a glass on my coffee table behind us, scaring us enough to ruin our enchanting and always fleeting lovefest. Stella quickly turns around and glares at Missile before turning her attention back to me.

"Is War Soul okay?"

"War Soul will be fine. Bleeding all over my sheets though."

"Please, I know how rarely you change your sheets. We really should burn them anyway just to get rid of the fleas' advanced, sophisticated society that they have no doubt created inside your bedspread."

"I don't want to. They just formed a democracy and erected a statue in my honor."

She laughs before heading into my bedroom to check on War Soul. God, I love her. She's better than all of us.

By two o'clock, everyone has arrived. Spiromaniac hushes us, calls to order the meeting of the Child Soldiers, and motions for me to begin the mission briefing.

"Tell your story, Liza."

"Okay, about three hours ago, War Soul and I assaulted Freedom's warehouse. We lost. But turns out that Freedom has a nuclear weapon in his possession. We don't know where."

"War Soul and I already knew he had a nuke," Hacker Plus interrupts.

"And why are we just finding out about this now?" Spiromaniac yells.

"Kid and Lady Metroplexer knew too!" Hacker Plus yells back, not answering the question.

Everyone turns to look at Kid Metroplexer, who appears about ready to punch Hacker Plus.

"My sister and I knew one of the North Korean suitcase nukes went missing, but we didn't know it was Freedom who bought it," he attempts to salvage his embarrassment.

"That's a lie! I texted Lady Metroplexer weeks ago!" Hacker Plus screams.

"Enough, please!" Stella begs. "I shouldn't have asked the question in the first place. Pointing fingers is pointless. I don't care anymore; we have far more pressing issues."

Thankfully, as Stella preempts the battle of blame, so does

49

she halt any further questions about my half-true story. No one needs to know about my conversation with War Soul or the deal I made with Freedom to keep War Soul alive. Half of the superheroes wouldn't believe me while the other half would agree with War Soul.

"Since we have confirmation from Freedom himself, we can't waste any time arguing over who knew what," Spiromaniac orders. "Our mission begins tonight. The suitcase nuke takes precedence over your homework or sleep or anything related to your civilian life."

Bamboo whines he has a test tomorrow morning at school.

"Because it's a nuke, that's why!" Stella shushes him. "Here's what I want to do: Hacker Plus, you find the surveillance footage from Freedom's warehouse. Find anything useful and see if you can track the vehicle that Freedom left in. Mentalmind will stay with you to help go through the videos. When War Soul wakes up, he'll join the two of you. The cameras will be heavily encrypted – can you break it?"

"I'll need a few hours," Hacker Plus responds.

"That'll do. Freedom wants something with Miss Nucleus, so Kid Metroplexer, you go with her and head downtown. We know of at least two pubs there run by the supervillains on Freedom's payroll. The criminals downtown tend to be better informed on his plans and might react better to seeing her. Bamboo, take Firestarter with you and hit all of Freedom's normal hideouts north of downtown. See if you can get any information from his associates. Bowhunter, Globe, and I will visit the hideouts south of downtown. Missile, you monitor the police scanner and alert us if needed. Make sure none of this gets leaked to the press and all of you make sure no one is recording you with their phones while you're in the field. Now go. Hurry. Be diligent."

Everyone eventually scuttles off after the fifth or sixth time Stella pleads with them to trust her decisions. And eating everything in my apartment that isn't moldy. Hacker Plus sets up in my living room, promising to check up on War Soul every half hour or so. If

War Soul dies in my apartment, it's going to be hell to get someone else to rent it.

It's after midnight, so we don't contact Metroplexer or his teammates in the Burlington Safety Organization. It's futile. He and the other older superheroes go to bed early, leaving most of the evening and night patrols to us. Part of being old, I guess. They'll justify it with adages like we children need to learn to solve our own problems or we children need to learn not to always rely on the adults, but they just want their full eight hours of sleep. Also, that's why seeing Freedom late at night is an odd occurrence – he prefers to stand with egotistical pride during full daylight, begging Metroplexer to show up and fight. That dude *really* hates Metroplexer, and Metroplexer, if he knows the real reason why such an animosity developed, refuses to tell anyone. Metroplexer is simultaneously the most famous and secretive superhero in the country.

Hacker Plus and Mentalmind close my bedroom door for their first pass at playing nurse with War Soul, leaving Kid Metroplexer and me alone in my kitchen. I make my way toward the front door – when we fly away, I'm hoping Grant doesn't mind me riding on his back. It's difficult for me to get excited for downtown butt-kicking when I've just been carried seven miles cradled in his arms. Especially after the day I've had. The past two days. My whole life.

Kid Metroplexer grabs my wrist.

"Hey, real quick before we go. What really happened at that warehouse? Tell me what really happened. You know I won't tell the others."

I shake my head. No one should know. No one needs to know. Except for Hacker Plus when she grabs the surveillance feed. And Missile. And War Soul. And then I guess everybody else. Fine. So reluctantly, I tell Kid Metroplexer the whole story. And Kid Metroplexer responds like he always does.

"Yeah, War Soul's a jerk, but I don't think he really meant what he said to you. He gets mean in the field and it's hard for him to drop that persona once he dons his costume – if you had worked with him more often then you wouldn't have taken it so personally."

"Grant, he punched me in the face. Twice."

His face contorts into confused skepticism.

"But you're invincible."

"He didn't hit me out of self-defense! I didn't have him in a headlock! I was just standing there."

He face remains unchanged.

"Did you say something snarky to him? You do that a lot."

"Go to hell, Grant."

Realizing that his defense of War Soul only made me angrier, he drops the subject. And then, in a gracious move on his part, he apologizes. Even if the apology was probably insincere, I'll take what I can get.

"You did the right thing, by the way. You saved War Soul's life, Liza. Everyone would agree with your choice, except for maybe Missile or Belial or Hacker Plus. But those ladies we're keeping a close eye on anyway. You can proclaim you've quit being Miss Nucleus all you want, but you'll always be a superhero. We're all going to be superheroes until the day we die, and with your powers, you may not even be able to die."

"What? Immortal?" I suddenly realize. "Oh, God. I think I just threw up in my mouth."

"Because of the alcohol? Are you drunk?"

His eyes go wide with dread as he instantly realizes the question he asked.

"Anyway," he quickly continues before we get into another argument. "I always thought you were a good superhero. Capable and principled when you wanted to be. I trust you. Our plan tonight involves hitting two bars at the same time. I'm going to drop you off in front of Patrick's. You remember the supervillain Lazerz? He owns the place. His name is Neil Young, a brilliant man with a background in, well, lasers, who made himself some fancy gloves – they, as you guess, shoot lasers – and now he has a decade long rap sheet. I can't blame him for being evil. With the name Neil Young and as anyone who's been through high school can attest, how could he not turn to crime? He has a small crew that usually hangs out there and Lazerz has worked with Freedom consistently for the past few years. I'm going to drop you off at Patrick's and I'm going to the Wading Pool. Got it? Ready? Are you psyched up?"

I nod. I'm not really psyched up.

"Liza, no, Miss Nucleus. Your mission is simple. I know you can do this. Go into Patrick's. Say hello. If they won't give you the answers you want, then beat the crap out of everybody in that bar. That, I know you can do."

He's right. This man, just like his perfect hair and perfect body and perfect set of superpowers, knows when and how to land a perfect final verbal punch. The motivational haymaker.

"Yes, you're correct," I agree. I can feel the beginning of enthusiasm. "That I can do. I really need a win."

He smiles.

"Miss Nucleus, consider yourself officially back in the superhero business."

I groan.

———

Kid Metroplexer drops me off in front of Patrick's. He cradled me in his arms, refusing to fly until I settled for the demeaning cuddling. He's not a horse, he obstinately stated.

For the most part, the streets have emptied. Just the alcoholics remain. Last call was an hour ago and by now I have no doubt word has spread to all the supervillain hangouts that they're being attacked by my coworkers. And it's no secret that Freedom owns Patrick's. They'll be ready for me. Good. I really want to hit someone. Anyone. Everyone.

Patrick's has a reputation as the dirtiest, grossest bar on a street of bars that can best be described as dumpsters with doors. Which is odd, because Freedom is almost certainly a billionaire. Every time the government confiscates his money, he escapes or is released from prison only to reemerge with a new cache of cash, treasure, drugs, women, and valuables. No one can figure out exactly how, but Hacker Plus theorizes he owns several large, legal companies he operates under pseudonyms and launders money through them – and of course powerful lawyers and slimy politicians who'll happily take a significant bribe. But as for Patrick's, I can only assume that Freedom enjoys making Metroplexer, our city's greatest hero (and upper-middle class citizen with a nice house and a beautifully manicured lawn), slush through the city's filthiest, smelliest locales if he wishes to find out where to re-arrest our city's greatest supervillain.

So here I go. Look, I know I've been a terrible superhero lately. But when I kick in the door to Patrick's, I'll prove that I'm just not a whiny sad sack. That Kid Metroplexer is right about me. That I do win on occasion. That War Soul is wrong. Despite every awful, depressing, miserable thought I have about myself and every annoying, irredeemable, disappointing mistake I make – I still want you to root for me. So let me give you a reason and an awesome redemption story to one day tell my grandkids.

I kick the door in on my fourth try, my dramatic entrance somewhat waned. I count five goons blocking my path Lazerz – his mad scientist gloves resting comfortably next to him on top of the bar. And now I'm going to find out where Freedom's hiding. Or the nuke. Or whatever he happens to know. I'm not really that picky.

"The rest of you can leave. I'm here for Lazerz."

No one moves. They all just kind of look at each other.

"C'mon, I'm Miss Nucleus. The superhero. Remember when I saved that cruise ship a few years ago?"

They look toward Lazerz. He shrugs.

"All these kid heroes sort of blend together," he replies, putting on his gloves. "Get out of here and go back to your baby crib, kid."

"First off, I don't sleep in a crib. I sleep in a racecar bed."

No one laughs. I shake my head.

"Fine, the hard way. Let's do this, motherfu—"

Lazerz raises his glove and blasts me in the chest. The concussive force sends me flying out the bar and into the street. I secretly hoped Lazerz' lasers were heat-based (to which the only damage would be a ruined shirt), but nope. There goes my grand opening. I guess I don't instill that pants-wetting fear in the criminals of this city.

I brush myself off. Undeterred, but embarrassed, I stumble back into the bar. I give Lazerz the middle finger.

He politely asks his henchmen to kill me.

I quickly analyze the situation. The bar itself is directly in front of me and there are pool tables equally spread on my left and right – the five dudes will have to attack me head on. Good. All of them are definitely over six feet tall. Also good. Since I'm five foot nothing, I'll barely have to duck. Plus, they don't know the extent of my invulnerability. I hope they're all drunk. I wish I was drunk. Oh, and a Fiona Apple song is playing from a speaker somewhere in the corner. Odd choice for a supervillain bar.

The first guy rushes toward me, throwing a sloppy punch when he gets close enough. I take a step to the right, watching his fist go harmlessly past me. I counter with a knee to groin – which I miss by a few inches – but I hit him hard enough in the thigh for him to pause. A strong punch to his gut brings his face close enough for my follow-up jab to his nose. Down he goes.

A pool stick hits me across the forehead. I stagger a step or two, but I stay standing. The second dude attempts another swing, but without his element of surprise, I easily duck out of the way. Surging forward, I get close enough to him that he can't effectively use the long, unwieldy weapon. He reeks of booze. This time I nail the crotch shot. I shove him into a pool table, and just to make sure he stays down – with all the momentum I can muster – I land an exquisite kick to his forehead. Thankfully, that one year of soccer I played when I was six-years old is still paying off.

The next henchman pulls out a switchblade. This is where I

shine. He charges at me, thrusting his knife into my stomach. But the blade won't break my skin, and in his confused pause, I get in more than enough strikes to take him down. If you want to be a criminal, you should at least have the forethought to Google which superheroes you might fight. It clearly states on my Wikipedia page that I'm stab-proof.

The final two decide to take me together. The guy on my left attempts a low, sweeping kick to which I jump back far enough for him to miss. The other guy throws a right hook to my head. I stoop down to avoid, but before I can counter, he hits me in the jaw with a hook from his other hand and I drop to the ground. I await their next move, but they both pause for a moment. I see one of them pull out a pistol. Fine by me. I scramble on the floor for the broken pool stick as a bullet bounces off my shoulder. I swing the stick at the shin of the man closest to me, but I don't strike him hard enough to stop him. A second bullet ricochets off my forehead. I have only a few seconds before they realize the gun won't hurt me. I jab the end of the pool cue into the abdomen of the guy without the gun. He steps backwards, a bullet bounces off my chest, and I manage to stand back up. Another shot careens wildly above me into one of the bar's speakers. Fiona Apple's voice slowly morphs into a slow, sad Kermit the Frog.

Round two. I swing the pool stick at the man on the right. He catches it and chucks it away. Okay, not great. I lunge for the other guy's gun. He shoots off another bullet as we struggle for it, but I manage to get in close enough for me to get off an elbow to the ribs. The gun is mine now, and I celebrate with a shot to the guy's thigh. He tumbles to his knees. I fire twice at the remaining goon's shins. The shattered bones overwhelm both his desire to fight and his ability to stand. A few quick kicks to the back of both their heads – fine, a lot of kicks – and victory is mine.

As I'm reveling in my conquest, a laser blast misses my face by inches. I point the gun at Lazerz's shoulder and pull the trigger. Click. No more bullets, though that's probably for the best – I have terrible aim with firearms.

A second laser blast hits me in the chest. I sail over one pool table and crash into another. I crawl under the broken table, grabbing a pool cue from the wall above me. As I spring up, Lazerz's next shot brushes my shoulder. I throw the pool stick at him sideways, like how one would toss a discus. I don't have anywhere near the skill to nail him if I chucked it like a javelin – and the pool cue ricochets off his chest. He remains standing. Okay, so I don't have the skill *or* the strength.

Thankfully, he starts talking.

"I figured you out, whore. Miss Nucleus can't be hurt, am I right?"

"Words still hurt, though," I respond.

He fires off a few more lasers in my direction. I dodge the first one as it destroys most of the wall behind me. The next blast smacks into me, sending me into the collection of pool cues along the edge of the wall.

"Are we at an impasse, Miss Nucleus? I can't hurt you, and you can't get close to me. How shall we settle this, whore?"

"Stop calling me that. Are you cool with rock-paper-scissors?"

I drop to the floor quickly enough for his next shot to miss. I pull out my phone. If there's one thing I'm well aware of, it's my limitations. Eventually Lazerz will crash me through a wall or the bar will collapse, and I don't want this fight to spill out to the street. I can't risk civilian casualties or whoever unscrupulous happens to be out this late.

He switches targets, aiming instead at the closest pool table. It slams into me, pinning me against the wall. Doesn't matter, I can still use my fingers. Autocorrect ruins most of the message, but I manage to send off my text. "Come her knead help platypus." And now I stall.

"Hey, buddy. Lazerz. I think we got off on the wrong foot with me knocking out five of your friends. I just want to talk. Look,

I'm a legal adult. You should know I find gloves by far the sexiest man accessory. How about we split a craft beer and find out if opposites attract?"

I brace myself for more laser blasts, but no more pool-related objects smash into me. What's he up to? My face is pressed against a pocket of billiard balls and I can't see over it. Finally he speaks again. His voice comes from the same location as last time. If he was smart, he would have just run.

"Is this what you say when you're losing? Your final strategy is to prostitute yourself?"

"Well, that's rude."

"You know what? I'll be happy to split a drink with you if you'll show me your—"

A whoosh of wind. There we go. Within seconds, the pool table holding me down is flung across the room pinning Lazerz to the bar as he screams unintelligibly about his newly broken arms. Mid-scream, the supervillain drops. Hard. Kid Metroplexer's hand reaches out to pull me out of this mess, and I happily accept.

"Not bad, Liza. Look at those men. They're huge."

"Thank you. Fantastic entrance. Don't we need Lazerz to talk though? What if he has brain damage?"

"Please, I'm better than that. He'll wake up in a few minutes."

"That's enough time for a celebration beer. I don't think anyone will mind if we take a brew or two."

"We're on duty, Liza."

I moan. He rolls his eyes. I shoot a look toward the bottles lining the bar, but Kid Metroplexer silently shakes his head. Fine. I have plenty of booze at home.

"Great teamwork, Grant."

He grins.

"I'll fly these five men to the police station. I need to go back to the bar that I hit and finish up there, and then I'll have to go to the station for the police report. Listen, Lazerz knows something." He lowers his voice and ominously whispers, "Find out what he knows.

Take all the time that you need. Do whatever it takes."

I hate this part.

———

Lazerz wakes up tied on top of a pool table. I took each of his broken limbs, and using some rope I found in the bar's storage closet, I secured each of them to one of the table's legs.

Obviously confused, the supervillain yells out – the kind of shouts we would all make if we wake up from a nap to find out we can't move. He struggles. Let him. I can do knots, not to brag. Sitting in a chair a few feet from him, I crack open a beer. It's not stealing – these are blood beers, right? Like when the police find drug money so they spend it on a new coffee maker. And I have his gloves in my lap. I've inspected them and there's a lot more circuitry inside these gizmos than I thought. Y'know, my apartment doesn't have a supervillain trophy room, but now is as good a time as any to start. I bet you War Soul has a trophy room. Didn't he once mention he's always had a crush on Lady Metroplexer? I bet he has a lock of her hair in there that he sniffs after missions. Actually, my parents' wedding anniversary is coming up soon; they would definitely appreciate mad scientist killer laser gloves.

"Where are you, whore? Where are my gloves?"

"Don't call me that. I'm close by. Me and your gloves."

"What's your plan? Are you going to torture me until I tell you where Freedom's hiding?"

"No, I don't really torture. I'm going to sit in this chair, catch a buzz, play some games on my phone, and we'll see if you're willing to talk in a few hours."

He laughs. Supervillains are always so cocky. Is it delusion or arrogance? I'll ask Metroplexer for the psych breakdown one day.

"You think I'll talk after a few hours of nothing?" he replies. "I'll be bored of being tied up and tell you everything?"

"Oh goodness, no. I've already texted my friend Hacker Plus, and she'll have all your personal information to me in an hour or two. Your name, your family, your medical records, your high school yearbook photos, and of course, every e-mail, phone call, and text message that you've ever made to Freedom. Hacker Plus' technological expertise isn't as vast as she makes us think it is, but that girl's a firecracker when it comes to invasion of privacy. Then I'm going to send all that to the police with a message from you, saying that in exchange for a plea deal, you're willing to cooperate and sell out your employer Freedom."

Lazerz struggles harder. I put on one of his gloves and point it at the ceiling, but I can't get it to fire. How many buttons are inside this thing? After a few minutes, Lazerz begins to beg.

"If you give that to the police, I'm a dead man. Freedom will have me killed within the hour."

"Most likely. But I'm just not the type of twisted person who'll cut off a finger every time you refuse to cooperate. But don't worry, I'll tell you when Hacker Plus gets back to me. We have time. You hang out while I hang out. You tell me Freedom's location or anything about the nuke or why he wanted that Liberate drug, and I'll deliver you to the police myself – no personal information of yours gets sent anywhere. Your arms are definitely broken, by the way. They made awful sounds when I tied you up."

Lazerz laughs. Not like a giggle, but that kind of insane self-satisfied cackle that angry people get when they see a video of a teenager stealing an old woman's purse before immediately falling off his skateboard and cracking his head open on the curb. The kind of laugh that comes from witnessing immediate karmic vengeance.

"Liberate? I received word from Mephista that Freedom made one of you baby superheroes swallow the pill. That's you, isn't it? You're the test subject, aren't you? Oh, fantastic! This changes everything! I've decided to let you send all my personal information to the police. Let's wait for this Hacker Plus to reply to you. Oh, you have no idea."

Something's wrong. What's so important about this Liberate? What's going on? Freedom wanted Metroplexer to swallow the pill, but why? No, Lazerz wouldn't let me send Hacker Plus' findings to the police – it goes against every slimy self-preservation instinct these supervillains possess. I've never met one who would pick death over prison. They're narcissists. Egomaniacs. Every supervillain I've ever talked to boasts about how soon they'll be back on the street. So fine, Lazerz. Let's wait this out.

Three thirty in the morning, I ask Lazerz to give me information. He refuses. Four. Four thirty. Five. Same thing. At five fifteen, my phone gets a text message. Finally. Hacker Plus took her sweet time.

No.

It's from Freedom. Just three words: "A new game."

Lazerz begins to chuckle. What does he know? What do I not? Have I just made a huge mistake? Lazerz speaks up for the first time in two hours.

"Is that Hacker Plus? Am I done for? Woe is me!"

He laughs. Why is he laughing?

"It doesn't matter who sent you that text, honestly. I'm a former scientist, Miss Nucleus. Drugs – especially pharmaceuticals – don't work immediately. Pills can take hours before they take effect; the human body is vast and complex."

My blood runs cold, but not because of the pills.

"Stop gloating! Tell me what Liberate does!"

"Override code eight six one nine seven. Find out for yourself."

The two gloves on my lap glow brighter. I toss them, but not fast enough. The gloves explode.

My world goes black.

―――――

I went unconscious. My vision's a blur. I've never gone unconscious before in my life. How long have I been out? What's going on? What the hell is going on? I glance down. Red. Blood. I'm bleeding. I'm bleeding! What the hell? And then I feel it. The pain. I've never felt physical pain before. This is pain? Is my body being torn apart? Am I on fire? I want to cry. Why can't I cry? That's my blood soaking my hoodie. I'm dying, aren't I? Is this what death feels like? Please, let me die. I want to die. My vision stays a blur. I fall back into unconsciousness. Good. Finally. I pray I never wake up.

4

I wake up in a hospital bed, both my arms handcuffed to the railing. Two armed guards stand in front of the room's entrance. Freedom sits in a chair across from me, reading the newspaper. I'm disappointed – for many reasons.

Everything hurts. I can't move anything without a searing, tiny explosion throughout my body that takes every bit of restraint I've got not to scream out. How does anyone possibly fight crime with this constant, guaranteed pain? Bamboo once mentioned to me that he gets stitches at least once a month for his injuries, and my goodness, do I have a newfound respect for him. And he must be insane.

A guard alerts Freedom that I've woken up. Freedom – who I can best describe as dressed like a dad at his kid's touch football game – calmly folds the newspaper before putting it in his back pocket.

"Hello, Miss Nucleus! It's me, Freedom! Remember me? You've been out four whole days. I think you'll be happy with how the doctors pieced you back together – they said you would most likely wake up today. You're probably still sore, but no lasting damage fortunately. Plus, you get to see me!"

I turn away, saying nothing.

"Miss Nucleus, let's not be cranky. I had to break up with my girlfriend yesterday when she asked me if I was ever going to shave my soul patch, yet I'm doing my best to stay positive. And you can too. Do you prefer Miss Nucleus or Liza? Hmm? Silent treatment or still a bit muddy in the brain? My dear, I'm not happy about you being in the hospital either. Lazerz could have killed you in the explosion, and I like to think of anyone who's playing one of my games as family. Well, not so much like siblings or father-daughter, but more like I'm a young boy and you're my beloved pet hamster. I include you in family photos and you get a sentence in the annual holiday letter and I'm always delighted when I see you running on your adorable tiny hamster wheel. That kind of family. Oh, but do you prefer I call you Miss Nucleus or Liza?"

He takes a long deep breath.

"Look at me, child."

I refuse. The guards make a move to force me, but he stops them.

"Miss Nucleus. We'll stay professional and I'll call you Miss Nucleus." His next sentence is spoken slowly with an emphasis on each carefully chosen word. "You. Will. Look. At. Me. Because. There. Will. Be. Consequences. To. Other. People. If. You. Don't."

So I do. We lock eyes, and his immediately soften – the two of us sharing that uncomfortable, lingering gaze I remember from the last time we spoke.

"I'm going to need your cooperation here, child. I have a few items I need you to confirm. Answer honestly, please, because as I told you, we're pretty much family now. And I know that primal rewards like hamster food or hamster water or oodles of money or even just plain old fear aren't going to motivate you like they might others. That's okay – I'm used to negotiating with superheroes. Thus, you're going to run in your little hamster wheel for me because for every question you don't answer, my guards will go out into the hall, grab a nurse or doctor, and blow his head off. Or her head off – let's be equal opportunity here. Got it? Answer me."

"Yes."

"There you go! William, take off Miss Nucleus' handcuffs for me, will you?"

64

The guard walks over, fiddles with the cuffs, and they fall to the floor. Freedom sits at the foot of my bed, grimacing.

"Not your personality, definitely not your personality. But your features. You remind me of–" And then he stops, deciding not to continue this line of thought.

"Well, Miss Nucleus, we're in West Burlington Regional Hospital. I own the place under one of my pseudonyms. Do you like it? Of course you do. My men collected you from Patrick's. You really didn't need to wreck the place. Sure, my men attacked you, but what did the bar ever do to you? Buildings don't commit crimes, people do, yet you superheroes just love to destroy my buildings. And Patrick's was special to me. The place always smelled like a urinal doused in cheap cologne for some unexplained reason, but it always made a decent profit. Lazerz died when his gloves exploded, but I would have had to kill him regardless for almost killing you, so no big deal. We rescued you just in time. But the doctors here did a great job on you, right? The staff was paid extraordinarily well so as not to tell anyone, especially police or other superheroes, that you're here. And we kill the ones who squeal. Standard stuff."

"Why am I still alive?" I ask.

Freedom stands up, sighs, and meanders over closer to me. He strokes my sweaty forehead with the back of his hand. I'll never be clean again.

"Miss Nucleus, you're part of this game between Metroplexer and myself. We're in this together – you and me. Look, I spent months cooking up a scheme and gathering all the necessary parts. Months! I had to learn to speak Korean to get that nuke from North Korea. I wasn't about to get ripped off by some translator, and Rosetta Stone is not easy for someone of my age. Then your boyfriend War Soul messed it all up. I planned to secretly slip Metroplexer the Liberate pill – that's why I made you grab the pill on the sly instead of men just storming Harold Industries – but I know you superheroes. You all like to blab, and if your boyfriend knows about the missing suitcase nuke, then so does Metroplexer. Plus, your little operation four days ago when you and your fellow Child Soldiers wrecked seven of my properties. Those poor, defenseless, profitable buildings. So I have to delay this whole Metroplexer thing for a couple days to switch around some details. But I don't want to waste my all the time and effort and lives that went into my plan. I worked hard on it. I told you it was brilliant. It is. Thankfully, the Liberate works. Thank you for your participation."

"Unwilling participation," I correct him.

"I don't care."

"This doesn't feel like a game to me. And why the Liberate?"

Freedom waves at a guard, the one that's not William. He leaves the room for a brief moment before coming back with a gun pointed at the head of a scared nurse.

"My dear Miss Nucleus, a game doesn't have to be fun to be a game. A game only needs a winner and a loser. Worry less about my vocabulary and more about your current situation, please. But why the Liberate? You probably figured out by now: you're powerless. Hurray for Liberate! How does it feel? I mean, I wouldn't know, but I bet it sucks. Since I'm not done with you yet, if you don't mind, I'd like to ask you some questions about your past. We need to make sure everything's accurate."

The supervillain motions to the nurse.

"What's your name, woman? Jasmine? Pretty name. Like the Disney princess! I remember really sympathizing with Jafar when I watched that movie for the first time – that probably should have been a bad sign, I guess. So as long as Miss Nucleus is as honest with me as I am with her, you'll be safe. Got it? Stop whimpering, Jasmine. It's distracting. First question for Miss Nucleus, to make sure your brain is working. Your full name is Liza Lindsay Lewis?"

I nod.

"A triple alliteration, huh? Parents really need to think names through. Great. Let's continue. You were institutionalized at a mental hospital when you were twelve. Correct?"

I nod again, even though that was two separate questions.

"The doctors diagnosed you with major depressive disorder with suicidal tendencies, correct? You've been on medication ever since? Correct?"

I nod a third time.

"Got it. Now you see, I didn't know this about you until after we got you in the hospital. I had Charles look into your past, but we figured with your invincibility that you didn't have any hospital records. Oops. That complicates everything. Now that you can be hurt, if I let you go, you'll kill yourself. Won't you?"

I remain still. My eyes glance toward the window.

"Miss Nucleus. Answer my question. For Jasmine."

The nurse starts to sob. Freedom shoots an annoying look in her direction. When he gazes back at me, I answer affirmatively. I'm free from my powers. I don't know how long this Liberate will last, but I will. I will kill myself. My first thought when I wake up every morning and my last thought when I go to bed every night.

"Yeah, that's what I figured. You don't have to convince me that life is miserable, trust me, but I can't have you offing yourself, and not just because I like you. I'm still angry at Lazerz for almost blowing you up. I think we can both agree that we're glad he's dead. Listen. The Liberate drug obviously works, but I need to also learn the length of time your powers are eliminated. Since I have to alter my plan, this detail suddenly becomes very important. Go ahead and feel the top of your head. I know you have a bunch of cuts and bruises, but push deeply in the top of your skull. Inside all that hair."

On the top of my head, I feel a large, protruding bump. Definitely something surgical. My face scrunches as I touch the painful wound.

"There you go! My dear, I've been playing supervillain for fifteen years. Accomplished far beyond what I ever expected. But I've run out of time. My relationship with Metroplexer and this wonderful city needs to be wrapped up. Tears will be shed. Ladies will weep openly in the streets. Men with good taste, too, hopefully."

"Why do you hate Metroplexer so much?" I inquire,

dangerously pushing my luck. "Is it jealousy?"

Freedom doesn't smile. Just a cold, piercing stare.

"No. Are you serious? Not jealousy. Don't ask stupid questions. Look, I can get my hands on more Liberate, but that'll be my last chance. That's why studying you is so important. My adorable hamster in her adorable hamster cage running on her adorable hamster wheel. This Liberate pill will be my only chance to kill Metroplexer. Both the Messianic superhero and the dull, low-key suburban therapist he pretends to be. And before he dies, as he and I watch together hand-in-hand, the nuke will rip a permanent, incurable hole in his most precious Burlington jewel – precious in ways I cannot and do not wish to possibly understand."

He turns to William.

"That was a beautiful sentence, wasn't it? I should have you guys write down my words and put together a poetry book. Do you agree?"

William agrees, but I doubt he has much say in the matter.

Poor Jasmine whimpers again uncontrollably, and Freedom – obviously annoyed – asks Jasmine if she has become a liability, someone he has to worry about. She shakes her head between sobs.

"Jasmine, I don't kill often. Only for good reasons, and if I worry you'll tattle on me, well, that is a good reason. Or you just being obnoxious works too. I'm almost done talking to Miss Nucleus, and then you can return to work. I'll have my men slip you a few thousand dollars, but I need you to be quiet."

The nurse doesn't say anything, but she stifles her next few sobs. Silently, Freedom watches her before eventually turning his intense gaze back to me.

"Let's get back to that scar on your head. The doctors guess that the Liberate will stay in your system for about two weeks or so, and as your body breaks down the pill, you'll slowly regain your invulnerability by the second week. You were unconscious for four days, but those still count. I need to see this progress for myself. I taught myself Korean to do my own nuclear negotiations, for example – I'm not terribly trusting. To make sure you do your best to stay alive, the surgeons implanted the trigger switch for the nuclear weapon onto the top of your brain. If at any point your brain switches off – like say, death – then the nuke goes off. I'll be honest, I'm proud of this conundrum I've put you in. Once again, you get to pick between another two terrible choices! I know you want to kill yourself, but if you do, then you also take out fifty thousand people when the bomb annihilates a chunk of the city. Plus, who knows how many others would succumb to their injuries or radiation poisoning or cancer a couple of years down the road?"

I ask the only question that matters to me.

"If the Child Soldiers or the BSO find the suitcase nuke before you detonate it, I'm allowed to go jump off a building?"

"I suppose so," he shrugs. "But good luck with that. I'm detonating the nuke soon anyway, so who cares? Well. Hang on. I've played so many games in these past years that they've gotten stale. Boring. If I have to call a bunch of audibles already, what's one more fun twist? You know what? A week. I'll detonate the nuke within a week. Go use that information to play with your friends and see if you can grant me another surprise in our game. I told you I enjoy surprises." He pauses. His face scrunches in a frown that seems to disagree with his words. "Most surprises. Not that surprise when your boyfriend raided my warehouse. Or that surprise when my ex-girlfriend declared she hated my soul patch. Anyway, you're free to walk out of this hospital today and go live your newly mortal life. William, knock out Miss Nucleus for me. We need to leave and I don't want her doing anything rash. Just hit her or something."

Before I can react, William marches toward my bed. His fist slams into my forehead. My world fades to darkness.

———

My depression has hovered at a suicidal level for years, which made my invulnerability ironic. But I still fantasize. Constantly. Daily. Occasionally on the radio, I'll hear a sad song – ones where they announce they'd rather feel heartbreak than nothing at all. But what's wrong with feeling nothing? For those of us with the clinical stuff, the chemicals are all messed up in our brains. Life is miserable – against our will. If we can't be happy, whether because of life choices, medical issues, living situations, or just terrible genetics, I bet you 98% of us would rather be numb than depressed. The other 2% are totally lying. So I might be a borderline alcoholic, fine, but alcohol numbs. And I know I'm supposed to be a good role model – I'm supposed to tell you to stay in school and drugs are wrong and to practice safe sex. But I'm trying. Not as hard as I should, but I'm trying.

Yet when I saw my own blood for the first time in my life, when I felt my body shutting down, I was thrilled. And now the choice has been taken out of my hands.

I'm released from the hospital a few hours after Freedom and his groupies leave. But since they signed me in with a fake name and my cell phone got caught in the explosion, I leave the hospital alone, wearing a plain white t-shirt, blue scrub pants, and a pair of cheap flip-flops I begged from a nurse. And fine, I do know a few numbers by heart if I can borrow a cell phone, but I have very little desire to explain where I've been the past four days. Half embarrassment and half reluctance to answer a never-ending barrage of questions or detailed explanations of the supervillain's convoluted scheme. I'm stuck penniless with an impossibly long walk home. Thankfully, I manage to charm (nag) one of the more sympathetic doctors out of $10. That's enough for bus fare. No, I should do brunch. I deserve brunch.

I pick the first diner I see. I couldn't bring myself to check out what I looked like in the hospital bathroom's mirror, but I suck up my dread and march to the diner's bathroom – especially after seeing the faces of passersby as they walked by me. My arms and chest are covered in blistering burns, while bruises mark the rest of my skin. My face is a road map of lacerations squeezed between its own share of cheek burns and bruises along my jaw. And worst of all, my hair appears like a shrub cut by the world's worst gardener. The waitress cautiously and nervously approaches me in my booth, and I can't blame her. But, thankfully, she takes my order.

I eat my soggy waffles and drink my coffee in silence. The waitress forgets to bring me creamer, but I'm just going to make the sacrifice and drink my coffee black.

So now I must find the nuke. Within a week. And if I find the nuke after the next five or six days, it'll probably be too late. I'll be almost back to full invulnerability by then.

But how do I even begin to search without Freedom knowing? Freedom has hundreds of city workers and tech guys on his payroll. He employs psychic supervillains that he can throw around to locate me. What's to stop him from simply bombing the mall or parking garage or wherever I'm lucky enough to stumble upon the weapon?

Yet speaking of the mall, I've missed the past few days of work, so I must assume Kid Metroplexer and the others are looking for me. Thankfully, I only talk to my parents once a week at most, so at least they won't be concerned. Though Stella must be worried sick. Moments like these, I hate being sober. This is why I don't want to call anybody.

Still, I need to give myself some credit. I'm not useless. I can be helpful during the city-wide search. Maybe fight some bad guys. Even if I'm currently about as tough as a random sorority sister who recently fell down a flight of stairs, I have five years' experience in analyzing, planning, and implementing plans of action. Well, maybe not those exact words, but I've been in enough awful situations that I can usually predict how the battle will go, how the criminals will act, and how I can adjust my fight strategy for different locations. I've apprehended hundreds of criminals. I've fought in more than fifty supervillain battles. I mean, about twenty or so by myself and then another thirty with the other superheroes – although they did most of the work. Plus, I'm Freedom's pet hamster, so he probably won't try to kill me immediately. Right? Hopefully right.

But currently, as I sit alone in this diner eating cold waffles and lukewarm coffee, I'm scared for the first time in my life.

———

Spiromaniac and War Soul's condo, the official headquarters of the Child Soldiers, should only be a few miles from the diner. War Soul's uncle rents it to him and Spiro moved into the second bedroom a while ago to escape living in her parents' house. My body hurts everywhere and I'd rather go to my own place, but without a phone – and I chose hunger over bus money – I don't really have any other options. Do pay phones still exist? I'm susceptible to germs now, and aren't those things coated in feces and Ebola? I'll just gradually limp to the condo.

My new sensation – an overbearing fear – won't go away. As I walk down the street, car horns scare me. Loud arguments worry me. Screeching of tires freaks me out. Why are there so many people on the sidewalk today? How many of them are secret agents hired by Freedom? I'm suddenly wildly aware of the sounds of the city. Do normal people fear this much? Does everybody on this block live with this fanatical, constant terror? What is life like for people who can be hurt or smashed or killed at any random, unforeseen moment? And what about superheroes? Half of us don't even have any superpowers.

Then I make a mistake. I glance down an alley.

Two men stand behind a dumpster. In a scene I know from dozens of times before, the man on the right has a wallet in his hand while the other man grips the guy's other arm. A mugging. If I intervene and fail, fifty thousand people die in the nuclear blast. But... Are there cops around? No, of course not. I'm not going to risk so many lives on one man's unfortunate luck. Who goes down an alley by himself anyway? But... Fine! Okay, fine. Go make your mistake, Liza. Carry out your superheroic obligation.

I walk down the alley. The first rule of superhero-ing: make the bad guys focus their attention on you.

"Hey, over here," I yell. "You, the guy grabbing that dude's wallet. Can I talk to you for a minute about the Church of

72

Scientology?"

They both stare. I continue to walk toward them. I must look like a crazy person. A hundred percent homeless. Maybe a drug addict. Definitely someone who would eat out of the trash. The mugger loosens his grip on the other man, silently watching me.

"Could either of you boys give me a hug? I've had a really rough day. But heads up, I don't smell great."

The mugging victim backs up. The other man steps out from behind the dumpster. Yup, he's holding a gun. And with all the noise out on the street, no one would hear the shot or give it more than a second thought. But he wouldn't dare shoot at me. My back is to the street. He can clearly see I'm not carrying any weapons—

The gun goes off in his hand. In my direction. Oh my God, what have I done? Why are the criminals in this city so damn impulsive?

I wait for a nuclear explosion in the background as I drop dead. Nothing. I take two seconds to see how lucky I am, and then pain explodes from my ear. I touch it – a mistake. No more earlobe. The three of us glance back and forth between each other, no doubt contemplating the horrible decisions that led us to this moment. No time to delay. Go, Liza. Go!

I lunge forward, utilizing the second rule of superhero-ing: hit the bad guy as hard as you can. Unless you have super strength, then it's more of a love tap. My fist explodes in pain as I connect with his jaw. Holy crap, punching people really hurts. Why do superheroes do this on a regular basis? After my second strike, the guy backs up. I'm in no condition to fight him. But deciding between brawling with a tiny, hurt, stinky girl or running off before something else can go wrong, he bolts. Thank you, Xenu!

The rescued victim doesn't waste any time to rush out of the alley and disappear into the crowd on the street. So be it. I'm used to the civilian's rush of adrenaline usurping proper manners and thank yous. Blood from my ear onto my borrowed t-shirt as I lean against the dumpster, waiting for my hand to stop throbbing.

My incredibly stupid move to save a guy's twenty bucks aside, I feel good about myself. Proud. Even in my darkest hours and my strongest moments of self-loathing, I have to hold on to my desire to do the right thing. The superheroic obligation. It's typically the only thing I like about me.

As I walk down the sidewalk, I'm not as scared anymore. I should stop by a convenience store and spend my last dollars on Band-Aids.

———

I reach my destination about an hour and a half after I left the diner. I'm still limping a little. If I walk too fast, pain ignites in my legs, shooting up and down like fireworks. But the sight of Spiromaniac and War Soul's apartment complex gives me my second wind. I enjoy being there. The Child Soldiers throw parties there once a month, to which criminals get a free night to wander the streets unabated as we vomit off the patio. I'm not judging – that's how I spend my nights at least twice a week.

Despite the incredible dysfunction among the twenty of us, we hide it surprisingly well. The people of Burlington love the Child Soldiers. The press loves the Child Soldiers. The police tolerate the Child Soldiers. In public conferences, Spiromaniac speaks for the group. Stella's mask hides most of her face and she lowers her voice an octave when she speaks in costume, but she's charismatic, funny, passionate, and always way too friendly. As opposed to me, who once received an intervention from the Child Soldiers about my curmudgeonly attitude. Well, I say they can go to hell.

We even have our own rogues' gallery of supervillains. Wizardman – an old man who wears a robe made of fireworks and whatever else he can arson – proudly announced himself as our official nemesis soon after the Child Soldiers' official beginning. But over the past year or so, he's developed a growing dementia and has been confined to a wheelchair, so superheroes feel really hesitant about punching him. Good, I say. The people of Burlington watched the Child Soldiers grow up and everyone felt uncomfortable watching a senior citizen attempt to set fire to a colorful group of teenagers. Stella told me a few weeks ago that an illusionist named Denial and some bog animal calling itself Poisonous proclaimed themselves Wizardman's successors, but no one – superhero, supervillain, or otherwise – seems to care.

I ring the apartment doorbell. I hope someone's home. What time is it? Most of the Child Soldiers don't get out of school until around four. I knock on the door. No answer. I ring the doorbell a second time. I hear some noise from inside.

"Let me in! It's Liza! Please?"

I knock again. Thankfully, the door unlocks, opens, and Stella pops her head out. Her eyes go wide. I don't even have time to speak before she embraces me. I love this woman with all my heart.

"What happened to you? Whose blood is that? Why do you look like that? Is this a prank? You know I don't like pranks."

"Yeah, so I've got some news."

"Oh my God, Liza, we were so worried. We've been searching for you every day. I contacted your parents. Kid Metroplexer won't stop blaming himself. Are you okay?"

She begins to cry, and that makes me cry too.

"I'm okay. Sort of. We need to get everyone together."

She cries harder.

"We will, but come in first. Are you hungry? Tired? Look at you! What happened? I was so worried about you. We all were. I was so scared, Liza."

She stops crying. I wipe away both our tears.

"I was scared too, Stella."

Stella marches me into the living room and motions for me to sit on the couch facing the TV. She plops herself down on the recliner next to me. I talk first.

"It turns out I'm not invincible right now."

"I can see. How?"

With no choice but to tell her the truth, I tell Stella the real story of the night at the warehouse – how I got the Liberate pill, swallowed the pill, saved War Soul, the brawl with Lazerz, and the explosion at Patrick's. She takes a moment to ponder before she replies.

"I'm really angry at you for not telling me this sooner."

"What?" I exclaim. "I lost my powers! I was blown up! I've been held anonymously in a hospital for four days by the country's most notorious supervillain! And you're angry at *me*?"

"Yes!"

"Why?"

"Because you're my best friend and you lied to me! You lied right to my face and thought nothing of it!"

"I didn't lie to you; I just didn't tell you the entire truth."

She gets up off the couch fuming, pacing in front of the television. I might have said the wrong thing.

"Liza! I get lied to all the time by the members of our team. I still care about them. But you? I *love* you. Emphasis on love. Well, not that kind of love, but you know what I mean. You need to apologize, because unlike them, you can actually hurt my feelings."

"I'm sorry," I shamefully respond. "I love you too. Emphasis on love, but *that* kind of love. I apologize, but I need to do it with tongue."

She laughs, tells me to be quiet, and heads to the kitchen.

"I forgive you, but don't do it again. Do you want a Fresca? Fruit Loops? That's all we have. Tap water if you want it. I promise to wait on you hand and foot like the queen you so very much deserve to be."

"Can I take a shower?"

"Done. Use my bathroom. What else?"

The two of us go through a verbal list of current necessities. I'll need clothes and some makeup – maybe just some foundation to cover some of the cuts and bruises. I'm going to have to call my parents, especially since Stella told them I was missing. Then we'll need an emergency meeting.

"I'm already sending out an emergency text to everyone,"

Stella announces. "Three hours should be enough time for all of them to get here – except Anne, sorry, Fisherwoman, because I think she's still trying to avoid the Coast Guard. It's not fair, Liza. She takes out all the bad guys and watery terrorists and scary fish monsters for them and all they do is try to arrest her. They don't even send her a thank you card or a gift basket or anything. I bet you they're jealous. Embarrassed. Everyone will be here soon and you'll update everyone on the nuke thing. You can wear some of my clothes if you want."

"Thank you, but you're a good six inches taller than me."

"When you're in the shower, I'll go buy you a shirt and pants. And socks and shoes. I'll make sure everything is super cute. You can use my phone when you get out."

"Thank you again."

Spiromaniac places her hand over her heart.

"Godspeed and good luck, Liza."

"May all your dreams and desires come true, Stella."

Patting me on the shoulder, she grabs her wallet and heads out the door.

I head to the bathroom and search for a clean towel. As the shower heats up, being curious, I make the mistake of holding up my arm to take a whiff. It's bad. Like I just completed a triathlon after forgetting to put on deodorant bad. I spot a bottle of perfume by the sink. Spiromaniac won't mind if I spray a squirt or two after the shower.

Twenty minutes later, naked, smelling great, and wrapped in a towel far too small for me – I think I may have accidentally grabbed a large hand towel instead of a bath towel – I walk out of the bathroom attempting to make sure one of my boobs doesn't pop out.

I adjust myself and look up. War Soul is sitting on the bed.

"Hey."

My legs barely handle the superhuman speed of my dive back into the bathroom, slamming the door shut.

"What the hell? Damn it, War Soul! What are you doing here?

Why are you in Stella's bedroom?"

"I live here. Spiromaniac texted me about fifteen minutes ago to head to the condo if I was in the area. You know, just in case. I thought–" he pauses. "I figured you had clothes in the bathroom."

"Why are you sitting in the bedroom? Why do you think Spiromaniac left the apartment? Clothes, man! Go watch TV or something – get out of here!"

"I'm sorry. I needed to speak to you."

"No! Go away!"

I hear the bed squeak as he gets up.

"Liza. Stop it. I'm not backing down. I'll talk to you through the door if I have to. It's important."

I slump onto the tile floor, my back resting against the cabinets below the sink.

"Talk then. Go, War Soul."

"Good. When I awoke in your apartment, Hacker Plus showed me the surveillance footage from the warehouse's camera. I saw what you—"

He hesitates. I hear the faint sounds of several deep breaths.

"You saved my life. After everything I said to you. You saved my life. I don't– Why would you do that? I don't under– Thanks. But why?"

While he awaits my response, we sit in silence for what feels like a lifetime. I collect my thoughts. After days of contemplation, I'm still not entirely sure how to articulate my reasons. But I can try.

"War Soul. Tell me your real name."

"Nick."

I close my eyes.

"Okay. War Soul. Nick. I don't have a lot of redeeming qualities. You pretty much nailed my faults. I want to blame all of them on my illness, but most of my awfulness is because of my own actions and terrible decisions. People have died because of my choices or my mistakes. More than the average superhero, as I found out from you. The guilt crushes me, man. But for all the crap that is my life and career, I still want to be a good person. And I know that everyone says that, and I know that doing the right thing is always so much harder, longer, and less rewarding than a selfish decision – even something super small like holding onto my empty soda can until I can find a recycling bin. But if I can't curb my self-loathing, I have to try something, right? I'm not super eloquent right now. And I don't like you. Not anymore. But I promise that if I have to pick between saving your life and risking the entire city in a nuclear explosion, I'll take the risk. Because it's the right thing to do, right?"

I hear nothing from the other side of the door.

"Nick, may I ask you a question?"

Silence.

"Nick. War Soul. If our places were reversed, would you have made the same choice?"

Silence. I can stay strong. I stifle a sob.

"Answer me!" I demand. "After everything that has happened. Would you have made the same choice?"

The quiet hangs for a long time. I adjust my towel. What should I do? Make a joke. I'll make a joke.

"If you don't answer soon, you're going to have to listen to me pee."

That was a stupid joke. I can't take this anymore. I suppress another sob. Countdown until my voice cracks.

"Please, Nick," I whisper.

"Liza."

A final long silence.

"You know the choice I would have made."

The bedroom door closes.

Ten minutes later, Stella knocks on the bathroom door and hands me the clothes she bought. She was right; they are cute.

———

I used to have a notebook where I kept everyone's names and superpowers (mainly so I don't embarrass myself when we all hang out). I threw it away six months ago when I quit, but I can probably do this from memory.

Kid Metroplexer and Lady Metroplexer have all the basic powers and qualities we all wish we had. Invulnerability, super strength, super speed, flight, incredible confidence, natural leadership abilities, beautifully chiseled abs. Maybe some other stuff they aren't telling us.

Spiromaniac says she tragically discovered her superpower as a toddler – I think she may have been born with it. Let's say someone breaks her arm, she can then reflect the same pain on someone else. Therefore she fights like a crazy person – purposely taking punches, stabbings, even an occasional gunshot to reflect back on the people she's fighting. Thankfully, she superhumanly heals in her sleep, making a good night's rest more than enough for her to be back in action within a day or two. Thus her name: the spiral of life and her insane fighting style. I guess. Look, most of us picked our names when we were in middle school.

War Soul is probably the best hand-to-hand combatant in the city. He claims both his dads are military special forces and they started training him the second he started walking. His only superpower is his super awful personality.

Hacker Plus has abnormally low muscle tone, though you can't really tell unless you're looking at her up close. Luckily, she turned out to be a technological prodigy and serves as our main source of information and any additional digital investigations we need. Also, she's the president of her school's Computer Club.

Featherblade and Icarus stole two experimental jetpacks from the army base where their parents worked. The sisters figured out how to operate and repair them, and now they soar around the city complete with a load of tazers and stun guns and whatever else they find. They're also the only ones who wear masks that cover their entire faces, since the army is still looking for the thieves who stole the jetpacks after all these years.

Globe communicates with nature. I think. I listened to her explain it all once, but I was drunk. And I got a C in biology. I know she's the only one of us who can connect with or use magical stuff. She does have six arms though, which I probably should have mentioned first.

Firestarter can't be burned due to a scientific miracle. So she douses herself in gasoline, lights herself on fire, and charges at criminals and supervillains. Trust me, it works more often than not.

Mentalmind possesses a genius IQ. Like one of the top in the country, and maybe the world. She can go out in the field and hold her own with the best of us, but her main job is to plan our attacks against the tougher supervillain strongholds. That woman can plan brilliant strategies in hours that the other nineteen of us would never consider even if we all worked together for days.

Bamboo and the Amazing Punchfist are non-powered martial artists. They lack War Soul's military training, but they spend every free moment training or signing up for various city-wide combat tournaments. They're both undefeated, records they maintain by refusing to fight each other.

Forestchild spent the first eight years of his life as a feral child somewhere deep in the Canadian woods. He became a small celebrity once he was discovered and rescued from the wolf pack he belonged to, but public interest quickly faded. He still can't speak very well, but he moves in such a strange instinctual, animalistic way that bad guys can never seem to hit him. Also, Mentalmind made him some steel claws for his fingertips. That dude cuts to the bone, much to the dismay of anyone who decides to fight him.

Bowhunter has some small degree of invulnerability, but I don't know how he received it. And he owns a crossbow.

Fisherwoman is rarely in town. She uses a customized speedboat to patrol the coasts – the nearest coast being a hundred miles away. I can't verify whether this story is true or not, but a rumor started that once when she fought Globe's supervillain father, he attacked her by controlling a pack of sharks and at least two giant squids. She took all of them down – but like military vets and the mentally-scarring things they've seen, she won't talk about it. But I've seen her boat before. That woman has more harpoons and spear guns stashed in her boat's deck than a hundred divers combined. Needless to say, she's not a great conversationalist.

Friendleader took a batch of mystery goo to the face when he was a child. Now he can wipe or implant false memories. So yes, the women stay as far away from him as we can. But to be fair, he saves us hours of questioning and paperwork down at the police station during our missions that require a more, I want to say, invasive touch.

Missile and Belial lived next door to each other as kids. They realized their abusive childhoods gave them something in common, and their friendship blossomed. The two of them will only work in the field with each other and skirt around any discussion of their superpowers. I do know their crime scenes are usually so bloody and horrifying that the police make it a policy not to send rookie police officers.

Fearboy never really talks about his superpowers. I don't really want to know. I've caught him several times leering intensely at me during meetings or briefings, so I do my best to stay away from him. I'll assume his power is to make the ladies around him queasy and uncomfortable. He doesn't get invited to parties.

And then you have me, now an injured civilian with clinical depression and a nuclear detonator lodged in my brain.

As the hours go by, the superheroes trickle in. Belial arrives first, bringing her dog despite the no pet policy in the condo. Spiromaniac and Belial argue before Belial agrees to leave her Pomeranian on the porch. Bowhunter and Friendleader arrive next, having skipped school once lunch was over to see an afternoon movie. Featherblade and Icarus join us with their giant suitcases in tow. They always look like they're about to leave for a week-long vacation, but it's the only way the two of them can lug their jetpacks through the city unnoticed. Forestchild brings a salad with him. Despite refusing to eat anything but raw meat until he was eleven, he recently converted to vegetarianism. I think Mentalmind convinced him to stop eating meat after she showed him a bunch of websites. She shows up soon after Forestchild. Hacker Plus apologizes for being late, then takes back her apology once she realizes how many superheroes aren't here yet. She makes Bowhunter and Friendleader go to her motorcycle and bring up all her computers. Bamboo and the Amazing Punchfist enter through the porch, the two of them spooking Belial's dog enough to receive an unwanted lecture about animal safety from the dog's pissed off owner. We catch Missile pouring herself a bowl of cereal – no one saw her come in. But no one can miss Firestarter's arrival. She smells like a gas station. Globe enters the apartment dragging Fearboy behind her. From what we can figure out from between her ranting and his yelling, Fearboy sent her some very inappropriate messages a few hours ago. She proclaims that she'll get her vengeance – or at the minimum, screenshot the messages and send them to Fearboy's mom. Kid Metroplexer and Lady Metroplexer make their entrance last – and loudly – insisting they were held up at the police station after following a lead they picked up a few days ago. Lady Metroplexer makes her rounds while Kid Metroplexer (after wrapping me up in a hug) advises Spiromaniac on some costume additions he's thinking about for her. Grant's been obsessing over fashion lately. Spiro ignores him and continues to pour snacks for her guests until Grant comments that she would look much better with bangs. Her death glare sends a chill throughout the room. As each person arrives and catches a look at me, I spot momentary glances of sympathy, pity, or bewilderment. War Soul won't look at me at all.

With all of us present and strewn across the living room – save Fisherwoman who always seems to be out hunting her white whale – the meeting can begin.

I tell them everything.

———

"I'm not going to just sit around and hide! I'm going to help. Me running around the city is just as dangerous as me hiding in a location where Freedom or any other supervillains could easily find out where I am. I can defend myself. You can't stop me."

The meeting has turned into a shouting match between War Soul and me, despite Spiro's frustrated calls for order.

"We're not asking you to hide for the next two weeks. We'll move you around to different places. They'll all be secure. There are seventeen other superheroes in this room all looking for this nuke. We can find it. You're going to go into hiding. This isn't a debate, and I can definitely stop you if necessary."

"*We're* not asking? No, just you. I already told you this isn't open for discussion. I'm going out and I'm going to help find this nuke. Just try and stop me."

"You're not a superhero right now, you're a liability!"

I can see War Soul regretting that statement the second it came out of his mouth. I'm sure he meant it, just not out loud. The only sounds in the apartment come from the air conditioner. I can hear Bowhunter breathing – he's always been a loud breather. The others shift uncomfortably in their seats.

"Sit down, War Soul," Stella intervenes. "I told you to stop and I'm not going to talk over you again. I'm the one who gets to make these types of decisions. Liza, then you'll need a partner. Someone who will spend twenty-four hours a day with you for the next week. Someone who can protect you. Okay?"

I see many of my coworkers look toward the ground, but there's only person I can spend that much uninterrupted time with who I won't strangle by day two.

"You. Never leave my side, Stella."

Spiromaniac quickly agrees. I see the faint hint of a smile. With that, the superheroes pile out of the apartment, each to continue the search that began four days ago. From what I can tell, Mentalmind put together some sort of formula to maximize covering as much ground as possible. Spiromaniac and I are the last ones to leave. She locks the door before turning to face me.

"We'll find the suitcase nuke, okay? Even Metroplexer and the Burlington Safety Organization are searching during evenings now. Screwdriver contacted me personally to discuss how and where we're investigating. How cool is that? I ate dinner with one of the original BSO members. Though I brought Mentalmind with me and she did almost all of the talking. But still, dinner."

"I've always wondered, do you think the BSO approves of us?"

Spiromaniac thinks for a second.

"Well, they don't have a choice, do they? It's not like we're going to quit if they suddenly tell us not be superheroes anymore. They have to say publicly they approve of us, because they know the only way to stop us would be through violence. Imagine that PR nightmare."

"Seriously, I can imagine. Breaking news: Metroplexer has just crushed six teenage superheroes. We have received word that Screwdriver attacked the remaining Child Soldiers with sentient construction equipment."

We walk down the stairs and toward the street. With most of my injuries covered up by Spiro's makeup, we can go incognito into the night. Neither of us are wearing our costumes, though her superhero costume is the only one worse than mine: a cloth face mask, jeans, and t-shirt emblazoned across the chest with a black spiral.

"Liza, my love, what do you want to do tonight? You've had an awful past few days, so how about we leave the nuke search to the others for tonight? It'll be fine with so many out in the field, and I'm exhausted from dealing with all of them. What do you want to do? Get food? Hey, how about karaoke? That would be fun! You aren't one of those people who claim they have to be drunk before they'll sing, right? I hate those people. No one expects anyone to be good, so there's no pressure. What about that tonight?"

"Sure, why not? That's not a bad idea."

"Wonderful! Hey, the best karaoke place is in the Bandwood Casino. They have private rooms. If you're worried about anyone hearing us, all those slot machines and card tables will drown out any noise we make. Oh, Liza, this is going to be so much fun!"

The two of us get on the bus headed toward Bandwood. The casino, located on the edge of town, won the Burlington Post newspaper's award for best buffet in the city. A fantastic idea by Stella. I'm going to sing karaoke, then gorge on crab legs until I birth a bloated food baby.

When we get off the bus, I freeze. The flashing neon lights of the casino, the beeps and boops of the machines inside, the cars pulling up and people hurtling out, the fountain in front of us electronically wired for the water to shoot in the air timed to a classical song playing nearby – the overloading of my senses almost causes a panic attack. I can't move forward, forced to sit on the bus bench outside the casino. Just like on that street outside the hospital. The loud chaos and the random fear echoing in my brain. Thousands of lives depend on me. Stella sees my eyes darting around and grabs my hand.

"Hey, you've got this. It's going to be worse when we go in. Hey, don't look around. Focus on me. Don't hate yourself for losing control. I'm by your side, so there's no need to panic. You can handle this, I know you can."

A few deep breaths later, I nod. She squeezes my hand.

"We'll stay here until you get used to all the noise."

"Thank you, I'll be okay in a second."

"You aren't an anxious person; this is just a new emotion for you. In the meantime, can I ask you a personal question? It's about what happened recently."

"I guess so."

"Everyone likes you, did you know that? I bring this up because a few months ago, Hacker Plus hacked into everyone's police, hospital, and government personal files. She even found all of our school report cards. Without any of our permission or consent. When I found out, that was the biggest fight we ever had and I'm still furious at her. But because of her lack of personal boundaries, she brought up your mental illness history when we were searching for clues to find you these past couple of days. I've known for years, but I don't think many of the others knew about your depression. I think some of the Child Soldiers didn't believe her. Lady Metroplexer was certainly skeptical. Because I've seen you put on a façade so many times during meetings and parties – a Liza that's not the real Liza – and I really think you could get a lot of support from us if you would open up more. Am I the only person you've been honest with? You've known most of them for four or five years; why keep them at arm's length? You've skated around versions of this question before with me – please don't do that this time."

How am I supposed to answer that? Spiromaniac remains by far the most optimistic, positive person I've ever met, and how can I explain my own misguided self-expression to someone like that? Someone who's beautiful and amazing and generous and despite everything terrible going on around her or any bad choices she makes, that girl's faith in herself will never crack. No matter what.

"That's, well, that's a really hard question to answer, Stella. Let me try an analogy. You and I have both been on dates where the guy spends large portions of it going on about his terrible ex-girlfriends. I've stopped dates with men before, telling them there's no good that's going to come from this. You want to talk about your exes? Sure, go ahead, but tell me you've dated rocket scientists and astronauts and Miss America winners. Because if the two of us date, then that means I've joined the same ranks as those attractive, intelligent, fantastic women. This guy chose those winners and now he chose me. And I chose him, of course – it has to work both ways. But when a guy talks about his awful previous relationships, after a while I begin to judge him. I think, well, you're the one chose to date all these terrible people, doesn't that mean there's something wrong with you? I would never want to date this guy. That's why I don't want to open up. Ever. I'm that bad first date going on about my personal incurable misery, unable to be cheered up or convinced otherwise, and no one wants to be around that person. At a party, for instance, we get upset or full of dread when we see that person – we just want to have a good time and here comes this bummer. I'm just trying to do everyone a favor; everyone has their own problems to deal with."

She says nothing for a short while. We sit there together, watching the people laughing and stumbling as they walk around. She never lets go of my hand.

"Can I try?" she asks.

"What?"

"If you gave me an analogy, can I try one too? I want to counter your argument."

"Go ahead."

Her nose scrunches up and her eyebrows move closer together as she ponders her answer. She grips my hand tighter.

"Hold on, I think I can do a dating analogy also. Imagine you've been dating this guy for a while now. You've had your relationship ups and downs, but the two of you have a strong, devoted bond and you don't see yourself leaving this man anytime soon, or even ever. Then one day, he tells you about his own past tragedies or mistakes or whatever else. You might get angry at him for not telling you sooner. You might not believe his excuse that he was scared your feelings for him would change if you knew that about him. And sure, there's always the chance that your feelings do change about him, but the most likely scenario? That bond the two of you have isn't going to be broken by an admission like that. Because he didn't cheat on you or love you any less, he just has, as you put it, personal incurable miseries. You might even love him more because he trusted you with his biggest secret. The same way works with friendships. You might push away some of your buddies, but the odds are on your side, Liza."

That analogy came from the top of her head? That analogy was improvised? How? I have to practice my excuses daily in the shower — all sorts of analogies and comebacks and quips and anecdotes and subject changes. Well, not daily. I don't shower daily. But here's an excuse I have rehearsed.

"Stella, I don't have anywhere near the level of self-esteem to believe that kind of thinking. I'm trying, I promise. I'm trying. Just be patient with me. Very patient. Like until we're elderly and have nurses spoon-feeding us. And I'm going to murder Hacker Plus when I see her again. But I like karaoke quite a lot and I adore you. I adore everything about you. I've heard Bandwood Casino has an Elvis impersonator that can marry you and me."

She proudly swats my hand away.

"In your dreams. I only date people who've dated rocket scientists and astronauts and Miss America winners. Talk to me again once you've built up that roster, my love."

I laugh – for the first time in days. I'm back to normal for good or for bad. We stroll into the casino, her walk converting into a skip by the time we pass the slot machines. Tonight will be delightful. And I'm going to rock "Criminal" by Fiona Apple.

Stella goes to the karaoke counter, asking for the room with the loudest microphones. No, I change my mind. I'll start with Fiona Apple's "Shadowboxer." You know what? I'll do both. Well, if Stella is paying, she should get first pick.

"What song are you going to sing first, Stella?"

She gives the man a few twenty dollar bills.

"Me? What's that one song from Hoobastank? The famous one. The one you bought that t-shirt at the mall that one time."

Another reason I love her.

This night will be perfect. Everything will go right, just like the—

The casino's lights flicker off and then back on again. We hear what sounds like gunfire close by. The casino patrons pour out in a stampeding panic. Stella and I stand back-to-back, frantically looking around for the source of the noise. She pulls out her mask from her pocket and puts it on. People scream as they run past us. The slot machines continue to blast noise. There's a techno song blaring around us. We can't pinpoint anything over all this racket. If we have to fight, we'll be fighting deaf.

89

A hiss can be barely perceived above us before a female voice booms from the loudspeaker.

"I heard the good news, Miss Nucleus. What a wonderful blessing! I decided I couldn't leave town just yet, not when we can conclude our unfinished business!"

The accent sounds familiar. She repeats my name several times, drawing out each syllable. A definite cackle.

"Time to die! Just like that poor woman at the bank!"

Oh God. Oh no.

I know that voice. Desperado.

5

Spiromaniac immediately shoves me to the floor. A bullet rips through the muscle of her shoulder, and reflexively, she points to where the bullet came from. Spiro drops to the ground as both she and Desperado share a scream of pain.

"She has a sniper rifle!" I shout. "What's our plan? What the hell are we supposed to do?"

"Our plan? We need to leave!"

The two of us scurry to the side of a slot machine, hoping the machine's cover will buy us a few extra seconds. Desperado will recover soon and begin shooting again. Her voice reverberates from the speaker.

"Spiromaniac! Damn you! Well, I brought friends too. Boys, surround and kill them. I'll give $10,000 to whoever kills them!"

Okay, this is bad. Really bad. What's our situation? The casino is loud as hell, and we won't be able to hear anyone sneak up on us. We're stuck a good two hundred feet from the exit, but the last twenty feet is entirely open space and we'll be slaughtered before we can make it out. Desperado's sniper bullet came from the second floor balcony, and we don't know how many henchmen she brought with her. We're trapped.

"We'll never make it out alive if we just run straight for the exit," I decide. "We'll have to circle our way around the casino and pray we don't get shot."

"I agree," Spiro replies. "Hopefully, Desperado won't shoot

her men and we can use that to our advantage."

"Hopefully."

"Stay behind me."

We see the first man turn the corner – a suit and tie. That usually means professionals. And a pistol. Spiromaniac tackles him before he notices us, and he begins to struggle with her. I look for a weapon to help.

The man shoves Spiro off, and he fiddles for his pistol. I pound him with a stool. Spiro hits him with a jab and he goes down. She throws me his gun. I help her up, but not before we hear a gunshot from above us and Spiro's cheek splits open. Blood coats the left side of her face.

"Dammit! It's fine; it just nicked me. Desperado's back."

She reflects the wound back at the supervillain. We scatter just in time for another sniper rifle bullet to shatter the closest slot machine. A man approaches from the left, but he leaps back after I fire a few wild shots in his direction. Spiromaniac yanks my arm.

"Give me the gun!"

She snatches it out of my hand, firing the last two bullets – direct hits in the man's knees. He drops in pain, and I scramble toward him to seize his pistol. If we stay still for too long, we're dead. If the men surround us, we're dead.

Too late. A second guy turns the corner within striking distance.

Spiro smacks him in the wrist, knocking his firearm away. He pulls out a knife. I shoot a few more bullets in Desperado's probable direction on the balcony, praying I delay her from taking a shot. As long as Desperado doesn't interfere, Spiro will be fine. Because that woman can fight. She dodges, counters, and every three swipes or so, she purposely takes the knife swipe – always getting sliced somewhere minor and non-vital before throwing the wound back at her attacker. He flinches each time, leaving him defenseless and open for a solid face punch or kick to the abdomen. When the guy grabs her shirt and pulls her in close, she retaliates with a vicious headbutt

— a fight move I thought was only used by drunken soccer hooligans. The defeated henchman hits the ground hard. No one has a higher pain tolerance than Spiromaniac. She bolts in my direction, barely dodging another shot from Desperado's rifle. Bonnie must have figured out I don't know where she is.

We still have halfway to go before we hit the exit of the casino. Desperado's voice comes over the speaker.

"Men, back off. Enough of this. Switching things up."

We reach the end of the slot machines. Just before we launch ourselves toward the cover of the poker tables, the table closest to us explodes in our direction, pouring scraps of metal and wood onto us.

Bonnie brought grenades.

We pause, waiting for the flash of pain indicating we're hurt. Nothing. At least nothing serious. The two of us push the remains of the poker table off of us.

I stand up. Let's try a non-violent approach.

"Bonnie, you know if you kill me, the nuke goes off, right?"

"Of course I do," her voice resounds back.

"At least fifty thousand people will die, and thousands more will be injured. And I know damn well that Freedom doesn't want me dead yet. You're stupid enough to willingly defy that man, Bon?"

She bursts into laughter.

"I don't care about Burlington. I don't care about America. I don't care about Freedom. I spent my entire childhood working my ass off for your country's glory and how does the Land of the Free and the Home of the Brave repay me? They deport my family! They deport me! I hope you and this city rot!"

Spiromaniac yanks me to the floor, Desperado's bullet barely missing me. We continue our long, covered crawl beneath several tables when Spiromaniac's eyes go wide.

"I got it. See the stairs to our left? The bullets have come from somewhere in that direction. Desperado won't be far from those. I'm going for the stairs."

Another explosion sends poker tables arcing through the air

in neon swirls.

"Liza, once I get to Bonnie, you run for the stairs after me. I'll need your help; I can't take her alone. Not with these injuries. No time to argue or explain again. I'm going now."

I'm still not entirely sure what she meant, but Spiro breaks into a sprint anyway, using the wreckage around us to conceal her location. But Desperado will see her coming up the stairs. I'll have to distract her. So I leap up.

"I'm right here, Bon!"

Two men charge from my right. I forgot about the henchmen. I fire the remaining bullets in the gun, missing them completely before throwing the weapon in their direction. Another miss. The first guy slams into me, sending us both to the ground. The two large men think they can take a tiny girl in a fistfight. Let's prove them wrong. Probably. Like fifty-fifty. Focus your rifle scope on me, Bonnie.

The second man reaches me quickly enough to pin down one of my arms, but I jab the fingers from my free hand into his eyes. As he adjusts to his temporary blindness, I shove my hand in his mouth and pull down hard on his jaw, giving me a chance to land a quick elbow to his nose. But before I can celebrate my badassery, I catch a punch in the face from the first guy. The agonizing pain kicks in and my vision goes blurry, but my flailing (and clawing) momentarily scatters both of the attackers. I scramble back to my feet. I still don't understand pain. How does my face feel both sore and numb at the same time? Do people ever get used to be punched in the face? Spiro gets punched in the face several times a week and she's never too bothered by it. Maybe it's a skill someone can learn?

I hear Desperado shout. Spiromaniac must have caught up to her. I need to hurry – I doubt Spiro could take Bonnie even if Spiro wasn't injured. But first, I need to end my own fight.

The fiercest jab I've ever thrown smacks the second guy in his already broken nose. The remaining dude jumps at me, but I'm a small target and he aims too high. I kick his ribs until he begs me to stop. My fists hurt like hell. Why are my knuckles bleeding? My feet ache. Like the same ache as if I just finished running a marathon (or in my un-athletic case, maybe several blocks). Seriously, I miss being invincible sometimes. If you ever have to fight, being invincible rocks. I highly recommend it.

I sprint up the stairs to the balcony just in time to see Spiromaniac take a kick to the chest. She topples back, pounding her head against the wall. Desperado spots me. Her shiver-inducing chuckle sucks away any confidence I thought I had collected so far during this battle.

"Miss Nucleus, I didn't want to take any chances. I knew this would be my only chance to kill you, so I called in a favor and brought a friend." She pulls a radio off her belt. "Hey, buddy. Can you join us now? You can eat these horrible girls if you want."

A roar shakes the building and every inch of my body.

"I've learned if you show the stupid monsters a little kindness, they'll do anything you ask," Bonnie announces. "Remember Bonecrusher? No, wait, sorry, Bonesnapper. You remember him, right? No, not him, it's genderless. It, not him."

Each stair rumbles as the monster climbs.

Bonesnapper. A two-thousand pound creature with ungodly super strength and a body stacked with unbreakable plates. Think of a Stegosaurus if the dinosaur's plates covered its entire body. And the Stegosaurus walked on two legs with two arms. And had the muscles to pass off as a Mr. Universe contestant battling a horrible skin conditions.

Give me back my invincibility and throw in another six or seven random powers and I still don't stand a chance. This monster regularly fights Metroplexer to a standstill. Metroplexer, a man who can lift a small office building with nary a grunt or a strain, has to punch Bonesnapper three or four times before it even begins to show signs of slowing down.

No one knows where Bonesnapper came from, whether it used to be a person or a botched demon summoning or a mutated armadillo. One day, the monster just showed up in Burlington and wiped out a quarter of our shopping district before Metroplexer managed to throw it in the ocean. Around once a year, the creature makes its way back to the city from whatever forest or swamp or tundra or Arctic hellhole it was tossed into to rampage Burlington once again. Also, where is Metroplexer? Or his kids? When the monstrosity shows up within city limits, an emergency call always goes out. There better be another giant monster crisis across town they're dealing with.

I can smell Bonesnapper before I turn around. Its rancid breath sinks into my every pore. The balcony begins to crumble with each step it takes. Desperado barks behind me.

"Bonesnapper, kill the smaller one!"

Spiromaniac's voice screeches behind Desperado.

"Liza, run! Run!"

I don't even get to move before its giant fist backhands me, sending me flying over the balcony. I land onto a blackjack table, and it collapses inward from the force of my landing. My world spins. My hearing fades into a buzz. Dust stings my eyes. I roll off, slowly and clumsily picking myself up. My legs aren't broken. My arms aren't broken. Thank God. My ribs might be though – I heard a nasty crack in my chest when the creature slapped me.

Bonesnapper lands a few tables over; its roar once more shaking the foundation of the casino. I can't outrun this thing. I can't fight this thing. Another strike like that will likely separate the top half of my torso from my bottom half. I run regardless.

It chases after me, and as I reach the wall of the casino, I leap to my left in a hopeful fake out. Effortlessly, the monster bursts through the wall. Looking outside and realizing my mistake, I dash after the monster.

Police cars have swarmed the outside of the building, lights blaring and sirens blasting in the darkness. This is bad. Giant monsters tend not to react well to sensory overload. Its howl causes the remainder of the loose casino wall to collapse.

"Don't shoot! Don't shoot it!" I scream.

Bullets fly from all directions. I plunge to the ground. And, of course, the bullets harmlessly bounce off Bonesnapper. But they do make it angry. I tried to warn them. If Bonesnapper charges the crowd, potentially hundreds of people will die. So I have to do something stupid.

I crawl and grab a loose brick from the wall's destruction. The firing slows, as only the most brazen police officers still believe bullets can harm the monster. I chuck the brick at Bonesnapper's head.

"Hey! You! It's me you want, right? I'm over here!"

Thankfully, it glances my way. I slowly back up, making sure it'll follow me. I have a plan. A terrible plan, but a plan nonetheless. I grab a broken steel rod, a casualty of the monster's momentum, and as soon as Bonesnapper begins lumbering after me, I race back inside.

I wish you could see the speed with which I leap over the shattered remains of a once decent casino. The faster I run, the faster the monster follows. Luckily – and I use that word loosely – Bonesnapper stops to sloppily throw a baccarat table at me, the only reason I'm not turned into paste at the monster's feet. As we reach the midpoint – where Spiromaniac and I first stood when the casino fell into chaos, I turn to face my opponent.

"Are you sure we can't settle this over a game of Texas Hold 'Em? I'll teach you the rules."

I get one chance. This is the scariest moment of my life. I have to slide between his legs. Action movie stars do this all the time. I stuff my steel rod through the right side of my belt.

Bonesnapper vaults toward me, reaching down to grab me. I slide – well, actually more of a sort of ducked, desperate dive – under his legs. I miss, my shoulder slamming into its shin, causing me to twirl around. But I'm on the other side. No doubt severely bruised, but the adrenaline numbs most of the pain. Using the extremely short window I created, I grab onto the plates covering the monster's lower back.

So a while back, the Child Soldiers and I fought a muscled moron named Steroidite – his actual supervillain name and not something I made up. Dude bragged he could easily deadlift 700 pounds. As he flexed, muscles came out of muscles that came out of more muscles. And Lady Metroplexer hit him so hard in the stomach that he crapped his pants – also something I didn't make up. We took him to prison with his pants full of shame poo, and there we learned an amazing fact: his arms and torso were so big that he couldn't actually reach down to wipe his own ass. We looked this up on the Internet, and it turns out that some of the largest, steroid-iest bodybuilders have this same problem. Google it yourself. And thus that's why most superheroes opt for the gymnast physique. And my entire Bonesnapper plan relies on this bodybuilding fact. This disgusting, horrific fact. I cling onto the plates on his back as the creature frantically tries to throw me off. The smell emanating from this part of Bonesnapper proves that I've got the right idea.

Using all my upper body strength for a single pull-up, I begin to scale the monster. Thankfully, four years ago I went rock climbing.

Once I snatch onto the neck plate, Bonesnapper manages to snag my left leg with his gigantic hand – and with a single squeeze shatters every bone below my thigh. I almost pass out from the pain. Tibias are useless anyway, I lie to myself. Spiro has survived far worse and I can too. As the monster lets go of my leg, changing tactics to crush my other leg, I shift over to the opposite side. I can barely see through the tears pouring down my face.

With a final pull, I throw my left arm around Bonesnapper's neck. I only get one chance – I'm now very much vulnerable. More vulnerable. I yank the steel rod from my belt.

I figure not every part of the monster is indestructible, right? There must be a weakness somewhere. If I'm wrong, I'm dead. And I want my epitaph to read, "Well, at least she tried."

Using the last of my strength, I shove the sharpened steel rod into Bonesnapper's eye. And in the greatest thrill of my life, the rod pierces it. I push harder. Bonesnapper flails, its screams of anguish rattling every bone, muscle, and organ in my body. The steel rod goes all the way into the socket. The monster snatches my left arm – breaking all those bones too – throwing me off his body and onto the floor nearby. But too late. I stabbed your brain, you bastard. And if you're not a bastard and Mama Bonesnapper tries to avenge your death in a Grendel's mother-type situation, I'll stab her brain too.

Bonesnapper drops to its knees, its body writhing and wriggling. Finally, it collapses. Lifeless. Most likely. It's not like I can examine the body – I'm stuck lying on the floor, the left side of my body a mangled mess. As I slowly sprawl onto my back, I spot Spiromaniac and Desperado still on the balcony.

Spiromaniac can't take Desperado in a fistfight. The girl can't reflect the blows back as quickly as Desperado strikes. When a strong kick knocks Stella against the back wall, I see Bonnie take out her pistol. I can't do anything. I can't help her. I'm useless.

No, not useless.

"Hey Desperado, dodge this!" I shout my bluff.

But Desperado looks back for a brief moment to check. And all Spiromaniac ever needs is a brief moment. In what I can only assume is a last ditch desperate gamble, she pushes off the wall and tackles Desperado, sending both of them off the balcony. The two twist in midair. Desperado hits the ground first, luck on both Spiro's and my side today.

Spiro – I don't know exactly how much cushioning Desperado provided – climbs off the supervillain, notices me, and begins a slow wiggle in my direction. Bonnie lies motionless, either unconscious or dead. I'm hoping for dead.

Spiromaniac reaches me after a minute or two, placing her head next to mine. Her previously bright clothes drenched deeply in maroon. Sputtering blood from her mouth as she speaks, a weak smile sprouts from her face.

"Well, that sucked."

I try to laugh, but I end up in a coughing fit instead.

"We won, Stella."

"Feels good, doesn't it?"

We say nothing for a few moments, and I nudge her to make sure she didn't pass out. She groans and then raises her least injured hand, holding it over my forehead.

"I have a secret power, Liza. Shhh, don't tell anyone."

She pauses to wipe the blood dripping down my forehead first. And then a warmth rushes over me. Not a warmth – euphoria.

"I can heal others, you know. Don't tell anyone. Bad guys will want to use—"

Her voice trails off. I nudge her again. Her forearm knocks away my hand, her groans interrupted by a cough.

"Let me nap. I'll be fine in the morning. I got most of your injuries."

So the two of us lie there together. The police storm the building as Spiromaniac nestles her head against my neck. Metroplexer leads the cops, floating above us. His eyes are locked on Bonesnapper's corpse. About time you got here.

––––––

"Liza Lewis, the superhero known as Miss Nucleus, and Sarah Lopez, an alias found on a fake identification card in the belongings of the superhero Spiromaniac, know the official Burlington Police Department stance on the use of citizens' actions in defending others from criminal behavior. They know they should have waited for police intervention. They know that what they did could have possibly endangered lives. They know that their actions could have had disastrous consequences by not following proper police protocol. But with only minor civilian injures, the apprehension of Bonnie Wang – currently on the FBI's Ten Most Wanted Fugitives list – and the death of the creature known as Bonesnapper, the police department agrees that Miss Lewis' and Miss Lopez's actions were not executed with reckless behavior or malicious intent."

Captain Hanson stops the recording.

"Liza, tell me what the hell is going on. I see a cut on your face. How is that possible? Why is Spiromaniac sleeping on my couch? She looks like hell – I pulled a lot of strings to keep you both out of the hospital and I demand some answers. Answers I deserve."

Spiromaniac moans a bit before rolling over. A single snore ensures us that she's still asleep. Captain Hanson's jacket acts as her makeshift blanket.

"We don't need the hospital and you know that. The hospital would have done DNA tests to figure out Spiromaniac's real name before a moronic intern unintentionally posts it on social media and a supervillain blows up her family. And the only supervillain in my entire rogues' gallery is currently in the hospital with a broken back and shattered pelvis. I hope she's paralyzed."

He angrily shuts me up. Then once again – with far less patience this time – he asks me what the hell is going on. I tell him everything. Spiromaniac told us to only go to the policemen that we can trust. The incorruptible. The ones who don't need bribe money. The ones who still cling onto the idealistic, simplistic view of justice. And Captain Hanson is one of those. He has never been investigated by internal affairs for anything unlawful. His wife is the most successful, expensive divorce attorney in the entire city. This man takes two weeks' vacation every year just to pour over cold cases in hopes of new leads. He's a good person whose only flaw is a mustache that smells like it was soaked in an ashtray over the weekend. And thus I tell him everything.

Not surprisingly, he needs a few minutes to process all this new, frightening information. Every ten or twenty seconds, he asks me to clarify something I said. Yes, Freedom is behind this. Yes, there's a new drug that takes away superhuman powers. No, I'm not accepting any police protection. No, refusing police protection doesn't endanger the city's safety. The last thing I need is an entourage. Dude, half the supervillains in this city are bulletproof anyway, and it's not as if any of your officers would go full Secret Service and jump in front of a bullet for me. Yes, Spiro will be fine by tomorrow or the day after. She's the perfect bodyguard. I once saw her arm get chopped off with a buzzsaw during a brawl in Home Depot – she picked up her arm, shoved it in her stump, and had Featherblade cauterize the wound with a blowtorch to stop the bleeding. Spiromaniac slept twelve hours and played ping-pong with that same arm the next afternoon. That woman's unflappable and won't attract attention like the Adonis children of Metroplexer would hovering a foot or two above the ground as we walk down the street.

Then he asks the questions I've been dreading – just because I know there's no way to answer this question without an argument.

"How come you haven't reported any of this to the police? Do you realize how many lives you've endangered? We have two thousand police officers employed by the city. Two thousand men and women could have been looking for the bomb. Instead, your thirty superhero pals have been the only people looking? What the hell is wrong with you? We have the manpower that you don't."

Solid argument. Hard to argue with. But I will.

"To start, there are only twenty-four superheroes in this city. Twenty in the Child Soldiers and four in the Burlington Safety—"

He slams his hands on the table, his face growing bright red as he suppresses the urge to yell at me or whatever else would attract a horde of police officers with their faces planted against the outside of his window.

"Captain, we can't tell anybody. Nobody. We both know that Freedom has paid off police officers in the department to be his eyes and ears. Both times Freedom talked to me, he mentions this stupid game he's playing with Metroplexer. I can imagine anything that ruins his game, like say, two thousand police officers looking for a bomb, will only result in a premature explosion. And you can't even tell the officers you trust. They'll want to get their families out of town. Those family members will contact their own relatives and friends to escape. Someone will inevitably tell the media – maybe even with the misguided logic of trying to save as many people as possible. But the moment this gets leaked, the city's destroyed. Ruined. Mass evacuations will bring this city to a standstill. Riots, looting, arson, murder, really anything any normal person would do when they become trapped in a city where a nuclear weapon can go off at any time. Burlington instantly becomes a ruined young adult fantasy novel-esque dystopia."

He says nothing, leaning back in his chair. Captain Hanson mumbles to himself about trying to quit smoking before lighting up another cigarette in his office. I continue my plea.

"Every superhero is taking an eight-hour shift each day following leads, looking for clues, and searching locations. If one of us has to go to school or a job during the day, he or she works the night shift. Even all four in the BSO with their careers and stable marriages take to the streets every evening, and they normally go to bed as soon as the sun begins to set. Despite the massive manpower of the police force, supervillain schemes are superheroes' specialty. And this is a supervillain scheme – we have the resources, the knowledge, and the ability to smudge the laws if we need to take more drastic action. We'll find the bomb. But if the police get involved then we're guaranteed a disaster with a minimum fifty thousand dead, many more injured or irradiated."

The captain grinds out his cigarette in the ashtray on his desk – a cigarette smoked abnormally quickly – and pulls another from his pack.

"The nuke trigger is in your brain?"

"Yes, I told you that."

He takes a few puffs before finally speaking. He never makes eye contact.

"Leave my office. Don't you dare drink. If within this next week I find out that you've been drinking, you'll permanently lose my support and I'll use the full police force to find the bomb. Do we have an understanding?"

"Yes, sir."

"Wake up Spiromaniac and get out of my office."

6

Audio Transcript for September 13th, 11:00 AM

Licensed Therapist: Dr. Mel Johnson

Patient: Liza Lewis

JOHNSON: You reek of alcohol.

LEWIS: That's not true. I spritzed my clothes with the air freshener in your bathroom. By the way, honeysuckle nectar is not a real scent.

JOHNSON: Yesterday, the news stations applauded you and Stella. You two successfully defeated two incredibly dangerous supervillains with zero civilian casualties. I saw your victory with my own eyes, and I can't overstate how impressed I am with both of you. Yet you told me you use alcohol to numb pain. So why are you drunk?

LEWIS: I'm not drunk. I'm overly buzzed.

JOHNSON: Did the two of you celebrate your victory last night?

LEWIS: No way. She slept nine hours, and I still have some cuts and bruises leftover after she healed all my internal booboos with her secret magic healing powers. I woke her up an hour ago. She's reading a magazine in your lobby.

JOHNSON: I didn't know she could heal others. Then why are you drunk?

LEWIS: Oh, keep that healing thing a secret. My bad. Look, I'm no BSO member like you. You guys handle the stuff that threatens the whole city or state or country or whatever. My normal bad guys are bank robbers and ambitious thugs and once I fought a ninja. All my supervillain fights are because I happened to be in the area, not because the city shone a spotlight in the sky of a giant whiskey bottle. And now I'm responsible for tons of lives. It's scary and alcohol is my coping juice. Also, now I can be hurt – which holy crap, do normal people get hurt all the time? Because I now totally get the difference between my depression and Bonesnapper snapping all the bones in my leg.

JOHNSON: Okay, let's build on that. What is the difference between your emotional pain and your physical pain?

LEWIS: Well, the suffering is different. I mean, both make me cry and scream and both would have me prefer to just stay in bed forever. But, and I know I must be biased, I'm sort of okay with physical pain. It's sort of a triumph, you know? Idealistically, we superheroes are supposed to suffer so innocent people don't. That's why we fight the toughest bad guys, right? People and monsters the police can't handle. And so, well, okay. Look, I mean, this stuff. When we do this. Okay, I lost my thought process.

JOHNSON: Because you're drunk.

LEWIS: A bit impaired.

JOHNSON: What's the difference between physical and emotional pain to you?

LEWIS: I can be proud of physical pain. Like a boxer who receives a bunch of punches before knocking out his opponent. Because there's a pride in standing up for yourself and giving it your all. But all that emotional (bleep)? Crying on the carpet in my living room isn't giving it my all. And unlike fighting supervillains, I can't fight the depression. I've never been able to. My thoughts just become a blender mixed with self-loathing, worthlessness, regret over bad life decisions, and the main ingredient: an overwhelming desire to jump in front of a train or hang myself off a stairwell or take three bottles of sleeping pills. And now I can. And now I also can't.

JOHNSON: Liza, you come to me every week. I'm your therapist. Just the fact that you show up on my couch – even though I know full well you'd prefer not to – means that you're fighting that depression. Mental illness may not be curable, but the proper medicine and treatment will allow you to always be able to stand up however hard the depression hits you. You'll stagger. You'll need help. But you can always keep on fighting.

LEWIS: But I don't want to fight! I've never wanted to fight!

JOHNSON: I think that choice has been made for you.

LEWIS: Don't you get it? How much do I have to accomplish before I stop hating myself? Do I need to save the city from nuclear annihilation? Punch Freedom in the penis? Make a bajillion trillion friends who will love me unconditionally? Find true love and have my husband move me out of my flea-infested dungeon of my apartment and into his magic unicorn castle? What's the end game here? What do I have to do to like myself? Because I don't know. I already read the self-help books you recommended. Nothing, man. Tell me the solution. Please. I beg you. I pay you to tell me. Please. And I need a tissue or I'm going to blow snot and tears all over your sofa. I think I need to throw up.

JOHNSON: Take a tissue. You're currently in pain, but it's not forever.

LEWIS: (bleep) you.

JOHNSON: That's uncalled for. You will eventually feel better. You can give yourself permission to feel okay. Solutions are possible. But currently? Saving the city from a nuclear attack certainly wouldn't hurt. After that, we can move on to – as you said – punching Freedom in the penis and finding true love. But let's start with the suitcase nuke. One problem at a time. Please don't throw up on the couch. Lean over the trash can, please.

LEWIS: Life is unfair.

JOHNSON: Very much so.

LEWIS: Okay. Okay okay okay okay. I'll throw up in your trash can. But I want to apologize. I mean it. Not just because I'm drunk. Don't you tell me to lay off the booze. I already said I'm sorry for the booze. This is something else. I'm going to be honest with you.

JOHNSON: Liza, I've never thought you were lying.

LEWIS: I think my depression manifests itself equally through both crying and anger. I think I lash out at those I'm jealous of. Which I'm slowly beginning to realize might be everybody.

JOHNSON: You know as well as I do that you have many endearing qualities– Oh, okay, aim for the trash can. Don't apologize, I'll clean the carpet. No, don't use that towel. I'll have my secretary get the disinfectant. Liza, I think we've had a long enough session for today. I'll only charge you half-price. Remember what I told you: your current goal is to find that bomb. Because that will make you feel better about yourself. Saving the city always makes me feel better about myself. Tell Stella I say hello. Good luck. I'll see you next week.

———

"Liza. I can definitely smell it on you. You were sober when I woke up. You never left my sight except for twenty minutes before we left so I could use the bathroom and take a shower. Liza, in those twenty minutes, how much did you drink?"

Stella and I are standing on the sidewalk outside Metroplexer's office. She's not happy with me.

"I only had like two shots. No, wait, two shots and a beer. Okay, I see that look in your eyes. Three shots and a beer. Stop looking at me like that. Three shots, a beer, and another beer I didn't get time to finish because I heard you coming out of the bedroom. But that's it. And you can only smell the alcohol on me because I spilled a beer on my shirt while I was trying to pour the rest of it down the drain."

"So what are we supposed to do now?"

"Lunch?"

"That's not what I meant!"

Spiromaniac has seen me drunk at night dozens of times, but never when the sun is shining. Never before noon. Nowadays, I'd pound coffee as a substitute for a morning buzz, but my nerves are a bit more on edge lately. Plus, I had to stop a robbery at the last coffee shop I visited.

"I'll make it up to you. I apologize," I promise.

"How?"

"I have a flask in my back pocket. Full and untouched. Do you want it?"

She pauses.

"Are you kidding me? Are you an alcoholic?"

"I'm not an alcoholic. I'm a drunk."

"Can I be completely honest with you?"

"That seems to be the theme of the morning."

"I don't know what to do anymore," she sighs. "I know it might be a bit disingenuous of us because I and the rest of the Child Soldiers occasionally drink as well, but even with all your good qualities, I know the Child Soldiers unfairly view you as unreliable. Because of the alcohol problem. After what happened six months ago, we figured you'd be working extra hard and be extra responsible to make up for your mistake. But you didn't. The opposite happened. Listen, we're definitely all your friends no matter what, but don't you think if you gave up the booze and worked more on repairing your reputation that you…"

I'm too drunk to pay attention to her lecture anymore. My mind drifts to those high school football trophies Metroplexer has in his office. I think about those trophies every time I see him. I knew he used to be a big deal based on some of my vindictive past research, but how could he possibly be proud of those? He couldn't not cheat with his superpowers, right? Did he have to fake a fall every time he got tackled? The linebacker may as well tackle a wall. Metroplexer could have run a 40-yard dash in the time it takes for the coach to blink. Metroplexer should have been on the drama team instead for the amount of acting he must have done to play high school football.

"Dammit, Liza, why won't you answer me? I love you so much and I don't like you like this!"

She grabs my forearm and drags me closer to her. I rest my chin on her shoulder and grip my arms around her torso. My alcohol-stained breath smolders along the side of her cheek as I whisper into her ear.

"Can we kiss?"

An exasperated scream comes from Stella's mouth. She yells at me for not taking a real problem seriously. Eventually, like in all arguments against an unwilling party, Stella's arguments – rooted in emotional well-being – fade into nothingness, the realization that she's wasting her time. The quiver in her voice recedes.

"Can you just promise me that you'll at least work on gradually drinking less over the next few months?"

"Yes ma'am."

"Great. Fantastic."

I hold my hand out in a gesture of diplomacy. Reluctantly, she shakes it. A firm, proud handshake.

"I'll drop the subject, Liza, but this is not the end of our discussion. Hold on, let me take some deep breaths. Okay, there. How about The Fire Pit for lunch? I hear they put fried eggs on their burgers and I want to try that."

"Awesome. Me too."

We walk (I stumble) to the restaurant. I wait for her to get a few steps ahead of me each time before I take a quick swig of my flask. Let the other superheroes think I'm unreliable – my need to not hate myself for a few nauseous hours takes precedence. But I'm sorry for the way I treat you, Stella. Forgive me.

―――――

At lunch, Stella reveals our latest developments regarding the nuke hunt. No one knows where it is still. So there really aren't any developments. All the obvious spots have been thoroughly searched. Most associates with a previous connection to Freedom have been interrogated. Morale is low, and since the BSO is taking the night shift today, the Child Soldiers decided to take an evening off for sanity's sake.

In a frustrated hypocrisy for Stella – a hypocrisy she feels incredibly guilty about – the two of us are off tonight to get blitzed. Sure, she'll spend most of the night trying to avoid me, but that woman still has to go home with me. Both of us very drunk. While we eat, she desperately explains to me the difference between drinking at night in social settings and drinking during the morning at home.

We arrive at the party around ten. Kid Metroplexer has sent me numerous texts every hour or so telling me how excited he is to see me – especially to make sure I'm okay after that battle against Desperado and Bonesnapper – and that he wants to hug me and tell me how amazing I am with what is going on. And, also, if I could pick up some alcohol, please. He wants everyone to applaud us when I show up to celebrate our victory. But if I could bring a bottle of vodka and maybe two or three cases of beer that would also be awesome. But mainly to see me. And honestly, I'm excited to go to this party. And not just to avoid the negative stigma society puts on me getting plastered alone in my apartment while I watch reruns of *Seinfeld*.

While Spiro self-righteously proclaims that none of these superheroes trust me to fight alongside them – almost certainly both true and a genuine plea for me to wait to start drinking at least until the sun goes down – the capture of Desperado and the death of Bonesnapper must have repaired some of the damage to my reputation, because for the first time I've ever been to one of these parties, I'm mobbed immediately as I arrive. Bonnie Wang irritated us for years, and if she broke her back like the rumors say, our long national annoyance is over. And as for Bonesnapper? If we were given a choice to either fight Bonesnapper or pee our pants on live TV while standing next to our parents, our deepest childhood crush, and the person we lost our virginity to, every single one of us would pick the latter. But tonight, when my coworkers raise a beer to my honor, I feel like an actual superhero – regardless that I'm currently not. At least, not with the Liberate still inside me.

Then we party.

Missile and Belial play Featherblade and Icarus in darts. About twenty minutes in, Featherblade nails a bullseye. In retaliation,

Belial throws a handful of darts at her and the party halts abruptly to pull the two off each other. Icarus threatens Belial's dog and nothing can then stop the bloodshed from staining War Soul's new couch. The four of them get thrown out of the party before midnight. But when they sneak back in thirty minutes later, we're all too drunk at that point to care. I did hear the next day that Missile and Belial siphoned fuel out of Featherblade and Icarus' jetpacks.

After some flirty banter between Globe and Bowhunter, the archer brags about his wrestling prowess at school. Instead of Globe complimenting his muscles or athleticism like he expected, she calls his bluff. Loudly and in front of everyone. So in order for Bowhunter to save face and also have a legitimate excuse to grab her inappropriately, the two move the chairs and tables out of the way to wrestle. Globe has six arms so Bowhunter gets destroyed, but halfway through the party, no one knows where the two of them went. So, success, I guess?

Kid Metroplexer talks quietly to Missile after the dart incident. I can spot his usual seduction stance from across the room – he leans back against the wall, one arm nestling his low-calorie vodka martini while his other arm lies to the side. His knees are slightly bent to look subtly nonchalant. You can see his eyes make contact with Missile's for just the briefest time before he drops his gaze – a false humbleness. He looks like a model in any teen magazine and he knows it. Not surprisingly, Missile eats it up. Too bad Grant doesn't know that Missile's last boyfriend broke up with her when she clawed him across the face for refusing to clap after she sang along to a song on the car radio.

Forestchild, like always, remains a wallflower. The former feral child still doesn't understand fashion and while we keep reminding him that asking other fifteen year olds on the Internet for clothing advice won't lead anywhere great, his Hawaiian shirt and fedora combo only serves to further socially isolate him. I told him once that fedoras are only for 1920s bootleggers and 1940s newspaper reporters, but he hasn't taken my advice. Once every few months, I drunkenly text him that baseball caps and t-shirts never go out of fashion. He never responds.

Bamboo, Firestarter, Mentalmind, the Amazing Punchfist, and Friendleader play cards in one of the bedrooms. Bamboo keeps suggesting strip poker but Friendleader keeps shutting him up. It's not tough to figure out why – Bamboo looks like a tanned sculpted marble statue with his shirt off and a nude Friendleader can best be described as furry and emaciated. But the fun of competition wears off quickly as Mentalmind, being the genius she is, dominates every game they play. She even destroys them in Uno, and that game's like 80% luck.

In the kitchen, Hacker Plus, Lady Metroplexer, and Spiromaniac swap stories about other people at the party. I'd join them, but I think Stella would like a few hours not forcibly attached to my side. Lady Metroplexer and Spiromaniac are impossible not to like, and when you add Hacker Plus' tendency to make inappropriate comments about those not listening, the three of them giggle for most of the night. Then Hacker Plus throws up on Lady Metroplexer which stops the laughter cold.

Fisherwoman sent a text to Spiro a few hours ago, telling her that she couldn't make it. Fisherwoman came upon a wounded walrus somewhere near the Arctic Ocean and she's nursing it back to health. The Arctic Ocean is over fifteen hundred miles from Burlington. I have no idea how she got there.

Fearboy doesn't get invited to parties.

And my role in this party slowly becomes defined. I'd be an odd number for the darts game. I'm not about to wrestle anyone. Kid Metroplexer'll get pissed if I interrupt his attempt to get laid. I know that if I play cards, there's a good chance in my generously impaired mood that I'll take my shirt off within the first hand or two of strip poker whether I lose or not. Because this has happened twice before. So with everyone else preoccupied, that leaves me giving fashion pointers to Forestchild, which I'd rather spend the night having Missile claw me across the face.

But one glance around the room, while I nurse my second beer (and one previous martini, shot of tequila, and whatever Firestarter used to make her "punch"), I realize I have only one other person to talk to. A person who approaches me with almost superhumanly speed. A person who traps me as I exit the bathroom so I can't escape our conversation. A person who smells like a football coach after being doused with a Gatorade cooler filled with only cologne and rum. A person who steps into his metaphorical Thunderdome for the toughest battle of his entire nineteen year life: to seduce me.

War Soul saunters up wearing an uncomfortably tight polo shirt – I can count his individual abs through the fabric – and jeans so constricting that they leave nothing to the imagination. I'm not great at math; I'm going to guess somewhere between three and nine inches.

"Hey, Liza. How are you doing? I heard about Bonesnapper. You're amazing. I knew you had it in you. I'm into tough love, you know? Your beer looks empty. How about I get another one for you? I found this great craft beer brewed in the Appalachian Mountains that I think you'll love. And then we'll talk. How's that sound?"

"Hey, Nick. How're you doing? Remember a few days ago when you punched me twice in the face?"

His face wrinkles and he takes a step back. Women don't talk to him like that. Women fawn over him. Women race to be the first to listen to his stories and pretend to be interested in his hobbies for the chance that they'll get the privilege of having his tongue shoved down their throats.

"How many times do I have to apologize to you about that?"

"You haven't apologized once yet," I remind him.

His eyes dart to the side. War Soul has to juggle a dangerous game. How can he retain his pride and maintain his narcissism while still attempting to sleep with me?

"I only hit you because I knew it wouldn't hurt you. The last thing I would ever do is want to hurt you."

"Yesterday, you admitted that you would let Freedom kill me to get him to reveal the location of the nuke."

He pauses while he considers his next sentence. In a desperate attempt to make up for his verbal blunder, he thrusts his hand onto the wall behind me. As he leans, his face now beckons within kissing range. I regret a lot of my choices tonight.

"You're invincible. I knew Freedom couldn't kill you."

"*Was* invincible. I can be injured now, so if we hook up tonight, I'd appreciate it if you don't break my jaw or shatter my collarbone or whatever else you consider foreplay."

"You're saying we can hook up?"

His face gets even closer.

"Okay, War Soul. Stop. Nick. Since I clearly don't have much of a choice or escape route or anything resembling a good time, we can hang out. We'll talk. Like normal people. I'll drink your craft beer. We'll sit on the couch and converse, okay? And if you so much as drape your arm around me, I'm going to break my beer bottle over the coffee table and stab you in the neck. You still want to hook up? Then get to know me first and let me get to know you – you erratic, egotistical, abusive craphole of a person. Can we agree to this? Understand that if your face gets any closer to mine, I'm going to karate chop you in the neck."

He backs up and I can see the disappointment streak across his face. War Soul peers around the room, searching for a girl that he'd have an easier time enticing. Seeing none, and not hiding his displeasure, he shrugs.

"I'll get you a craft beer and we'll go to the couch. We can talk or whatever. But I'm not abusive, okay?"

I nod – maybe a bit too sarcastically.

We sit on the non-bloody sections of War Soul's couch. His beer choice is surprisingly decent. He starts off with a question.

"Do you hate me?"

"Kind of, yeah."

"I'm sorry, Liza. I really am. My dads were special forces and they treated my mistakes with verbal abuse and violence. They meant well, but they really messed me up. I've tried really hard to not act like them, but—"

"Stop," I interrupt him. "I don't want to hear a sob story. Look, I've been thrown in a hospital looney bin. I'm supposed to take six pills a day just to stay stable. I cry almost every morning even if I have nothing to cry about. Okay? Are we done? Do I need to continue with more sad facts about my life? We're at a party and we're drunk. Can we just talk like normal people?"

"Sure."

So we talk.

He raves about the new Vin Diesel movie. I agree. War Soul listens to my slurred personal theory that movies should be one of two categories: good or fun. A movie can be good, but not fun – like all those Oscar movies. A movie can be fun, but not good – like say, every Vin Diesel movie. Either one is perfectly fine by me. If a movie is both good and fun, then all the better. War Soul approves, though that may just be his way to get me to like him. We discuss the newest superhero movie *Technonaut*. Nick argues that the movie lost him with the logistics of a package arriving from a truck at the exact moment it needed to despite all the rush hour traffic. But the movie was about two robots falling in love and it was the package delivery that lost him? He laughs. I begin to loosen up. I tell him a story where, during a Fourth of July celebration, I wandered around the party confused at the people's expressions when I didn't know I had been lit on fire by a rogue firework. He tells me a story about a basketball game he played while babysitting his young nephews where he accidentally knocked himself unconscious when the ball bounced off the rim. He doesn't like blueberries – I can't even comprehend that. War Soul reads my palm, surprised at my shallow fate line. My proclamation of being an undefeated thumb wrestling champ becomes untrue. I destroy him in a beer chugging contest.

His company isn't irritating for the hour or so we talk and drink. More drinking than talking.

War Soul and I have known each other for five years without so much as a single conversation not about work. Every time we hung out, he spent most of his time barking orders at teammates who didn't ask him to lead or trapping attractive women in corners in an attempt to flirt his way past their objections. But the women rarely object, and I can now see why. But he punched me in the face. And his body – it's the most amazing male physique I've ever seen. I want to slice him in half and climb inside him like a tauntaun. Why does War Soul's face look like that? Did I just say that out loud? But he punched me in the face. Twice.

The party begins to wrap up. Kid Metroplexer and Missile left long ago. Belial, Featherblade, and Icarus made up and are celebrating their friendship with improvised raps about their genitals. Spiro invited Forestchild to join her and Lady Metroplexer in their dance off. The five card players moved on to Scrabble. Anytime a player can't get more than twenty points for a word, they take a shot. Four of them pass out sometime near the end of the party; Mentalmind remains disappointingly sober. Hacker Plus took over the laptop to play DJ, and her lack of talent for picking songs did not go unnoticed or without complaint.

War Soul's and my future sits in limbo. As I announce I should probably go, he goes in for the kiss. Our conversation was fun, and I let him kiss me. Once. But as he immediately moves on to more handsy maneuvers, I stop him.

"Nick, you want me to be blunt, right?"

"Not really."

"I'm sorry. This is awkward. But we're not going to sleep together or date or snuggle or hold hands or go putt putting or anything else. You're super attractive and you were nice to talk to, but I just can't get over the warehouse stuff. You hit me, dude. Sorry, but there's no rebounding from that. Are you okay with settling for being friends? You've already slept with half the women who were at this party anyhow."

He pauses, frowns, and then begins to get off the couch

before turning back to face me.

"Do you still hate me, Liza?"

"Not as much."

"Then tonight was worth it."

———

Thankfully, I wake up in my apartment. Half my body lies off my bed and I spot Stella sleeping on the floor next to the bathroom. I'm not wearing pants and she's not wearing a shirt. I can't figure out where, but I definitely smell vomit. Why do I have a memory of the two of us attempting to capture a wild animal? Is there an angry wild animal somewhere in my apartment? As I step off my bed, my feet collide with something wet draped across the carpet. I examine the damp trail – it leads to my bed. Did I pee my bed? Is that why I'm not wearing pants? The search for Freedom's nuke can wait – laundry becomes my highest priority.

After Stella wakes up, she recalls us chasing a raccoon down an alley on the walk home, trying to coax it with granola bars she kept in her purse. But the mysterious disappearance of her shirt provides us with more questions than answers. Most horrifyingly, while we can both definitely smell the puke in my bedroom, we can't find it anywhere. I'm supposed to work this afternoon, but I call in sick – I can't believe Kid Metroplexer will show up either.

Stella stumbles to the kitchen, opening my refrigerator. I already know she's going to be unhappy.

"Do you have Gatorade? Something with electrolytes?"

I don't answer, still dizzy from attempting to sit down on my toilet. She asks again before I disappoint her.

"Why would I have Gatorade? I don't exercise. And what are electrolytes? Some sort of magnet or something?"

My neighbors from across the hall loudly slam their door, Stella unleashing a groan that is vaguely similar to the sounds she makes when she's stabbed or shot.

"Stella, you heal a thousand times faster than the normal human the moment you pass out. How are you hungover?"

"I don't know!" she screams back at me. "No one knows how their powers work! I'm sorry I'm not a geneticist, Liza!"

As she lies down on the living room couch, I overhear her offhanded remark on how poorly I sweep. Flushing the toilet, I close my eyes and grow to hate the everyday sounds of a world going about their business.

We eat lunch at one in the afternoon. Our current superhero predicament dictates that we spend our day achieving two objectives: finding the nuke and keeping me from dying. Lunch helps the latter.

"Okay, let's go over what we know about the bomb search."

Spiromaniac pulls out a notebook. If our morning was ruined taking turns to throw up in my bathroom, unable to venture much farther than the restaurant a block from my apartment, then hopefully the shame will be lessened a bit if we discuss the hidden nuclear weapon.

Spiro stuffs French fries in her mouth, chewing quickly to avoid talking with her mouth full.

"Liza, didn't Freedom already have the bomb hidden before he even initially contacted you?"

"Yeah. If he detonated the nuke, he'd do it to cause maximum damage to Metroplexer, right? He wants Metroplexer to witness the explosion before Freedom kills him, I think."

She takes another bite before continuing.

"Metroplexer lives in Franken, and that suburb borders the southwest part of Burlington. If Freedom set off a nuke, he'd ideally want it to annihilate everything Metroplexer has worked for."

"Like his house, his yard, and his pool. But the other heroes must have combed that area pretty thoroughly by now. The bomb would have to be somewhere that we wouldn't ever think to look. Somewhere no one thinks Freedom could get access to, or at least, somewhere he would be stupid enough to place a bomb."

"A place with tons of surveillance and people."

"Exactly."

We take a minute to process our line of thought, but mainly

to eat whatever's left of our afternoon lunch. And by eat, it's more of a shoveling motion hoping the other doesn't notice. The first meal after a hangover is no time for manners.

"Liza, none of us have talked to Freedom except for you. Can you remember anything he said or hinted at that could help us? A clue he told you that he didn't tell anyone else?"

"Nothing groundbreaking. Except he told me in the hospital that besides killing Metroplexer, he wanted Metroplexer's 'most precious Burlington jewel' wiped out as well. That's an odd choice of words, yeah? I remember how odd those words sounded, but to be fair to me, the Freedom says lots of odd things."

"Most precious Burlington jewel? Like a place he cares about? The place he cares the most about?"

We write down locations Metroplexer would have some sort of emotional attachment. His house. His therapy practice. The apartment his son and daughter share. The home he grew up in on the outskirts of the city. But wouldn't all of those have been searched by now? We start getting desperate. Metroplexer's favorite grocery store. The tailor shop he buys his capes. The dealership he leases his Mercedes. The department store his ex-wife used to manage.

But the word "jewel" would imply somewhere our superhero finds valuable. Somewhere that would devastate Metroplexer – not just in material goods – but in something from his personal history that would have defined his self-esteem or legacy or the location of his happiest memories. And from what Kid Metroplexer told me, happy memories would definitely eliminate Metroplexer's childhood home.

But I barely know Metroplexer. We've never had a normal conversation. Our therapy sessions focus entirely on me. Even his own children have repeatedly expressed disinterest in whatever private life their father lives. Then. Hold on. Wait. I'm the only superhero who's also his patient. I'm the only one of us who's ever seen inside his office. And in his office—

"Oh my God. I know where the bomb is."

7

Metroplexer's athletic prowess in high school is a well-hidden secret that has cycled sporadically in hushed tones around the superhero community. Most of the facts and details I know about Mel Johnson, the civilian, come from clippings of old newspapers that I researched when my new, curious therapist first began asking me about my personal history. Y'know, to turn the tides on him.

The stories begin with Mel Johnson entering the ninth grade at Tamberlyn High School, trying out for the school's below average football team. He had come into his powers sometime during his elementary years, but Mel wasn't stupid even at that stupid age. He could probably tunnel down under the surface of the school before tossing it up into the sky, but secret identities meant secret identities. And he was five foot, four inches. So he joined the team as a kicker – the perfect position that none of the stars of the team would question of a child prodigy. Mel nailed a few field goals, casually mentioned playing soccer when he was young, and the kid began to rock special teams. The next year, Mel stood four inches taller and packed on another thirty pounds, so he became a running back. Despite all the records he set that year – this child dodging linebackers with seemingly superhuman reflexes – his biggest victory came as the gift of puberty. His junior year, at six feet and 200 pounds, he annihilated his old records. Now no one asked many questions when he could shove off a defender with just a light tap from his shoulder. Expectedly, the team won the state championship. In his senior year, his final growth spurt adding another three inches, he walked onto the field at 220 pounds of pure muscle. Nothing could stop that man. Hand the ball to Mel Johnson and watch him score a touchdown. Throw Mel Johnson the ball and watch the crushed dreams of anyone foolish enough to attempt to stop him. They would make Mel Johnson quarterback for the fastest, most accurate spiral in the state. Place him as the kicker and he'll punt ninety yards. Or linebacker. Or center. Wait, where's the center? And the tight end. Is the tight end on defense? I don't know a lot of football positions, but you get my point. The team dominated the high school state championship. ESPN magazine wrote an article on him. College recruiters were willing to practically sell their firstborn child if Mel Johnson would play for their school.

But Metroplexer wasn't foolish; every other week new rumors would pop up about these new, scary "superhumans" in our safe American cities. Metroplexer must have known what this fame would lead to. He couldn't keep up these athletic lies forever, sullying everything he accomplished for his high school in an inevitable massive scandal. Like when Barry Bonds broke Hank Aaron's homerun record, but all those steroids gave his proudest moment that dismissive asterisk. So Mel Johnson announced he was done with football, enrolled in a local state school, and earned his doctorate in psychology. Oh, how the football world speculated on Mel Johnson turning his back on the game. What could have caused him to do this? Why would he throw away such incredible gifts? Whose fault was this? But the number one question asked by every Burlington sports fan discussing this insanity with his or her Burlington sports fan friends: what the hell?

Twenty-nine years later, pretty much no one remembers the name Mel Johnson – except Tamberlyn High School, who venerates Mel Johnson and the team of 1988 as deities whose warm light sadly abandoned the school when future generations of unworthy students failed to revere and worship the most triumphant days of Burlington's sixth worst high school. Now the greatest high school football player who ever lived makes his living berating me for my growing alcoholism and my refusal to be more honest with my parents. So when Freedom wants to blow up the most important time of Mel Johnson's life, my guess is he'd go after Tamberlyn High School football.

If you do the math, Metroplexer's entrance into the costumed world of crime fighting didn't happen until the man hit the age of thirty two. I don't know what took him so long. Let's assume he was busy with his education and raising a family and maybe a hidden opiate problem? Trying to get personal information out of Metroplexer might as well be like trying to learn about the porn habits of a United States congressman. You'll just get hit with a never-ending wave of denial, deflection, and self-righteous exasperation. How could anyone realize the extent of Metroplexer's silent pride in his these athletic achievements – albeit unfair achievements – when he refuses to candidly talk about his high school experience, even to his own children? And a more important question: how did Freedom know? Well, assuming the bomb is actually in the school.

———

"I've created two fake student IDs. You're both in the system, but you'll still have to talk your way in."

Hacker Plus briefs us on our newest mission – the mission that sparked from my sudden, hopeful epiphany. We stand outside Tamberlyn High School, two miles from Metroplexer's childhood home.

Fortunately for me, I graduated high school last year. Barely. With my evening superhero duties and a clinical depression/puberty combo, not much homework or studying got done. But it's not like I was a genius either. I'm average at best. IQ no more than 100. Or maybe 95. That infuriated my teachers – they knew from parent/teacher conferences all about my genius scientist parents, and thus my teachers simply assumed I wasn't trying. A combination of laziness and apathy. I could see that look in all my teachers' eyes when they realize a student who, without any hobbies or passions or work ethic, is doomed to a mediocre and insignificant adulthood. Except I was a part-time superhero. And yesterday I killed a giant monster. So there, Mr. Hunter of sophomore English. Guess who had the last laugh? Mr. Hunter hasn't killed even one monster.

For academic comparison between Stella and me, she once told War Soul, during an argument about busting local drug rings which turned into a braggart tangent, that she had made the honor roll since kindergarten. So yes, War Soul, she wouldn't, but she totally could cook high quality meth if she wanted to.

Hacker Plus sighs loud enough for us to hear through Stella's cellphone speaker, asking us if we understood what she's talking about. Condescension remains a constant theme with Hacker Plus.

"Why do we have to talk our way in?" Stella complains. "I'm not good at making stuff up. Why didn't you e-mail us our IDs?"

"Because I'm not a Kinko's. You're lucky I skipped school today. I still have a throbbing headache from last night, I feel like my insides have been mauled by a large animal, and you called me seven minutes ago. That's only enough time to put you in the system, not to actually create the IDs. Stella, you're Lauren O'Connor, a senior who just moved here last week with your family. Liza, you're Chelsea O'Connor, her sister."

"Are you kidding me?" Stella shouts. "I'm clearly Latina and Liza has the skin tone of a cloud. Why would you make us sisters?"

"Don't forget the physique of a cloud too," I add.

"Can you just trust me? I call myself Hacker Plus for a good reason. I've done this before. I learned from trial and error. School administrations automatically suspect any students arriving at two in the afternoon to be truant, and you really don't want to be questioned by the principal or cop. They care far too much. School receptionists care far less. If you're sisters, then you can just say your parents had an emergency or the car broke down or whatever. Seriously, Stella, we live in a world of hostile diversity; no one wants to be called racist. Just follow Liza's lead. You're a fighter, but she's a

123

talker – but only if she's sober. Is she sober?"

I tap the phone.

"I can hear you. Let's not be rude."

I'm not sober. I figured I couldn't save the city with a hangover, and what stops a hangover? More alcohol, of course. In my crime-fighting utility belt is just one single pocket for a flask.

Hacker Plus hangs up, mumbling something about a pizza being delivered. Infiltration missions don't mesh well with Spiromaniac. The higher risk of arrest scares her more than, say, a beating or a laser attack, which she would far prefer over having to be handcuffed and dragged to jail for a weekend. Plus, she's a terrible actor. Luckily for her, my years of lying incessantly ("Yes, I'm doing fine. I'm not sad. See me smiling? How are you doing? Great? Great!") make up for any of her shortcomings. My turn to lead.

"Okay, here's how this plan is going to work. We walk through the front entrance after we get buzzed in. We'll go to the front office, where we announce we're new students and don't have IDs yet and whatever else. Our family moved here for our dad's job – we're from Cleveland."

"I hate Cleveland."

"What? Why? No, forget it. We want to start classes tomorrow, but for today, especially since the school day is almost over, we'd just like to tour the building. Would that be okay with the school? Oh, we'll need someone to walk us around? Fine. Then, using our years of superhero training, we'll lose our guide. And by that I mean we'll duck down a hallway and run really fast. The bomb will almost certainly be hidden somewhere football related. Any questions?"

"Yeah, I have tons—"

The school bell rings to change classes.

"No time, follow me. Let's use the chaos."

We're buzzed in through the intercom and head to the Tamberlyn High School front office. The receptionist leans forward in her chair – a woman I'm assuming probably hates her job but must remain optimistic and friendly because of the whole-children-are-precious-and-our-future mantra.

"Hello," I announce as we walk in. The woman doesn't look up, so I knock on the desk to get her attention.

"Yes? What is it?"

So she's neither optimistic nor friendly. Fine.

"Oh, okay. Well, we're new students. Our family moved here a week ago for our dad's job and—"

"Names?"

I can hear Spiro grit her teeth. Sometimes one comes across a man and woman you can't fib your way past. These people by default don't like you, and no matter how many Edible Arrangements you send them, the bile that has warped their own lives is always targeted directly at the person who dares to interrupt their menial tasks.

"I'm Chelsea O'Connor and this is my sister Linda O'Connor."

"Lauren," Spiro quickly interjects.

The receptionist doesn't respond beyond beginning to type.

"Yeah, Lauren," I respond. "My bad. Y'see, I know if you looked at us you would see how different we look, but that's because Lauren is adopted—"

"I see a Lauren O'Connor but I don't see a Chelsea. I do see a Shelsea. Is that you?" And in her first interaction between the three of us as actual human beings, she asks, "Is that your real name?"

In all her hungover, grouchy splendor, Hacker Plus typed my name wrong.

"Yes, that's me. Shelsea. My mom, she, y'know, she loved the ocean so much. Hence she combined her favorite words, shell and sea."

Now the receptionist's interested – not a great development in our brilliant, flawless plan. I blame Hacker Plus. And I shouldn't have finished off my flask of whiskey before we got here.

"Then why aren't you just named Seashell?"

"Okay. School is tough. You understand. She didn't want me

to get beat up by bullies, with their normal names like Emily and Kelsey and Michigan."

"You mean Michelle?"

Change the subject, Liza. Quickly.

"I was conceived on a beach, I'm told."

The receptionist drops the subject with a very visible eye roll. Spiro pushes me to the side, and despite a small tremor in her voice, she explains the situation to the woman. While Spiromaniac can't improv like I do so phenomenally, she can recite facts – information from Hacker Plus to convince the woman to give us a pass to register for classes down the hall in the counselor's office. We assure the receptionist that we don't need a guide. She acquiesces with directions instead.

"You see that? Perfect deception!" I exclaim as we step out of the hallway and out of earshot of our opponent. "Infiltration successful! Their defenses penetrated!"

"Their defenses were an angry old woman. And don't use that word in a building full of children. It makes me uncomfortable." Stella begs.

"Penetrate?"

"Yes, that word."

"You're a sicko for thinking I meant that connotation of penetrate," I accuse.

"I'm allowed to not like words! Diction is a pet peeve of mine, okay? Like when you complain about people who chew loudly."

"I don't know what diction means."

"How do you know what connotation means but not diction? Diction is the choice of words that—"

She cuts herself short when she sees my eyes wander.

"Liza, I have a suspicion that you may be drunk. Am I mistaken?"

"Stella, I have a suspicion that a stick penetrated your—"

She slaps me across the cheek. Not hard enough to bruise,

but hard enough to hurt. I accept my deservedation of that hit. Stella retorts that deservedation isn't a word, and sensing an upcoming statement from me that requires another smack, she grabs my arm. We join the hordes of students moving about the hallways before their next class starts.

As the two of us wander the halls, unaware of where to go but forced to march onward with the crowd, I take a quick second to look upon these children's faces. My mistake. My therapist believes my current method of dealing with emotional triggers – I take all these horrible feelings, push them deep down inside me, and then one day I'll die – to be unhealthy, but too late. Trigger pulled.

I watch these kids. Smiling. Laughing. Playing and kissing. How? How are any of them happy? High school for me meant an endless looping of self-loathing, self-doubt, and self-pity. Jealousy at those who had even an inkling of something better than me. But look at these kids surrounding us. They're happy, aren't they? How? Am I just whining? I worry I whine too much. Am I just bitter? Is this just my Vietnam flashback of teenage angst? Instead of phantom helicopter blades and breathing in the scent of napalm, I hear awkward, desperate teenage flirting and cologne that smells like perfumed farts. Aren't the kids who were miserable in high school supposed to be happy once they graduate and enter the real world? Then why not me?

Stella nudges me with her elbow.

"Hey. Are you okay? You look angry."

"I'm fine. Not angry," I reply.

No. No, not now. Stop it. I can always pity myself tonight. But we have a nuke to find. Cry later. I compose myself by taking all these horrible feelings and pushing them deep down inside me. No one is as happy as they look, right? Still, I bitterly wish a curse of a thousand pimples on every student I see.

"I'm cool. Thanks for asking. Let's move," I reassure Stella.

If my hunch is correct, we'll need to find the trophy case of decades old football victories. We get directions to the school's gym when three stragglers late to their next class tell us that the boys' locker room holds a bunch of awards. So the most destructive force in the city is most likely hidden in a room drenched in the sweat of unshowered minors. Why in the locker room? To remind the football team of past triumphs the absolute latest they can before charging onto the field? To give the coach something to point at during halftime motivational speeches? We go onwards, walking the hallways of a dilapidated school whose proudest years embraced a secretly superpowered teenager bringing their football team to national glory by cheating the ever-loving crap out of the game.

We enter the boys' locker room with no problems. Seriously, high schools, you really should up the security on these. First, Stella and I wait fifteen minutes concealed in the hallway until both genders have changed clothes, poured out into the gym, and began whatever game the teachers decided to humiliate the smaller, weaker students with today. It turns out the game of choice is badminton, which doesn't really require the hulking strength or size that I pessimistically predicted. Second, we pretend we're late for class, rushing with just enough hurriedness to make it realistic and not draw attention. If we break into a sprint then we'll get a noticeable whistle from the coach, and if we nonchalantly stroll then we'll get a whistle to hurry up – both making it impossible for us to sneak into the boy's pubic den. Spiro asks me not to call it that. And third, and possibly most important, the boys' and girls' locker room are uncomfortably close together. In the midst of picking the badminton teams, we only move another few feet past our gender's changing room and into the boys'.

Since both Spiro and I are legal adults, the adjectives I use to describe this locker room will have to be carefully chosen. I'll use my diction. Imagine a gym inhabited by the hairiest, moistest men that you can think of. Men who use whatever Old Spice deodorant sounds the most like a sexy centaur in place of anything resembling a shower. Now take these men, give them two or three sets of clothing that don't know the slightest feel of soap, and allow them to store these fabrics – ones that smell like a year's worth of unrestrained hormones – in a single, unventilated room. Then force these smells to linger in this room combined with the terror sweat of an impromptu towel whipping. This is the aroma that blasts our senses when Spiro and I enter the locker room. Thus, time is of the essence.

Near the showers, which I'm assuming from a quick glance consists of at least half mold, we spot the trophy case. The glass enclosure contains five trophies and three plaques, all from the late-1980s. In the corner, next to a photo of a football team wearing a menagerie of mullets, Jheri curls, and glam metal impersonations, we spot a large suitcase.

Carefully sliding the glass open, I carefully pick up the suitcase, carefully slide the glass closed, and carefully place the suitcase on the floor. It's heavy. Spiromaniac's voice trembles as she instructs me to undo the latches, and my hands shake uncontrollably, neither of us content to die in the room equivalent of an unwashed armpit. And there it is. I mean, we don't know what a nuke looks like, but what else could a suitcase full of electronic equipment and wires stashed in the Tamberlyn High School's trophy case be? Stella snaps a picture and texts it to Hacker Plus, whose return text confirms our suspicions: "GRAB IT AND GET THE HELL OUT OF THERE." We found it. We did it. Once we disarm the nuke, our troubles are over. I can kill myself. Metroplexer is right; this is good for my self-esteem.

Two students walk through the locker room door.

"What are you doing here?" one asks nervously.

"No time to explain," I answer. "We're perverts."

We shove past them before they can respond and walk quickly toward the school entrance.

We don't even make it out the school before Stella's phone receives another text message.

"Miss Nucleus, give me a call. Love, Freedom."

———

We ignore the Freedom's text. Let him find out the bad news tonight on TV instead.

The end is in sight. Thank God. Once this nuke gets taken care of, all that's left for me is to choose my method. I've thought about this a lot over the past few days. So many options. Drowning. Hanging. Prescription pills. Gunshot. Tall building. Tall bridge. Drug overdose, maybe? No worries, I'll have time to think about this tomorrow.

Spiro's phone blows up with texts from Hacker Plus. She's driving to the school to pick us up. She should be there within ten minutes. Contact Kid and Lady Metroplexer immediately. Contact Metroplexer too. Have one of them fly the nuke at least twenty miles outside the city. Don't bang the nuke against anything. Keep the suitcase level at all times. If the bomb goes off before Hacker Plus gets there, she'll never stop ghostkicking us in our ghostfaces for all of eternity.

A text arrives from Kid Metroplexer: the twins are on their way, but all of our phone calls to daddy Metroplexer go straight to voicemail. Not a good sign; during our therapy sessions, Metroplexer would pause the session during the few occasions he received a text or phone call. Impolite, yes, but he couldn't risk missing a superhero emergency or whatnot.

Spiromaniac slowly sets the bomb down in the parking lot. I feel like my stomach's about to burst through my throat. Before the two of us go into a full panic attack, the Metroplexer children arrive – wearing t-shirts and jeans and visibly uncomfortable at appearing for official superhero business in street clothes. And no one misses a Metroplexer entrance. They hit the ground with a bit too much speed, the impact on the asphalt powerful enough to cause the tiniest, precise, and self-contained earthquake. Every time. They know what they're doing. If they had their way, trumpeters would announce their arrival while adoring fans chant their names in unison. Once at a party, I angrily shouted this scenario to the twins, which Lady Metroplexer fervently denied. But it's not as if she softened her landings afterward, either.

Hacker Plus appears almost immediately after, her motorcycle careening into the school parking lot so quickly that she T-bones an innocent truck parked near us. Probably injured in some capacity, she tumbles off the motorcycle, scrambling over to us while pulling who-knows-what gadgets out of her backpack.

And then Spiro's phone rings. The five of us freeze, praying Metroplexer has returned our call. Stella whispers that it's an unknown number. But not to me it isn't. I clumsily snatch the phone out of her hand, pushing down on speakerphone.

"Miss Nucleus, I thought I told you to call me."

Spiro and Hacker Plus don't place the voice, but the blood in Kid and Lady Metroplexer's faces drain immediately. They're scared. I've never seen them scared before.

"Look, Freedom, oops. We've been a bit busy."

"I know! My compliments on finding the bomb! You've done wonderfully. I expected you'd need at least another day or two. My secretary interrupted my meeting a half hour ago to announce that you had gotten off the bus a block from the school."

"Thanks. Thank you. The game is over? We won, right? I'm going to hang up now."

Freedom audibly sighs.

"Almost. I pride myself on my manners and I figure the polite thing to do would be to congratulate you in person. A final challenge for our triumphant superheroes. I don't want this experience for you to be anticlimactic. Luckily, my associates and I will be there in a few minutes, so it wouldn't be very nice to remove the nuke from the school grounds. That'd be bad manners, don't you think? See you soon, Miss Nucleus. Tell the Johnson twins that I say hello."

Lady Metroplexer hyperventilates. Kid Metroplexer freezes. Hacker Plus undeterred, she opens the suitcase, unlocks her toolbox, and starts to type on her phone. Spiro shoots a fearful look at me. I have no idea what to do. Why are Kid and Lady Metroplexer so frightened? What the hell are we in for?

"Grant. Grace. We're going to fight Freedom, aren't we?"

Lady Metroplexer, through deep breaths, answers.

"Yes. Liza. Grant and I can't— you see, Liza, listen. The two of us will fight Freedom. Spiromaniac will fight his associates. I just—"

She begins to hyperventilate again. Kid Metroplexer continues for her.

"You need to know this," he insists. "We can't beat Freedom. The two of us together can't beat Freedom. Our dad loses to Freedom as often as he wins."

"What? But we've never seen a story on TV or in the newspapers that Metroplexer has—" Spiro interjects before Hacker Plus interjects her.

"Shut up. All of you. I Googled how to disarm this nuke. Don't look at me like that. But I can do it. I need five minutes. Minimum. Probably more like ten. I'll be busy saving the lives of thousands of people, so our mission is this: don't let me or Liza get killed. That's it. You don't have to defeat Freedom or his buddies. Just keep them busy for like, fifteen minutes. Got it? Good? We all good?"

A solitary black car slowly makes its way down the street, as if all the traffic has respectfully parted. The windows are deeply tinted. Lady Metroplexer, her hands wiping the sweat off her brow, is the only one to answer Hacker Plus.

"We're not invulnerable. Grant and I are not invincible like Liza. Like she used to be. We're tough, but we can be hurt. Killed. And Freedom..." She trails off. "Neither of us is as powerful as our dad. Not by a long shot. But Hacker Plus is right. We have a mission to complete. You have my word, and the word of my brother, that we will not let this nuke be detonated here. No matter what it takes. Leave Freedom to us."

Spiro searches through Hacker Plus' backpack. She pulls out two Tasers.

"Are these the only weapons you have, Jen?"

Hacker Plus grunts.

"Search deeper. I stole a cattle prod from when we busted that meth lab inside that farm. That's all. I'm not supposed to be in the field."

The car pulls into the parking lot, stopping a short distance away. Hacker Plus begins to disarm the bomb. The countdown begins.

One man and one woman step out of the driver and passenger seat. The man wears entirely gray: a suit, a shirt, a tie, and gloves. A silver cape drapes over his back. The woman carries a charred stick — a large one — and a green robe. Bedazzled too. I recognize those two. Other than Hacker Plus' tinkering, silence has crept in the battlefield. Even the wind halted and birds stopped chirping.

The man is Denial, a former stage magician and illusionist. Someone stole his assistant's sex tape, propelling her to a semi-successful reality show. Now he's resentful and angry. Not particularly dangerous either, but he has a buttload of tricks, most of them flammable. And the woman calls herself Mephista. I think she's an actual demon summoner. Like she tears open the fabric of our world to bring forth actual demons. That's what Globe says, but I don't believe her.

Spiromaniac speaks up.

"I can't win this fight either. Maybe I can take Denial, but that's Mephista, isn't she? I can't beat her."

Stella throws the cattle prod to me.

"Liza, you're more important than me. Don't you move from Hacker Plus' side. If you die, everything we've done is for nothing. Only engage the enemy if you have absolutely no other choice. And by that, I mean, don't you dare fight alongside us. Understand?"

"What about—"

"Do you understand, Liza?"

I nod. Denial opens the back door of the vehicle and Freedom steps out. Tight v-neck shirt, cargo shorts, and sandals. Once again, he sports the fashion of what I can best describe as a man who owns a beach house, but never actually wants to go in the ocean. Before he approaches us, he kicks his sandals off. The Metroplexers take a deep breath.

"Hello!" Freedom waves. Kid and Lady Metroplexer clench their fists.

"Miss Nucleus. Spiromaniac. Hacker Plus. My lovely Grant and Grace. Do you want to talk first or—"

With a sonic boom almost strong enough to knock everyone else off their feet, Lady Metroplexer slams into Freedom. The two of them hurtle out of eyesight, Kid Metroplexer a split second behind. Spiromaniac sprints toward the two remaining supervillains.

Here we go.

The battle between the twin Metroplexers and Freedom soon becomes impossible to follow. Streaks of light occasionally pass by above, but I can't tell you who's winning. And I didn't know Freedom could fly.

I focus my attention on Spiro, and once again, I'm watching battle poetry – she dodges all the dangerous attacks and effortlessly takes all the hits that won't hinder her. I see a playing card lodged halfway in her hip. She sports a black eye. An angry dove sliced open her forearm. Her torso's exposed with a firework-shaped hole in her shirt. And then Spiromaniac, ducking under a flurry of thrown knives like she just won the world's scariest limbo competition, nails the diving dove with one of her Tasers. That woman. My God. Compare her battle strategy to mine over the past years: "Are you done punching me? Great. So you cool with surrendering or do you want to tire out some more first?"

More streaks of light flash by above. The battle in the sky roars throughout the parking lot. After a ferocious haymaker from Freedom, Lady Metroplexer crashes downward into a light pole – close enough to the nuke to make my heart race – before she shakenly soars back to the clash overhead.

While Denial keeps Spiro busy, Mephista finishes her first incantation – a glowing portal opening beside her. And holy crap.

Turns out demon summoners aren't a myth. I owe Globe an apology. Imagine a seven-foot lizard, standing on two feet but made entirely of boiling black goo. The thing smells like rotting flesh, and the asphalt turns to ooze with each step the monster takes. Spiromaniac takes an evil gooey lizard claw to the back. She stumbles, and I see her attempt to reflect the strike back to the demon. Nothing. Confusion flashes across Spiromaniac's eyes. She was right – she won't be able to beat Mephista.

Freedom zooms to a stop at the far end of the parking lot. Kid Metroplexer hits him with a speed and a force I've never seen him use before. The supervillain is knocked back a few feet, but seems otherwise unfazed.

"Is this the best you can do?" Freedom bellows. "Oh, Melvin did a terrible job with both of you. Is this why he forbade you two from fighting me? He always was the smart one."

Any further taunts are interrupted as Lady Metroplexer strikes him from his other side with the same immense ferocity and power of her brother. Still, Freedom almost instantly regains his bearings from the sudden attack, his expression unchanged. He counters their blows with his own swipes quicker than the twins can react, and the child Metroplexers rocket across the battlefield. How much time has passed? Two minutes? Three minutes? Neither the twins nor Spiromaniac can hold out long enough for Hacker Plus to disarm the nuke.

But why are Denial and Mephista still fighting Spiro? Isn't Hacker Plus or myself their target? The nuke's the goal, right? Hacker Plus can't defend herself and my only weapon, at best, annoys cows. Killing Spiromaniac accomplishes nothing. Certainly Denial could hold her off for long enough that Mephista's lizard rips me in half or pierces the explode-y part of the nuke.

Wait.

Regardless of Freedom's intentions, why would Denial and Mephista *want* the nuke to go off? The nuke would incinerate them. They won't dare risk it. Who cares what Freedom wants with the bomb? His henchmen plan for long, illustrious careers in supervillainy. So, I march forward. Unafraid. Determined. Ready to save my damsel in distress.

I interrupt the summoning of Mephista's next demon with a cattle prod to the neck. The partially-summoned creature dissipates. She yelps, turning around to face her attacker. But she pauses. Damn right. I make my way toward the lizard monster. The demon takes a cattle prod to the back. Nothing. But the creature halts its assault on Spiro to discover its new attacker. I spread my arms wide. Slice me in half. Do it. The monster raises a claw before a rushed chant from Mephista dispels the sludge monster. Damn right again.

While I'm not a doctor, I think Spiromaniac's diagnosis at this point would be "messed up." She stumbles a few steps before steadying herself. Whether she's pissed at me joining the fight or not, she doesn't say anything. Taking just the briefest second to wipe the blood out of her eyes first, Spiro lunges at Mephista.

Denial, realizing how limiting his options just became, freezes. He faces two terrible choices: run and face Freedom's violently disappointing talk with him later, or lose and take my slightly less violent beating. Defeat is preferable to cowardice when one accepts employment from Freedom. Denial throws a half-hearted punch at me before the cattle prod sends him twitching to the asphalt. The cattle prod isn't possibly strong enough to permanently take him out of the fight, but he refuses to stand back up. Spiro quickly uses her second Taser on Mephista before she gets the chance to summon whatever else is in her demon rolodex.

We won. Just in time for Kid Metroplexer to smash into a car from somewhere high above. He's groaning, but not moving. Freedom lands in front of us, the ground cracked open from his force. A visibly hurt Lady Metroplexer drops nearby, collapsing to her knees. Her clothes are soaked in blood, her face swollen with a mixture of black and blue. Seemingly unconcerned with her injuries, Lady Metroplexer screams out.

"Where's our dad?"

Freedom takes a moment to fix his hair.

"You see those two morons over there?" Freedom motions to Denial and Mephista. "A quick business lesson, Miss Nucleus. Make your employees prove themselves before you pay them. Have them intern for a week or two. Because how many supervillains reside in Burlington? Fifty? Maybe sixty? And the city has, what? Twenty superheroes? No one knows how to fight anymore. On Denial's resume, he wrote that he decapitated a jewelry store security guard with a single card throw. Mephista claims she destroyed an entire Amazonian village with just one spell. They can't even take down two children. Thankfully, I'm rich. I'll hire better supervillains next time."

Lady Metroplexer screams her question again. Freedom ignores her again.

"Miss Nucleus, my sweet, beautiful hamster. I enjoyed watching you run in your little hamster wheel these past couple days, but you comprehend enough to know that running on your wheel won't actually get you anywhere. I didn't lie to you about our game; I promised you I wouldn't. Though I did leave some details out. I'm sorry. I rigged the game in my favor – I can't risk losing this one. Hacker Plus, stop fiddling with the nuke. Look at me when I'm talking. I will not ask again."

Hacker Plus obeys immediately, tools dangling in her hands.

Lady Metroplexer cries out a final time. Freedom shoots her an irritated glance.

"Shut up, Grace. Miss Nucleus, I'm sorry I dragged you into this game. I really am. But your role is done – earlier than I hoped, but done. You helped me learn quite a lot about the Liberate, and understand that this knowledge will not go to waste. You're the best; it's been an absolute pleasure to know you! You might be my favorite superhero."

His eyes lock onto mine. A piercing, unrelenting stare.

"I wished you didn't look just—" He stops mid-sentence. "Miss Nucleus, I want to thank you. For everything. I'm going to give you what you want. Your deepest wish. It's the least I can do. Thank you for playing, but I need to go."

Freedom casually grabs his sandals before flying off. Denial and Mephista lie on the asphalt near the car, abandoned by their boss. I always figured Freedom killed his failed employees, not left them for the police to potentially squeal.

The final bell rings. School is out. And then Hacker Plus screeches.

"The nuke! It activated!"

Oh. That's why he left Denial and Mephista here.

Lady Metroplexer stands up, her emotional breakdown temporarily subsided. She nods and turns to me.

"It'll be okay," she proclaims. "We're superheroes. This is what we do."

Lady Metroplexer's sonic boom sweeps us all off our feet, the nuke disappearing with her.

Seconds later, deep in the distance, the nuke ignites.

Oh, God. The nuke. Oh my God.

We need to leave before the crowd reaches the parking lot. Children and adults begin to scream out. Panic spreads throughout the school and will quickly seep into the nearby neighborhoods. Fear and confusion have overtaken reason. The bomb, removed from the city in its final seconds, grips the area surrounding us into an uncontained and indomitable chaos. We need to leave now. But we don't. We stay trapped in this horrific moment, refusing to move dare we push time forward. But we need to leave. Now.

Kid Metroplexer rolls off the caved-in car, staggering toward us. He remains stoic only briefly, the façade quickly fading. We turn toward him. Spiromaniac asks him the question. The one we all have.

"Can Lady Metroplexer survive—"

He interrupts.

"No. She can't."

He breaks composure, his uncontrollable cries filling the silence we dare not break.

8

This is what happens when I'm a superhero. People die. People who are far better than I am. People who don't deserve to die. Yet I still breathe, unharmed and ready to kill again. I shouldn't have returned as Miss Nucleus, but I did. And now Lady Metroplexer is dead.

Six months ago, Bamboo and the Amazing Punchfist caught a drug dealer. They broke eight of the guy's ribs. The two superheroes offered the man a deal: cough up his supplier and they'll go away, or keep quiet and suffer eight more broken ribs. The drug dealer gave up his supplier who lived in a nearby drug den in the Normand neighborhood – part of a collection of neighborhoods we cutely call the "stabbing" parts of town. Because three of us have been stabbed there.

They called me to investigate on their behalf. Not because they wanted to. None of us like taking down drug dens or crack houses or meth labs or anything similar. Drug addicts tend to be unpredictable, numerous, and surprisingly well-armed. In the worst-case scenario, word will travel quickly throughout a neighborhood and an angry mob of nearby drug addicts will gather proactively outside before we can finish the mission. Of course they're angry; that's where they get their drugs.

So for this particular mission, Bamboo and the Amazing Punchfist called me, because I couldn't be stabbed. And because Kid and Lady Metroplexer were out of town that day. I went to check out the place.

You see, when the Child Soldiers decide to do our superhero-ing, we (reluctantly) agree to follow the six tenets created by Spiromaniac to enforce some sort of perceived order. The Code of Superheroism. The How-to-Be-a-Superhero poster keeps the police a little more satiated and gives us a good reason to reject any creepy newcomers if we so choose. When Forestchild initially joined us, he invited his friend Polar Bear to join alongside him. But, while no one could fully prove it with enough evidence, Polar Bear almost certainly ate a dude. So the Child Soldiers used Spiromaniac's first and second rules to politely tell Forestchild he couldn't invite his friend while also ensuring the Child Soldiers wouldn't be forever known as the superhero team that once let a cannibal join their ranks.

Our Code of Superheroism:

1. Do not use more force than is absolutely necessary.
2. Be kind and generous to bystanders or hostages.
3. Always be ready to intervene if you see a crime.
4. Never give up if retreat means innocent lives will be lost.
5. Never expect or demand payment from those you help.
6. Laziness kills. Be meticulous and vigilant while in the field.

There you go. The ideals we all strive for. Except eight months ago, War Soul turned a drug dealer into a paraplegic for selling weed to children. Two years ago, Hacker Plus ruined a random stranger's credit score for telling her that she should wear sexier clothes. Three months ago, Featherblade and Icarus ignored an apartment fire to avoid missing an important test at school. A year and a half ago, Fisherwoman abandoned a kidnapped Coast Guard officer with his captors when a hand grenade blew up her harpoon stash. Five months ago, Belial snatched an iPad off the store shelf after she stopped an irate woman from screaming at the assistant manager – also, in violation of tenet one, Belial stopped the woman by grabbing her in a headlock and aggressively dragging her out of the store. And tenet six – that's the one I broke six months ago at the drug den.

I managed to escort all the druggies outside. Violently. Luckily, no crowd had gathered outside yet. The Child Soldiers' protocol for breaking up drug dens demands that I either collect all the illegal objects to turn into the police or I remove all traces of illegal objects from the area. The first option is to ensure convictions in court, and the second option only if a situation has escalated past the point of collection. The drug dealers were no longer a threat, but I didn't bring any baggies, so I opted for the second choice. Since drugs are flammable, I lit a controlled fire and called the fire department. By the time they arrived, the drugs were destroyed and the house unusable. I left the area as soon as I heard the sirens to avoid the paperwork – the police couldn't arrest the addicts if no drugs remained anyway, making the normal superhero paperwork back at the police station unnecessary. Mission accomplished.

Except the house wasn't just a drug den. They also ran a human trafficking network, where women – eventual sex slaves or prostitutes – would be held against their will in the house before the local gang sells them to their buyers. I never checked the basement, and twenty-three women burned to death.

I quit being Miss Nucleus, upped my daily alcohol intake, and unsuccessfully attempted to emotionally process the worst mistake in the entire history of Burlington superheroes.

All my coworkers eventually forgave me – because in spite of everything, the mistake was incompetence and not malevolence – but my shame prevented me from rejoining them. I soon took a job as mall security thanks to Kid Metroplexer, and I slowly began attending parties again. Plus, and maybe this influenced my under-aged coworkers' compassion, I was the only one who could nab large quantities of alcohol without rummaging through my parents' liquor cabinet.

But for the past six months, I've essentially rotated between a crushing, suffocating guilt and a desperate desire to blur my world into an alcoholic nothingness.

Then Lady Metroplexer died saving the city from a nuclear

explosion. I dreamt that night that I found a genie hidden in a lamp. One wish, he says. What do you want? And all my grief and dreams and powerlessness merged into a single overwhelming thought: I wish it had been me instead.

––––––

A family out camping and hundreds of animals died in the nuclear explosion. That's all, thankfully. Lady Metroplexer managed to get the bomb thirteen miles outside of the city before it blew, but that didn't stop every single news outlet in the world from infinite round-the-clock coverage. Even worse, Freedom released a statement taking credit resulting in the government officially classifying the tragedy as a terrorist act. The city burst into a panic, the citizens' fears not abated just because the nuke only exploded near the city instead of inside it. The police cracked down hard, sending every available officer to clamp down on any and all visible chaos. The people didn't feel safer, and for the next two days, businesses were closed and curfews enforced. On the third day after the explosion, the Burlington police commissioner decided that most of the more impulsive behaviors had been eliminated and the city resumed its normal activities. Well, as normal as any city would be if a small nuclear bomb detonated just outside its city limits.

Hacker Plus, having the foresight or paranoia, rushed home and within minutes, had deleted all camera footage from the school parking lot. She found all backup systems that the cameras fed into and deleted the footage there too. Then she searched for satellites or drones near the school that day and deleted of all their footage too. Next, she broke into the school's security footage and deleted everything from the whole day, erasing our faces so there would no chance of us being spotted. Finally, she hacked the receptionist's cellphone, finding adulterous texts and threatening to release them if the receptionist talked about anything that happened that day.

This meant that while word spread immediately throughout the school, community, and media that superheroes and supervillains were definitely battling over a nuclear weapon in the Tamberlyn High

School parking lot, no one was able to provide any substantial proof of who was involved. Except Freedom, since he openly announced his presence. And Denial and Mephista, who we left for the police after we fled. In a fiery speech the next day, the Burlington police commissioner condemned the superhero community for their lax enforcement of the laws. No longer would these untrained teenagers or costumed adults be allowed to run free in the great, proud city of Burlington. He argued if supervillains are superheroes' responsibility, then we've done an awful job. Any masked vigilante spotted in the city would face the full force of the law, and that included potential prison time. And for those of us aged eighteen or older, that meant being thrown in a prison full of felons we had personally put there. Which meant either a certainty of being shanked to death during lunch or years of protective custody alone in a tiny cell 23 hours a day.

So for the past three days, all superhero-ing froze. A possible ten-year prison term for assaulting a mugger suddenly didn't seem worth it. The one time I went back to my apartment to grab clothes and toiletries, I noticed police cars following me before I managed to lose them in the alleys. I moved in with Spiromaniac, sleeping on her couch – partly for safety reasons and partly because I didn't want to be alone.

Sadly, Lady Metroplexer didn't get a funeral. A flurry of texts by the Child Soldiers attempted to set up a memorial service, but no one wanted to risk a public meeting while the police had their brief martial law. We mourned privately. Metroplexer is still missing while Kid Metroplexer vanished within hours of the blast. Yet every so often, one of Freedom's associates would report to the local news that something violently tornado-like had destroyed their completely legitimate homes or business.

And worst of all, three days after the explosion, despite Freedom's and my own objections, I'm not dead. I had a ten hour window while Stella slept off her injuries, but I did nothing. She was gone an hour at the grocery store, but I did nothing. She spent an afternoon on a conference call with the other Child Soldiers, but I did nothing. I don't know why. But I can guess.

I stood in Stella's shower yesterday. I would need only to fill up the bathtub and then slice a razor down my wrist. Or sink deep in the water and drown. Stella wouldn't know. She couldn't stop me. But I couldn't. I once saw a psychiatrist (the famous Dr. J. Michael Straczynski, I believe) interviewed on TV. For those flirting with suicide, he asked us to consider a single quandary: go ahead and kill yourself, but only, *only* if you honestly believe that in your heart – no matter how broken or despondent – you'll never, ever have another happy day. Every single day for the rest of your life will never again have a single moment of joy. Then you can kill yourself, but only then. I shoved those words deep into my psyche and forgot about them; the words were irrelevant when I was invincible. But now. In that shower. The water a bit too hot. The sound muffled. My tears washed away. I couldn't remember a single day in my life where I've been happy. Not one. But...

And I tried to argue with myself. Won't your friends and family be devastated? Certainly, but if I'm crying every day from an incurable mental illness – a sickness that'll never, ever go away – wouldn't they want my pain to finally stop? Why would they want me to go through this suffering for another sixty years? And oh my God, what if my invincibility means I can't die from old age?

But I turned the shower off, dried myself with a towel, and went about my day. Still breathing. Stella smiled at me when I exited the bathroom.

I won't give up on suicide so easily. I probably have another week until the Liberate wears off and I'm fully invincible again. In that hospital room, Freedom said that the pill should last for two weeks. Plenty of time left to kill myself.

———

Despite a recent paralyzing hesitation of getting caught, the Burlington superheroes still have a mission to complete. Our work has not ended, which no one is happy about. I've never seen Stella yell at so many people, just a constant barrage of, "We've always known the risks! Wear a mask and the police won't know. If you walk away now, people will suffer. Stop it and act like an actual superhero. Kid Metroplexer is clearly on some sort of rampage; we'll deal with him later. You can't skip this meeting; just go to Starbucks and use their Wi-Fi. I loved Lady Metroplexer and how dare you for saying that! Don't you go to the police for any reason. If I hear you went to the police, I'll sic War Soul on you. He treats bone breaking as an art form."

But finally, our new mission has been announced:

1. Locate and rescue Metroplexer.
2. Locate and defeat Freedom.
3. Attempt to regain the police's trust.
4. Prevent whatever the rest of Freedom's "game" contains.
5. Be careful, not heroic. Please, no one else die.

Which of those can I do? Rescue Metroplexer – the city's most powerful superhero? Fight Freedom in actual combat? God, no. And I'm not going near the police. But, maybe, I have a lead on the fourth task.

Spiromaniac and I head to Harold Industries.

The company seems unaffected by any of the recently dire current events. The glass is always perfectly polished. The plants appear much larger than before, although I swear they're plastic. Our t-shirts and jeans still look out of place in the professional lobby of a professional business. But today, only one receptionist mans the front desk. The same one as last time. Carol. So, as what survival experts recommend when approached by a large animal, I'm going to stand my ground and make as much noise as possible.

"Hello, Ms. Receptionist. Carol. How are you on this lovely post-nuclear day? Remember me? It's been a week, but there hasn't been a day I haven't thought of you."

She looks up.

"Why are you here?"

She definitely recognizes me.

"I need to speak to my parents, the Dr. Lewises. This is of an urgent matter of important science matters. If you could please supply me and my dear partner with visitor passes, I promise to forever leave you alone until I need another visitor pass."

The receptionist lets loose a formidable groan, making sure I know how much I annoy her.

"I'll give a visitor pass to you, but I'm not giving one to your friend. Since the terrorist attack, we've tightened our security, and non-relatives of our employees with no business at our company will not be allowed any further than the lobby. Your parents can come down and talk to both of you, but she can't go up."

Okay, Carol, let's go. Stand my ground. Make lots of noise.

"This woman next to me – she has a name, by the way – is not just my friend. This is my confidante, my lover, and my wife. You can reject her, but know that's discrimination and you can promise I will let every news outlet in town know that your company does not recognize the marriage equality we legally have in our modern, accepting society."

The receptionist buries her head in her hands, letting out a second mightier groan. I bet her hatred of me rivals that of any supervillain I've ever fought. Maybe combined. She turns to Stella.

"Are you her wife?"

Stella meekly and unconvincingly nods. You put that girl in charge of any press conference about any topic, and even the harshest superhero critics can't deny her passion and eloquence. But she's the worst liar I've ever met. But I can lie plenty for both of us.

"Carol, my friend, can't you see how much we're in love? Please give us the visitor passes. I would hate for anyone to think of you as a bigot. Especially not *The Burlington Post*. And *The Burlington Morning News*. And *Buzzfeed*."

With a loathing in her eyes that would haunt a lesser woman, she gives us our visitor passes.

On the elevator ride up, a question pops into my head.

"Stella, you don't have to be my bodyguard anymore. Why

are you still following me around?"

She looks at me dumbfounded, emphasis on the dumb.

"Liza, we're a team."

"And lovers."

She rolls her eyes.

"Talk to me when you're eight inches taller and have some chest hair. Speaking of which and since we have a lengthy elevator ride ahead of us, what's your type anyway, Liza? You told me once and I don't remember."

I pause while I think. No, new tactic. Reflect the question.

"We're not really lovers? Are you breaking up with me?"

"Stop it, Liza. Answer me."

Unable to avoid her nosiness, I take another moment and think. I must have a type, right? Are my standards currently as low as my self-esteem?

"On a one-to-ten scale of attractiveness, where do I rank, you think?" I ask.

"An eight?"

I involuntarily laugh out loud.

"What? God no, Stella. Thank you for being a great friend. On a good day, I'd say I'm a six. I'd want to date someone between a, let's say, four and an eight. Lower than a four and I'd eventually resent them, but anything higher than an eight and my insecurities would drive them away. Anywhere in that range is fine by me."

"Your type is 40% of all the world's men?"

"Chest hair would be nice too."

The elevator doors open and we get off on my parents' floor. Nothing different. No security guards. One security camera. Maybe more aggravated receptionists in the lobby were Harold Industries' only security upgrade.

My parents' lab smells weird, but I'm always afraid to ask. They'll give an honest, in-depth answer, but I barely passed high school chemistry, much less professional scientists describing a state-of-the-art revolutionary new pill or gizmo. I counter them the same way when they ask me about my dating life. Ten minutes of me making up wishy-washy text messages I've been swapping with a bunch of guys bores them enough that they no longer ask.

My parents completely ignore me after Stella walks into the lab. My dad embraces her tightly enough to lift her off the ground. My mom bombards her with questions about her life, her parents, her superhero adventures, and anything else that comes to mind. Her diet. Her hairstyle. Her college plans. Her interest in floral design that she mentioned once to them three years ago. Spiromaniac, the master politician she is, answers every question enthusiastically, gracefully, and with the poise of an official press conference. I finally interrupt.

"You know, your daughter's here too. Not just the daughter you wish you had."

"Sweetheart, we haven't seen Stella in months. We're excited." My mom chides me. "Okay, Liza – my real daughter – how come you haven't called us since that nuclear bomb went off?"

"I still don't have a cell phone."

"But you called us a week ago on another person's cell phone. Was it your cell phone, Stella?"

She sheepishly nods. I drop the excuse and cut my losses.

"Sorry, mom. Dad. My bad."

"Liza, do you know what happened with the bomb?"

"Nope."

"How are all your superhero friends doing?"

"Great."

"What's going to happen to you all now?"

"Hide from the police."

"Do you want the leftover pizza on the counter?"

"Yes, please."

They ask Stella the same questions as she painfully skirts around each one. Except the pizza. She kindly refuses that.

Now my turn.

"This is superhero business, but I have a question for you two, if you don't mind—"

My dad interrupts, begging my mom to tell me the news.

"We first," she announces. "We got a new oven. Remember how the old one would only cook half the food? Well, this new one – did you know Amazon sells ovens? – is amazing. So many dials. I don't know what half the dials do. But we made a macaroni and cheese in there last night, and oh my goodness, Liza, it was the best macaroni and cheese we've ever cooked."

"Okay, but—"

"I know you're thinking, 'Why are my parents going on about an oven?' But when's the last time you've been over for dinner? Like a month? That's ridiculous. You're our only child. If visiting your aging parents isn't enough, now you have a new reason. You'll have the best meal of your life, and you know what? I know we shouldn't, but if you come over, after dinner we'll let you have one glass of wine. Red. White. Pink. Your choice. Does tomorrow night work for you?"

"Look, mom, I love ovens just as much as—"

My dad stops me. "Tell her about the pork we made. Tastes just like we cooked it on the grill. Maybe better."

I remain calm. How could I yell at people who mean so well? Especially the woman who pushed me out of her body alongside the man who stood steadfast next to her in the hospital as she cried and screamed and pooped. I've heard some women poop when they have a baby. But I interrupt them. Probably rudely. But time is of the essence – is also what Stella told me when we missed our first bus because I took too long to pee in the convenience store.

"Real superhero stuff going on. Important stuff. It's why we're here. I mean, besides seeing you all. I apologize for my abruptness, but what's going on with the Liberate drug?"

My dad seems bummed that I totally ignored all the oven and dinner talk, but he answers.

"That's a vague question, sweetheart. The scientists working on it are pretty hush-hush, and we gave you the pill we were asked to examine. They believed our lie that we had lost it, probably rolled off the table and crushed it somewhere. But – and before we answer with whatever we know – what did you do with it?"

"The pill? I lost it. I think it rolled off a table and—"

Spiromaniac nudges me with her elbow.

"Liza, tell them the truth. You know what they risked to give you that pill."

Fine. If we're to do our job – save lives, whatever – then we need my parents' full cooperation. They deserve to know. They're guaranteed their jobs by the lawsuit anyway.

"You're right, I'm sorry. Mom and dad, here's the absolute, non-exaggerated truth. I tried to stop a bank robbery by Desperado. It went badly, and she told me to bring a drug called Liberate to an abandoned warehouse."

My mom interjects. "But why you?"

"Because I don't keep my secret identity hidden very well. They knew that you two worked at the same company that produced the Liberate, so I was the obvious choice. At the warehouse, I was forced to swallow the Liberate."

"The scientists tell us it's a painkiller."

"Nope. The opposite. Took away my powers. Freedom wanted the Liberate to use on Metroplexer. He still plans to. So, and I know this is presumptuous of me, but Stella and I need access to the Liberate lab. Because we need to destroy all of it before he can use it on our town's most valuable player."

My parents look at each other, taking the necessary time to process everything I just said.

"Liza. You're not invincible anymore? Are you okay?"

"I'm never okay. But physically, I'm fine. Don't worry."

"You know that there's no way we can possibly get you into the Liberate lab, much less the dozens of laws being broken by you destroying the pills."

Spiro scrunches her nose – her thinking face.

"Hold on. There's a bunch of this that doesn't make sense. The Liberate team must know Liberate isn't a painkiller, and they know you would discover it's not when you examined it. Why would they give you a pill at all? When did you receive the pill?"

"The day before Liza came."

"I've witnessed far too many supervillain schemes to believe that's a coincidence. They must have known Liza would be coming, and the only way they would know that is if they received word directly from either Freedom or one of his lackies. I don't see any other way. Has the Liberate team ever been investigated for corruption or anything suspicious?"

"Not that we know of."

"Assuming the scientists were working for Freedom for whatever reasons – monetary or coerced – then who was the scientist who brought you the Liberate pill? Where is his lab?"

My parents pause. "Dr. Molinas. He gave us the pill. He's one of the researchers. And—" Another pause. "The lab is on the 23rd floor. Go to the end of the hallway on the left. Please don't hurt the man; we've known him for years and he's a good person."

They say nothing else. They've worked for Harold Industries their entire life, and I wonder if their corporate benefactor's possible corruption feels like a punch in their gut. Like when a significant other cheats – the bond of trust shatters. Permanently, in some cases. Like my boyfriend Tommy in seventh grade. I saw you kissing Rachel, you bastard.

Stella pulls her mask out of her back pocket, then a second one for me.

"We need to ask Dr. Molinas some questions. If the police arrive later, tell them you were threatened and had no choice. Thank you for your help. I'd like to come over for pork soon as well."

"Don't you hurt him, Stella!" My mom yells after her. "He is not a supervillain!"

Spiromaniac nods, but I'm not certain whether that was in agreement or to satiate my parents' fears.

Following Spiro's idea, the two of us wait outside the men's bathroom for an uncomfortable hour. We're scared to talk in case anyone overhears anything. Our masks lay stuffed in our pockets. They really should up the security in this building. For a corporation that profits from curious scientists, no one seems even remotely curious about two teenage girls in street clothes hanging out in the hallway.

Finally, we see Dr. Molinas – his nametag prominently hanging off his shirt pocket. A short man, unkempt hair, and the scraggly beard of a man who doesn't shave often. He doesn't give us a second glance, but we don the masks and follow him in. Thankfully, whichever distracted deity watches over us felt we finally deserved a break. No one else is in the bathroom. No one saw the three of us go in. There's a lock on the inside of the bathroom. Beautiful. And when our doctor pulls down his pants, Spiro shoves him against the wall. Men will be more receptive to physical threats if their penis is out, a drunk Kid Metroplexer once told us.

"Who are—"

Nope. Spiro's forearm pins him. He won't go anywhere, his chest pushed deep into the urinal. I lean up against the sink. She begins the standard interrogation speech. Like the Miranda Rights of potential violence.

"Dr. Molinas. We need to have some words with you. My name is Spiromaniac and this is my partner Miss Nucleus. We've been having a rough couple of days."

"I don't know wh—"

She pushes harder.

"No. We don't have a lot of time, so Miss Nucleus and I are going to do a quick Good Cop, Bad Cop routine. She will ask you a question, and then you'll answer. If you don't, I'm going to hurt you. Badly hurt you. Got it? And understand that we're aware what Freedom will do to you if you say anything. I don't care. So behave. Ask away, Miss Nucleus."

Spiro graduated from the War Soul method of questioning. Though if I were her, I'd move to the side. Sometimes they get so scared they piss themselves.

"Doctor," I begin. "We need all your Liberate. How can you get it to us?"

"I can't do any—"

Spiro snatches his hand. She casually mentions how easy fingers break. Though to her credit, War Soul would have broken Dr. Molinas' fingers before the interrogation started.

"Again. We need all your Liberate. How can you get it to us?"

"We don't have it! Don't you realize what that drug can do? Harold Industries only gave us the one pill that Freedom had me deliver to the Lewises. We aren't allowed to touch the stash – we can only study Liberate's data and the results of experiments already conducted, but that's all. After that nuke went off, the pills were moved to a Harold Industries warehouse that we sometimes use for excess product. The company is scared that the drug will be compromised."

Spiro lets go of his hand.

"But the drug is already compromised, isn't it?"

"Yes! The company screwed up! Freedom came to our homes about three weeks ago. He gave us a choice: $50,000 or death. What could we do? What other choice did we have?"

Spiro releases him, giving Dr. Molinas a quick moment of privacy so he can zip up his pants. She adjusts her lopsided mask.

"Please hand over your keycard," she demands. "We'll need it. Thank you. Okay, our standard spiel: you never saw us, this never happened, we'll come back if you tell someone, etcetera. You get it. So on to our final question: Dr. Molinas, where is this warehouse?"

He tells us the address. We tell him it may be a good idea for him to take his family on an impromptu vacation for a few days. Starting as soon as he washes his hands.

———

The warehouse's floodlights illuminate the loading area, but those are the only lights on the street. Dark and creepy. The warehouse sits just blocks from Patrick's, the ruined bar I fought Lazerz, and in the distance, voices and the sounds of traffic can be heard from other bars full of drunks and gamblers. Yet no one dares to venture to this spooky corner of the neighborhood. No one walks down the street. No one exits the warehouses. No vehicles are parked nearby. That's usually a bad sign. Supervillains love ambushes.

Our plan is simple: we use the keycard to open the door and take the initiative to secure the area of any hostiles. Once everything is clear, we call in Icarus and Featherblade – they're stationed on a roof close by. They'll fly in, take the Liberate barrels or containers or whatever, fly them to the lake, and drop them in. Problem solved. No fire or explosives or anything that risks dispersing Liberate dust all over the warehouse.

Over Spiro's cellphone speaker, Featherblade chimes in.

"Ready, ladies? If there's an army of bad guys in there, call us in for reinforcements. We bought a whole bunch of bear pepper spray online last week, and we really want to try it out. Pepper spray for bears, ladies. It sprays thirty feet. How cool is that? Super cool. Actually, y'know what? Call us in no matter who you're facing."

Spiro replies with an affirmative. Our masks both on (at her insistence), flashlights shining, and Dr. Molinas' keycard in hand, we open the door silently and step into the warehouse. Ready to fight. Ready to spoil Freedom's game.

Except the warehouse is empty. Just some boxes stacked by the door. Icarus asks if we see anyone. No one. But that doesn't make sense. Freedom must know about this warehouse, yet our turnaround from Harold Industries was just a couple hours – even if he knew about our talk with Dr. Molinas, he wouldn't be able to empty the entire warehouse out that quickly. Yet the doctor wasn't lying – Hacker Plus checked the lease and Harold Industries definitely owns this place. Then where is the Liberate?

We open a few of the boxes: packing peanuts, lab equipment, more lab equipment, stuff that is probably lab equipment.

"Liza, I think there might be something here," Spiro shouts.

Abruptly, Featherblade screams out from the cell phone.

"Uh, hey, you kind of need to leave now. Like right now. I

don't know if you triggered an alarm or someone was watching you but there's a whole bunch of cop cars coming your way. We're pulling back, and you got to get out of there! Ladies, I think you stepped into a trap!"

"Not a trap," Spiromaniac yells back.

The lights of the cop cars begin to shine through the warehouse windows. I pull Spiro's arm, but she won't budge. In front of her lays a suitcase. The sirens blare through the walls. I yank her arm again, but she shoves me away.

"Stop it, Liza. There's a note on top. What does 'seven of twelve' mean?"

The cops' speaker booms out.

"Surrender! Come out with your hands up. Escape is impossible. Lethal force will be used if you don't surrender."

Spiromaniac opens the suitcase. Our stomachs drop.

Inside sits another nuke.

Spiromaniac shrieks into her cell phone.

"Featherblade! Icarus! Don't go anywhere! You still carry explosives on you?"

Nothing.

"Answer me, goddamit!"

"Sorry! Yes, always. But the police are everywhere, Stella."

Spiro scans the empty warehouse.

"I don't care! The back wall. Use all the firepower you have and blow a hole in the back wall! The sirens will cover the sounds of your jetpacks. We have probably about thirty seconds before they hit us with the tear gas! Move it!"

Nothing again.

"Did you hear me?"

"Yes ma'am! On our way."

We stare at each other. Then the nuke. Then each other.

"What do we do with this?" Spiro asks.

"Take it with us!" I respond.

"What? No!"

"Do you trust the police to disarm it?"

"Do you trust *us* to disarm it?"

"Hacker Plus almost had it disarmed!"

"Hacker Plus tried to disarm it by asking Google!"

"We'll be careful!"

"As we run from the police?"

"I don't know!"

"I don't know either!"

"I'm taking it."

"Don't take it!"

"It's coming with us!"

The back wall explodes much louder than I anticipated. I grab the handle of the heavy suitcase. Spiro throws me her cell phone.

"Be careful with the nuke! Take the phone, Liza, I'll fight for both of us if it comes to that."

Tear gas canisters burst through the windows. We scramble out the newly created back entrance into a side alley, but we barely step into the night air before the police rush both ends of the alley. We're pinned behind two dumpsters, one on each side. Spiro whispers into my ear.

"Don't worry, we'll get out of this. We've been in situations like this before. Featherblade and Icarus know what to do."

But—

I can finally—

I'm so sorry.

I'm not passing up this opportunity.

I stand up. Spiro throws me a confused look. She can't stop me. With one hand on the suitcase and one hand on the phone, I walk into the open and rip off my mask. I can get the police to do it. I know I can.

"I am Liza Lewis. I am the superhero Miss Nucleus. In this suitcase is a nuclear weapon, the same type of nuclear weapon that exploded three days ago. Go. Take a look."

I slide the suitcase over to the officers. Slowly, they open it.

"What are you doing?" Spiro yells.

Too bad. Too late. I'm not losing this chance. I point to Stella's cell phone.

"In my hand is the detonator. Look at it. See it. And know this. I work with Freedom. He and I worked together on the last nuclear weapon, and we continue to do so with this bomb. There is only one way to stop me."

I walk toward the policemen. They shout at me. They pull out their weapons.

"There's only one way to stop this nuke from going off. You have no choice. Do it. Do it! Stop me!"

I continue to walk toward them. They shout louder. I don't care. This is it. Finally.

"What are you waiting for? Do it! Shoot me! Do it!"

I hold the cell phone in the air. My other hand goes up, and as my finger touches the screen, the police shoot. All of them. The bullets rip into me and I drop to the ground.

Finally. As they pile on me, my blood seeping into the concrete, I see smoke canisters fill up the alley. The roar of Featherblade and Icarus' jetpacks overtakes the policemen's shouts. Good. Stella will be safe. And I will finally get what I want. I lose consciousness. For the first time, I am happy.

9

I awaken handcuffed to a hospital bed. A sign above the door reads Burlington County Jail. But alive.

Of course.

When Stella was a toddler – and this is a story she has only told once when she was very, very drunk – she and her dad were playing in their backyard. At some point during the roughhousing, her father accidentally hit her in the head. It's cool, kids are tough. But instinctively and without knowing she could do this, she reflected the pain back onto him. No one knew she had these powers – not her parents nor herself – and in his surprise, Stella's dad fell backwards, smashing his head on the concrete and rolled into the pool. He drowned.

She has to save people, she slurred, to wipe the ledger clean of her father's death. She was two years old at the time – she's forgiven herself, her mother forgave her – but that kind of guilt sticks forever. Then she vomited into my bathtub. The next day when we woke up, Spiro asked me if I remembered anything about last night and I shook my head. Nothing, I lied. What did we do? What did we talk about? Is that your puke in my shower? She wiped her runny nose and went into the kitchen satisfied.

Will she ever forgive me for almost being another loved one to die in front of her? I can only imagine the helplessness she must have felt. And even so, I wish I was dead. More than anything.

A doctor, noticing I'm up, comes over.

"Awake? You should count your blessings. Lucky you."

"Yeah. Lucky," I mutter.

"You were shot ten times. Four in the chest, three in the torso, one in your leg, and two in the shoulders. But when we examined you, the bullets never penetrated past the skin, like you were nailed with paintballs instead. File says you have superpowers, so congratulations on being superhuman, I guess."

Superhuman. My invincibility's coming back earlier than Freedom predicted. Fantastic. Wonderful. I might still have time. A fall from a skyscraper could kill me. But here I am, in police custody. What charge will they file? Treason? Probably treason.

"Oh, I almost forget. You have a guest, Ms. Lewis," the doctor announces. "Shall I send him in?"

I don't speak, but the doctor sends the guest in anyway.

Captain Hanson walks up, dressed in his properly pressed police uniform, reeking of cigarette smoke, his mustache jiggling slightly with each step he takes.

"What the hell, Liza?"

"You know me. Spreading terror wherever I can."

He takes a seat next to my bed. My God. How many cigarettes did he just smoke? A carton?

"Tell me the truth. No more lies."

I still lie, but like, a white lie.

"My partner and I suspected that Freedom placed more nukes in the city. We went to investigate a possible location."

"Your partner being Spiromaniac."

"Who knows? She was wearing a mask."

"You tried to get yourself killed."

I stay silent. Why bother? What's the point? My invincibility's coming back. I messed up. I waited too long. I should have sliced my wrists in that shower. But I didn't. No one to blame for that but me.

"Liza. Stop it. Dry your eyes. I'll convince the district attorney to drop most of the charges. I can vouch for all the criminals you put away. I have your psychiatric hospital records and your official medical diagnosis. I haven't heard back from your therapist, but I'll keep trying. But listen, they're going to get you for obstruction of justice. I can't do anything about that. You're the first superhero we arrested under the police commissioner's new edict. If they try to make an example out of you, you're going to do a few months in prison. I'll try to get you probation. You'll have to spend a few weeks in jail regardless until everything can be sorted out. Can you afford a lawyer?"

"Nope."

"Then I'll talk to the lawyer they appoint you."

"Why do this for me?"

"Liza. Dammit, Liza. You frustrate me. You anger me. You consistently lie to me—"

"Yes, I do! So why would you do this for me?" I interrupt. "I have so many people who want to help me. You. Spiro. My parents. Dr. Johnson. Haven't you all learned by now? I will always disappoint you! I will always let you down!"

The captain glares at me.

"Liza, shut up and let me finish. You want to know why I'm doing this for you? Believe whatever ridiculous misconceptions you want about yourself, but I know you do far more good than harm in this world. And I'm definitely not going to let you harm yourself. Protect and serve, that's my job. That means protecting you."

"Protect?" I'm yelling now. People are turning their heads to see the commotion. "Don't you get it? We found the nuke in the Tamberlyn High School. We found it! We tried to disarm it. We almost had it. And Freedom decided to detonate it. And Lady Metroplexer saved the city! She protected Burlington! Not you. Her! She died to save all of you! It's only because of her that a large portion of the city isn't rubble and you have the gall to say that you're protecting me? I should be dead, not her. Never her. Go away. Leave me alone."

Barely audible, he whispers, "I didn't know she died."

"She did. Goodbye."

Captain Hanson walks out of the room, clearly sensing the conversation is over. He pauses in the doorway.

"Liza, you can't stop me from helping you."

Help? Protect? Go to hell. I don't want sympathy. I don't want help. I just want to die. And now I can't even do that.

———

A few hours later, the doctor discharges me from the hospital, proclaiming I'm ready for my new county jail stay. I'm processed, fingerprinted, strip searched, and shipped off down a long hallway with a guard on each side to the holding cells. At least until they can figure out what charges to file against me.

"Hey, sir. Other sir. Cool baton. You know who I am, right?"

"Miss Nucleus. You saved that cruise ship a few years back."

"Hell yeah."

It feels good to be recognized. Or have the guard repeat what he read on my file.

"You ever meet a superhero before?"

"Warthog saved my life once."

I make a gagging noise.

"Hate that guy. Did you get to lead him to his jail cell as well?"

"No."

"I'm nervous, sir. Will you hold my hand?"

"No."

"What about you, other sir?"

Nothing.

"Okay, gentlemen. Great conversation."

The Burlington County Jail – well known to be underfunded and understaffed – puts its (alleged) criminals into twelve person holding cells. They accept the added chaos for the money saved. I enter my cell, under the watchful eye of my fellow (alleged) inmates, and the door locks behind me. There are two beds. A few TVs and benches line the cell. One toilet. That's all. No privacy.

So what now? Do we begin a montage where despite tense

beginnings, a fellow prisoner and I wretch up the same pink meatloaf-y thing, and as we lock eyes, I learn that I'm not so different from these women after all? That the prison system is unfairly incarcerating non-violent inmates and people's minds can change once they learn that these women are women and not numbers and that the poor decisions these women made when they were young and dumb shouldn't haunt them for the rest of their lives? Or maybe I'm surrounded by a bunch of killers and we all realize that we have talents extending beyond murder when the new, unconventional warden forces us to put on a Burlington County Jail Off-Broadway performance of *Chicago*? But honestly? I'm not really in the mood. I've had a bad day. A bad life.

Let's do something stupid.

I march over to one of the beds – a gigantic woman lies on it reading a magazine.

"Hey, you!" I shout. "Get off my bed!"

The cell gets quiet. Good. I want this. I want to lash out. Immaturity and impudence be damned.

Slowly hoisting herself up, the woman turns toward me, much larger than I expected. Like large enough for the two of us to recreate that scene from *Empire Strikes Back* where Luke carries Yoda around in a backpack. I strain my neck looking up at her.

"Hey. I'm Liza. The superhero Miss Nucleus. You know me, right? The guard's a fan. Thank you for giving me this bed. I'd like your magazine too – I've never read *Modern Cat* magazine."

She inches forward, her breasts now very much in my face.

"Miss Nucleus. You're Miss Nucleus."

Her voice sounds like if a bear tried to learn English, which would make sense, since her breath smells a lot like salmon.

I can see the other women begin to move closer – a wolf pack rallying around its alpha. I figure if there's one guard watching outside the cell, they'll need to call for reinforcements before they can break up a fight. They'll probably need to suit up too, with those shields or helmets or Kevlar or whatever. That's a minimum of five to ten minutes. Well, c'mon, woman. Punch me. Fight me.

"Look at you. What are you, six foot four? Have I ever beaten up any of your friends? I don't think so. I probably would have remembered if I fought any Bigfoots."

Finally provoked enough, she strikes me. It feels like a strong poke against my cheek. The last remnants of my fading mortality. Okay. Let's get this started.

"Ladies and yetis, I am your new boss. You will obey me and bestow me an offering of one Cheetos bag a week. From this point forward, all TVs will be turned to the Game Show Network. I have episodes of *Family Feud* I want to get caught up—"

She slams me to the floor. The others join in to fight alongside their leader. Criminals aren't too noble during their power struggles. So I fight all of them. A giant pile of women.

But piles I can do. Those are my specialty. I can't be hurt and I won't lose consciousness – and after the woman's fist barely registered, I'm not worried. I punch and I scratch. If they hold my arms down, I knee and I kick. If they hold my legs down, I bite and I spit. Even fully immobile, I can still win. There's a reason boxing rounds are three minutes long: fighting quickly tires people out. I don't have to wait long. I break a nose and a woman retreats, my knee connects with a throat and a woman withdraws, I hock a loogie into a woman's mouth and she no longer desires to brawl.

And I feel better with each hit that connects. Quite a bit better, actually. By the time the guards arrive, only four women remain on top of me. Their leader isn't one of them. I snatch the *Modern Cat* magazine as the guards drag me away, but a guard slaps it out of my hand. The same guard who said he knew me – a betrayal I will never, ever forget.

I'm thrown in a six-foot-by-nine-foot cell by myself. A holding cell for starting a fight against all other eleven inmates within thirty seconds of me entering a cell.

A bed. A toilet. That's it. Just me and my thoughts – and I can't visualize a worse personal hell. Everything I do in my daily life –

from drinking to fighting to sleeping to drinking – is to curb my own thoughts. To stop me from thinking. And now I sit and I think. And I lie down and I think. And I think and I think.

I've made an enormous mistake.

———

Five hours in.

I wonder if I could ever be happy. A steady boyfriend? A job I can tolerate? The adoration of my peers? Would that work? No. I'm petty and insecure and jealous and needy and moody and require constant validation. No man could love me. No man should love me. I just want to be loved. Held. Reassured. I know I have faults. I know. I can't be left alone like this.

I bang on the door. I beg the guards. Nothing.

What if I accept I'll never be happy? Will that help? I need my pills. My anti-depressants. Where's Captain Hanson? My parents never took me to church. But I beg you, God. Save me. Rescue me. Hold me. Please. I go to sleep, and I pray I never wake up. But I know already. I'll wake up. I'll always wake up.

Ten hours in.

Presenting a poem from the inspirational Burlington County Jail Poet Laureate Liza Lewis:

Invulnerable invulnera-sucks.

Fifteen hours in.

Audio Transcript

Licensed Therapist: Liza Lewis

Patient: Liza Lewis

LEWIS: A mermaid is half-fish, right?

LEWIS: Yes, of course.

LEWIS: Both a mermaid's parents are mermaids, right?

LEWIS: What are you getting at?

LEWIS: How do we know a fish isn't a mermaid?

LEWIS: Because a mermaid is half-human and half-fish.

LEWIS: Biologically, if both a mermaid's parents are half-fish and half-human, then there would only be a fifty percent chance that a human *and* a fish half are inherited. What if the kid inherits both the fish halves? He or she is a fish, but still classified as a mermaid.

LEWIS: Both halves could be human, too. Are you saying mermaids could walk amongst us? Living in our cities? Eating our food? Watching us eat their children?

LEWIS: I'm scared.

Twenty hours in.

What would Quotientia do to stop Freedom and find the nukes if she was still living in the city? I haven't thought of her in a long time. In my beginning days of superhero-ing, she was the superhero I aspired to be.

The woman graduated college at fourteen years old. She spent her teen years as a traveling scientist investigating long-lost ancient artifacts. Using that research, she devoted her twenties to scientifically and magically terraforming the Amazon Jungle back from its aggressively decayed state. Eager to move on after saving thousands of Amazonian animal species from extinction, she dedicated her thirties hunting down the Grand Wizards – a group of several hundred Ku Klux Klan members who stumbled upon a device that turned them into actual wizards. On her fortieth birthday, she joined the BSO, and in her five-year tenure, crime decreased in Burlington by 30%. Quotientia retired a couple years ago to solve the mosquito crisis in Africa.

She has no superpowers.

I wanted to be her so badly, but I learned quickly that I didn't possess her innate drive or genius intellect. My parents keep telling me that hard work will always bring more results than talent alone, and I believe them, but—

Stop it, Liza. Metroplexer says I need to stop seeing myself as a victim. But—

Twenty five hours in.

Science report on important scientific science from scientist Dr. Liza Lewis, PhD in science: bologna will successfully stick to jail cell walls until guards yell at you to take it down.

Thirty hours in.

Audio Transcript

Licensed Therapist: Liza Lewis

Patient: Liza Lewis

LEWIS: But then what about centaurs or minotaurs?

LEWIS: Or harpies. Or satyrs.

LEWIS: We eat a burger and a minotaur could be sitting next to us. A single, silent tear running down its cheek. What if we're in an Animal Cold War? Animal sleeper agents all over the city. Waiting. Watching. Ready to strike.

LEWIS: We're doomed, aren't we? How can we stop this? What if we all became vegetarians?

LEWIS: Let's not go that far.

Thirty five hours in.

F: Kramer

Marry: Jerry

Kill: George

Forty hours in.

How long has it been since I had a boyfriend? A year? In my romantic relationships, I unfairly latch my entire future of possible happiness onto someone who can't possibly live up to the impossible standards I set for him. I'm aware I'm emotionally needy, insecure, and overly sensitive. But if I'm to believe I may have one happy day sometime in the future, I can't do it by myself. But that can't possible work out if—

I'm interrupted by a knock from two guards, who demands I come with them.

The two stoic men handcuff me and escort me into another tiny room. I'm told nothing else. Did Freedom order this? Is he going to slowly fill the room with concrete? Maybe lava? If anyone could grab lava and bring it halfway across the world to fill a small room, it'd be Freedom.

A few minutes later, I'm uncuffed and led outside. I get it – the lava is outside. But then I see him. Another person trying to help me. Standing in his tightest t-shirt and his tightest jeans, Kid Metroplexer meets me outside the jail. My hell is over. The hypothetical dark clouds that hovered over my very dark and dingy cell disappear. A merciful God granted me a small reprieve from forcing me to live in a miniscule world without the always desperately needed distractions. Or someone paid my bail. What was my bail set at? I'm totally a flight risk. I bet it was high.

Without saying anything, Grant motions me to take his hand before flying the two of us to the roof.

"My hero," I tease.

"No way," he grins.

"Why are you here?"

"Stella left me thirteen voicemails. Sorry, I was busy."

In the past five days, a strong, overbearing desire for vengeance took up much of Kid Metroplexer's time. He smashed almost thirty homes, bars, restaurants, office buildings, warehouses, parking lots, nail salons, frozen yogurt shops, and pet stores. Anywhere that was owned by a known associate of Freedom. Warrants and due process be damned.

The police didn't arrest him. No charges were filed. They knew better. Grant wasn't going to let himself be arrested and the police had absolutely no way of stopping him. And thanks to his demolition derby, he discovered three more nuke suitcases. So the police commissioner said nothing except releasing to media the criminal records of the people Kid Metroplexer apprehended and the sheer enormity of the nuke suitcases being intercepted from Freedom. Once Grant finally listened to his voicemails and read his text messages, he went to the commissioner and told him that I was working with him. Obvious proof being my possession of one of the nukes when I was arrested. For these types of negotiations, we usually bring the BSO superhero Screwdriver, who's an actual lawyer, but he wouldn't return any messages. So Grant brought Mentalmind, who spent her preteen days obsessed with criminal law. Thankfully, that was enough to get me released.

Kid Metroplexer presents me with a set of clothes and a goody bag that he grabbed from Stella's apartment. A comb with a strand of hair still on it. Definitely someone's used deodorant. Foundation makeup that is not my shade. My keys and wallet. A half-used tin of Altoids. And the chosen outfit: a blue polo, bright red pants, and flip-flops.

"Grant, these aren't my clothes. Stella is a good six inches taller than me. And why red pants? Why not jeans like normal people?"

"She didn't have any clean jeans."

"Who washes jeans?"

"Oh, and here," he exclaims, pulling out a cell phone from his pocket. "It's yours. Your number and contacts and everything."

Noticing my skepticism, he continues.

"Hacker Plus, sort of, she stole your identity, then posed as you to get you a new phone. She was very adamant that you owe her. I'm sorry. We're all pretty sure she's a sociopath. But hey, new cell phone, right?"

"Thank you for getting me out of jail. I'm grateful, and it means a lot that you would do this. Jail sucks," I muster up a half-hearted appreciative gesture before I decide to launch into my own newfound uselessness. "But when I hit up my parents for information, that was my only lead. I don't know what to do now. Unlike my previous task of not dying, I'm not much help anymore."

I ready myself for Kid Metroplexer's usual response – an arrogant monologue with a long explanation of the various duties superheroes can do that don't involve combat or investigation or anything useful. Like volunteering or donating money or anything else I want to punch him for. But he doesn't.

"What time is it?" he asks.

"Around eight, I think? The sun is setting."

"Liza, to put it lightly, I haven't been doing too well recently. But truly, you don't have to do crap. We just like having you around. Most of us. Well, some of us. I do. And the absolute last thing you want to do is talk about my sister, correct?"

"My God, yes."

"I know a place dark, quiet, and owned by someone who owes me. He won't care we're under-aged. Do you want to go get a drink?"

"More than anything."

———

Even if someone wants to recognize two teenage superheroes illegally drinking at a bar, the lights are dimmed to the point where I have to hold my hands out in front of me in order to touch my way to the bathroom. Think of a passed out trucker – that's the best way I can describe the ambiance of this place. Something smells off, like an elderly alcoholic who wet his pants but kept on drinking. People speak loudly around us, but the music gargling from the broken speakers emits a reassuring white noise of secrecy. Everyone leaves everyone else alone, the drinks are cheap (and watered down), and losers can be losers without judgement. Thus Grant and I are both drunk.

"I've told you this a bunch of times before at work," Grant exasperatingly tells me. "I wish you would listen to me when we talk. I'm a sophomore at Burlington Community College. School started a couple weeks ago, not that I've been going to classes lately."

"Shouldn't you just be happy that I'm taking an interest in your life?" I slur. "What are you studying?"

"Nutrition. Personal fitness. If I have to constantly exercise and diet to be a superhero, I might as well make a career out of it."

I motion to the four empty shot glasses in front of him. Then without saying a word, I obnoxiously wag my finger in disapproval. He shakes his head; the beginning of a superior smirk dancing on his lips.

"You're right, Liza. I shouldn't be drinking alcohol. But you see how I've only had shots of vodka? While you've had four beers? What I've drank is infinitely better than what you've had."

"Hyperbole."

"Beer is basically bread. It has loads of sugar, because carbs are sugar. Sugar is what ruins a body. I would rather eat three steaks than drink one glass of orange juice. Haven't you noticed you've never seen me drink a beer or wine or tequila? Only vodka or whiskey or gin or rum for me – they're distilled."

"But beer is tasty."

"Unfortunately, I picked a unitard for my superhero costume."

"You're a unitard."

"Truly, what does Stella see in you?"

I celebrate my hoodie costume by ordering another beer.

"What about you?" he politely asks. "When are you going to college? What do you want to study?"

"I'm not and nothing."

Pity. I get his pity face.

"Do you have any passions or dreams?"

"None right now. I'm rudderless. No plans to make Miss Nucleus into Doctor Nucleus."

Kid Metroplexer doesn't respond, but I detect the tiniest of eye rolls. He asks the bartender for another vodka shot when my beer arrives. I chug the bottle – the bad feelings go away faster that way.

He pounds back the shot, and I can see his determination rise steadfast in his belief that the sharing of personal information should be equal.

"No Doctor Nucleus then. What about Mrs. Nucleus?"

"Shouldn't you get on one knee if you're going to propose?"

I see his teeth clench.

"I forgot I'm talking to Drunk Liza."

"Sorry. My bad," I respond. "Look, I'm the dating equivalent of a garbage fire."

"Please."

"No, no no no no. Let me talk. I told that to Stella one time. She said that I just need to find a man who has the fire extinguisher. But that won't work. I'll always find a way to light myself back on fire. Instead, I need to find a cold, desperate hobo. Someone equally damaged who only wants to warm his freezing hands on my gross, stinky flame. That's what love is, Grant."

"I don't think that's true. Like, at all," he stammers.

"Okay. In all seriousness, buddy – no jokes – I'd be happy to get married. But you know me; I'm a mess. I mean, I'll date, if only because of the free drinks and the much appreciated company and how badly I desperately need love. But I'm only eighteen. When I'm thirty or so I'm sure I can find a man who's willing to settle for me. And don't do that thing where you tell me I'm wrong. That someone will someday and whatever."

He rolls his eyes. For real this time.

"Please. I want to tell you that you're wonderful just the way you are, Liza. That someone amazing is waiting out there for you and you'd make a great girlfriend and any man would be lucky to have you and all those other clichés. I just want it on the record that I said all that. Though, also in all seriousness, I can help you become more attractive to men, if you want. Physically, mentally, and emotionally. You're not overweight, and with a few exercises I've learned in my classes—"

"Nope. Don't you dare."

We sit in silence for a minute or so, both quickly ordering another drink when the opportunity arises. Fine. I'll be nice.

"Grant. What about you? Do you want to get married? What kind of woman are you looking for?"

"I'm definitely going to get married. I'll have kids and grandkids and life will be awesome. My ideal woman? She should keep herself in shape. She'll have a college degree. She'll be— No, you know how it goes. All the standard stuff. I'm not going to list everything. I'm a bit too drunk for that. But I still worry sometimes I'll never find her."

I poke him in his nose.

"Be quiet. You're perfect and you know it."

Angrily and unexpectedly, he bashes the table, almost cracking it in half.

"You think I don't know what I am? I know what I look like. I know how strong I am and how high I can fly and that my dad is rich and that I shouldn't complain or worry when my life gets compared to anyone else's, but I'm still allowed to, aren't I? I'm human."

A long pause. I always suspected him of being an alien, so that's cleared up.

"I'm sorry, Grant. I'm not good at making others feel better about themselves. Do you—" I brace myself. "I'm not great with words, but do you want a hug?"

He shakes his head, smiling.

"Don't you ever worry about me, got it? You worry about you."

Kid Metroplexer's emotional shield of invulnerability reappears. Something he and his father share in common. The bartender brings over our next round. Grant continues before I have a chance to fracture it again.

"Miss Nucleus, did you see what you did? You considered my feelings. I don't think I've ever seen this side of you before, with your usual weapons of jokes and sarcasm. We're going to celebrate our new level of closeness with alcohol. I'm going to tell you how pretty and funny you are and that you're totally a catch. How about a toast? To our future marriages."

"To our future marriages."

We clink our glasses.

As we notice a few of the bar patrons stumbling out, Kid

Metroplexer lightly places his fingers on top of my wrist, tracing the faintest of lines along my forearm.

"The bar closes soon. You want to go back to my place?"

One of my eyebrows shoots up. He continues.

"No, I'm just saying, if we want another drink then I have some liquor at my place. Say the word and I'll fly you to your apartment and we'll part ways, but we've both had such an awful couple of days and it'd be nice to unwind. With another drink, I mean."

Another drink. As if I can't see through his façade. I take a moment before I answer. Not for dramatic effect or anything like that, but I'm drunk and I need a moment to think. And look at him. He's as drunk as I am.

"Grant, I haven't showered in three days."

"You smell all right, trust me."

Fine. I need this.

"Let's go. Lead the way. When we fly, don't cradle me in your arms – I want to ride on your back."

"No," he refuses. "I told you I'm not a horse."

"Then fly me to my apartment. I ride on your back or no deal."

Reluctantly, he agrees to my demand.

10

I sneak out of Kid Metroplexer's apartment before he wakes up. Better this way, so as to avoid those awkward morning-after activities he feels obligated. I don't want breakfast or pillow talk or eye contact.

My irrational fear of the disapproving glances of strangers worries me when I step out into the street and face the full force of a throbbing sun. In my current state, I really shouldn't be seen in direct light. But no one looks. No one cares. Everybody's busy with their own problems, and I'm relieved for the selfish apathy. Still, I keep my head down and powerwalk home. I text Stella back and forth that I'm out of jail for an excuse to keep my head buried in my phone.

Fortunately, I can spend the morning in the non-judgmental walls of my apartment, talking to no one while shoving food in my mouth all by my lonesome. My apartment doesn't care about my body odor or my bloodshot eyes or that I vomited in a gas station bathroom on the way here.

So, because my life can go no other way, my front door's already unlocked. Freedom stands in front of my stove, cooking eggs. He takes a swig from a beer as he waves, signaling me to my kitchen table.

"Good morning! Quite a night, huh? Gosh, you kids grow up so fast, don't you? If you want my opinion, if you're going to cheat on your boyfriend War Soul, I think you can do better than Grant. Way better. I'd rather you tell me that you slept with a mime or a ventriloquist or even the ventriloquist's puppet. But Grant? No shower can clean you off from that. No amount of water or acid or fire can ever get you clean again."

"Are you drinking one of my beers?" I ask.

"You like scrambled eggs? Sit. Not a suggestion. Take a seat."

Two of his bodyguards are sitting on my couch, watching the TV news. Freedom, in his casual recently-divorced-father-trying-to-date-again attire, places a plate of eggs in front of me.

"William!" Freedom barks to my living room. "Get Miss Nucleus a beer."

"Are you sure? It's 9:30 in the morning, sir."

A splash of puzzlement washes across Freedom's face. He bangs his fist on my shove, breaking a chunk off one of the burners.

"Do you want me to kill you and your entire family, William? You're making a phenomenal case for the death of everyone you love. Do you not remember less than a week ago when I activated and detonated a nuclear bomb next to a high school? You remember that? Remember when I was willing to slaughter not just all those schoolchildren, but the hundred thousand people who lived in that area? Yes, William? You remember? Therefore, do you think I give one flying crap about the appropriate time for Miss Nucleus to have a beer? Get off your ass and get Miss Nucleus a beer or I will start this murder fiesta with your dog, Freedom Junior."

William obeys, moving at a speed far beyond that which one should jump through my claustrophobic disaster of an apartment. He opens the beer and hands it to me.

"Freedom Junior?" I ask.

"When someone works for me and gets a new pet, I get to name it. That's in their contract. But I name them all Freedom Junior."

"What if it's a female dog?"

"I don't care about the gender. I name them all Freedom Junior. I get to name all my henchmen's new things. William, refresh my memory. What's your daughter's name?"

175

"We call her Freddie," he sighs. "It's, uh, short for Freedom Junior."

"See? I told you. Forcing people to do stuff against their will – I love it. It's a power move."

"Or a fetish," I clarify.

"Or a fetish," he repeats.

When William returns to my couch, Freedom continues.

"Miss Nucleus, why do you have zero food in your house but twenty-two beers? I had one of my men count. We found a bottle of cheap whiskey under your sink, but I'm not letting that swill touch my lips. I had another one of my men stop by the grocery store once we broke in. These are good eggs, too. The expensive ones. Organic. I only added some cheese and milk – nothing fancy. Some salt and pepper, too. Want to eat? I know you must be starving."

"Why do you have bodyguards?"

"I like the company," Freedom responds. "I'm a talker, and I want people around to listen. You should eat."

When I don't move, he asks me to eat again. This time as a command. Slowly and angrily, I take a bite.

"Not bad eggs, huh? I took cooking classes in college."

"They're not bad, though the company is lacking."

He sneers.

"It's always cute when the hamster tries to bite."

I'm curious how used he is to disrespect. I can't imagine people are rude to his face very often. I mean, I just saw him break a quarter of my stove when William asked about timing. He watches as I awkwardly take another bite before he speaks again.

"Your apartment reeks. Goodness, child. Why would you purposely live here? This whole ambiance reminds me of an abandoned barn. You have to start cleaning up after yourself or else you won't be able to date a man better than Grant. That'd be a damn shame too, because I'd rather you date three rabid possums in a winter coat than that boy."

"I'm going to marry Grant just to spite you. My wedding

vows will be a middle finger in your direction," I reply between bites.

"That thought alone is enough to make me lose my appetite. Well, not quite – I'm too exquisite of a cook to have that ever happen. My eggs taste far more delicious than any disgusting scenarios you dream up. But can we skip the small talk? No talking, yes? Just listen. I need a favor from you."

He sits in the seat next to me and lays his arm over my shoulder, sending chills throughout my whole body.

"William! Ted! Turn down the volume on the TV. Miss Nucleus, the two of us have worked together on a level of mutual respect. This game of ours? It's over in two days. That's all the time I have left. I don't mean that because I'm bored. Though I am a little bored. The only man who has ever been able to stop me no longer can, and I wish not to waste my valuable time with children. Especially children with such terrible taste in boys. William. Ted. Turn down the volume on the TV or I'm going to open Miss Nucleus' window and chuck you across town."

They wisely decide to put the volume on mute. Freedom takes a moment to eat a few bites himself. Off my plate. With my fork. Where are all the supervillains with low self-esteem? I wish I had a fraction of the ego he possesses.

"Dude, Freedom. I get it. You're evil. Please leave."

Freedom sighs, the same sort of sigh an adult makes when a toddler tries to argue bedtimes.

"Evil? No. Seriously, my dear. Is it because I'm a supervillain? Well, it does have the word 'villain' in it. I can see why you'd assume I'm evil. Remember Prohibition in the 1930s? All those gangsters and mobsters who became wealthy by ignoring the law? They flourished, but not because they were evil. They wanted money, respect, and they didn't want to work that hard. Bootlegging proved to provide all three beyond their wildest expectations. The possible threat of imprisonment or death became worth the reward. I'm no malicious agent of chaos – like them, I'm just selfish."

He pauses briefly to eat. Off my plate again. Same fork.

"Can you get your own plate please?" I plead.

"No. I'm already sitting down, and if you're invulnerable, that means you don't have any germs you could transfer to me."

"I slept with Grant last night and I haven't brushed my teeth yet."

He pauses.

"William, make me my own plate of eggs. Listen. A decade ago, remember when I hijacked and destroyed that TramFast passenger train? You might have been too young. The disaster caused millions in damages and dozens of people died. I forewarned further harm if people kept using TramFast. You see, I had just bought the Shelfield train company. The frightened citizens fled TramFast, headed to Shelfield, and I made a fortune. That's the selfishness I'm talking about. Everything I do, I do to best service my needs – financially and emotionally. In the fifteen years I've been a supervillain, my reign has been an unqualified success. I've accomplished all my goals. I have hundreds of millions of dollars and own dozens of companies. I'm the most powerful and feared supervillain in the country, and my arch-nemesis is the country's most powerful and beloved superhero. I've lived a good life. A valuable life."

William loads eggs onto Freedom's plate from the shattered stove before cautiously handing the plate to his boss. I ready myself for another lengthy speech.

"But everything has to end. Even me. I'm telling you this so you can tell your friends. Superheroes are the worst gossips. A year ago, I was diagnosed with pancreatic cancer. Stage four. I took six months and traveled to the best doctors throughout the world. Those who could heal scientifically, magically, and spiritually. Nothing. The cancer has spread everywhere and there's no escaping it. I'm forty-five years old and I have less than six months left to live. I'm okay with that – I deserve far worse for all the negative karma I've built up. Literally, too, as one Buddhist monk put it."

I take the time to ask the obvious question.

"Then if you have nothing left to accomplish, why not just go to, say, Europe and happily live out the rest of your life? Why go through all this trouble here? Your historical legacy is secured. If it's because of Metroplexer, just pump him full of Liberate and kill him. Then go away, right? Why all the nukes?"

"He'll die. He will. I gave him enough Liberate to guarantee he'll die when that final nuke goes off. But look, Miss Nucleus, you know what makes me content? Satisfied? Not the money or respect. Well, the money and respect are certainly nice. Actually, the money and respect make me quite satisfied. But mainly, it's the drama. The adventure. I don't get any pleasure or contentment out of sitting on a beach or whatever else people do during retirement. Fifteen years ago, there were barely any superheroes or supervillains in Burlington, and definitely none of any fame or notoriety. When I stormed that mall, I brought with me the golden age of supervillains just as the Melvin did for the superheroes, and I want the story to end with us. I can't be content with this city or Metroplexer being around when I'm not. I told you I'm selfish, and I want a satisfying conclusion to my historical legacy. Sadly, I've run out of time. I'm going to die a few months from now in an Italian villa deep in the Apennines Mountains. Good job guessing Europe. But before all that, I need a favor from you."

"Why me?"

Finishing his meal, he brings his plate to the sink, motioning for one of his men to wash it off. Ted volunteers. He sits back down next to me. Once more, I catch him leering at me with that creepy, intense stare.

"Because you look like my daughter. Just like her."

My shocked eyes go wide.

"Stop that. Please, you are not my daughter. I watched her die a long time ago. But you look just like her." He pauses. "Definitely not your personality. You have all the charm and grace of an unconscious drug addict. But you look like her if she had been given the chance to grow up. If I'm obligated to speak to a superhero,

179

please understand why I continue to choose you."

Ever so briefly, Freedom glances off to the side, obviously contemplating something. He calls to William, then motions to the empty beers. William brings us both a second.

"Thank you, William," Freedom politely responds.

"Thanks, Will," I reply, turning my attention back to the supervillain. "Look, buddy, can we go to a photo booth kiosk at the mall instead? You can take as many pictures of the two of us as you want. I'll get our pictures framed out of my own pocket. I'll even forgive you for drinking my beers. How about that instead of whatever you actually came here for? A much better deal, right?"

Freedom finishes off his beer in the brief time I make my plea. He points at my beer – I know that signal. Now both our beers are finished.

"You may look like my dead daughter, but every time you open your mouth, I'm reminded that you are not. Stop that. I hate begging. Hate it. You remember Mephista? The demon summoner. She escaped the police that day the nuke went off. I rewarded her getaway by placing her in charge of guarding my barrels of Liberate, but I received word yesterday that she killed my guards and sent a message to one of my rivals about selling the barrels to them. Mephista wasn't happy that I'd have let her die in the nuke explosion. She wants vengeance on me and millions of dollars in her bank account. That can't happen. I gave her another chance and this is how she repays me? I'd deal with her myself, but I have a doctor's appointment today, and as you've seen and fought, my employees are frustratingly incompetent. You and the other Child Soldiers take out Mephista and you can have the Liberate as your reward. I don't need it anymore. Deal?"

I don't answer. He continues regardless.

"Yes, I'm sure it is. I'll text you her address in a few hours. I'd buy you a new stove, but I feel like the broken one more appropriately fits the décor of your dumpster of an apartment."

I still have a question to ask.

"Where are the rest of the suitcase nukes?"

"They'll detonate soon; you'll find out then. Goodbye, Miss Nucleus. I hope we don't meet again. Treat yourself better. Buy better beers."

Freedom calls out to his bodyguards, and the three of them leave the apartment. Good. I'm glad he's dying.

Booze-related nausea ambushes me and I rush toward my kitchen sink. When my world stops spinning, I take care of business.

I text Spiromaniac that I found out how we can locate where the Liberate is hidden, where Freedom might be, and that an emergency meeting needs to be called. I leave out all the stuff about Freedom's tumors, and thank goodness, Spiro doesn't ask any further questions. She fires off a group text demanding a meeting in three hours at her place.

Globe immediately fires back that she'll be late because of church. Missile comments that she's a Hindu, her powers come from magic, and why is she in church? Globe responds that while all that's true, her current crush is very much a Christian and Missile should shut her mouth without knowing the full story. Spiro asks them to please drop the subject. Missile hopes the pastor doesn't mistake the six-armed Globe for a menorah. Globe responds that a menorah's used in Judaism, not Christianity. Spiromaniac begs them to shut up. Missile, angry at having been corrected, responds with a very graphic picture of a pastor having intercourse with a rabbi. We're in a group chat. All twenty of us get this message. The next seven or eight outraged texts quiet both of them. I learned long ago to turn off sound or vibration on group texts or else my phone never stops spasming.

I decide to finish the remaining eggs, regardless that they were made by a supervillain who broke into my apartment. My hangover conquers my pride. Sure, my apartment stinks, but I'm too preoccupied by a worse smell: the lingering whiff of Kid Metroplexer stuck to my clothes. The reminder of last night. I'm not ashamed – he's attractive, he's a good guy, and I like to consider myself a modern woman who can embrace sexual experiences not attached to marriage or love or whatever else threatens to keeps us women down. But I'm not high-fiving myself either, if just for the wildly uncomfortable conversation we're going to have to have in a few hours. I'm sure he planned last night as a one night stand. He doesn't want to date me (and me him), but neither of us want that terrible "Let's not do this again" excuse we all have to sometimes give. Stop overthinking. We're adults. I text him.

"You were great last night. That was a fun one-time thing."

Now comes the excruciating wait. I should have added, "I really mean it," to the end of the first sentence. I should have phrased the second sentence as a question, something like, "Are you okay with making that a one-time thing?" That would have been better. But nope. I dawdle in my text limbo. When I get out of the shower, I see he responded. Just the time it takes to click on his message causes me more anxiety than every moment of my week-long vulnerability.

"I agree this should be a one-time thing. See you at the meeting in a few hours!"

Well, now I'm upset. Why didn't he do that feelings-saver thing where he pretends it was my idea to not go any further? Something like, "If you think this should be a one-time thing, I agree with you." That would have been polite. Also, was I not great last night? I tried my best, and that should garner me an obligatory response of "You were too," right? Even if I want to emotionally strike back at him, there's nothing I could say. He has supermodel good looks, not one weird mole or hair or anything, and his junk was significantly above average size. This is unfair. As I walk past my dirty t-shirt from last night, I briefly catch his scent again. I throw it in the trash. That'll show him.

———

I arrive first to Stella's apartment. For self-centered reasons, so I can get all her attention to myself before she becomes distracted with our teammates. And it works – bear hugs and relieved exclamation. I adore this woman.

"I missed you so much! I was seriously thinking about planning a jailbreak when Kid Metroplexer finally called me back. I'm sorry it took so long to get you out of jail – Featherblade, Icarus, and I were on the run for the next day until we could get back to our apartments."

"It's okay, I did this to myself. I'm so sorry for that night. I'm not sorry for what I did, but for the pain I must have caused you. I'm so sorry."

She takes a long pause before responding.

"I know you are."

And that's it. That's all I'll get out of her.

"Will you forgive me?" I ask.

Another long pause.

"No, I won't. I love you and you're my best friend, but I won't forgive you. And you owe me money since I had to replace my cell phone, you know, since a bullet went through the old one."

"Oh, okay."

I change the subject instead of pressing further into my unpardonable sin.

"I slept with Grant."

Her face twists like one would when eating a lemon.

"Ew, gross. Do you know how many women he's been with? Did you use protection? No, never mind. I don't want to hear any details. Can we never talk about this again?"

"Yes, please. That's why I like you so much."

She resumes her hugs.

"Liza, I'm not going to leave your side. Where you go, I go. Unless I don't need to or want to. But seriously, did you use protection?"

I groan, pushing her off as we head into the apartment. She laughs at her own joke. But, my God, does she make me feel great.

"I love you, Stella."

"Love you back."

A few minutes later, vegetarians Forestchild and Mentalmind

arrive carrying three mushroom pizzas for the group. Belial and Missile show up soon after, to which Missile angrily proclaims that she's allergic to mushrooms, to which Mentalmind proclaims that's why she got mushroom pizzas after Missile sent porn in a group text. Forestchild and Belial hold the two apart. Kid Metroplexer shows up next, and we avoid looking at each other. War Soul and the Amazing Punchfist come through the door arm-in-arm. When did they get back together? Hacker Plus pops in soon after, boisterously explaining that Bowhunter, Bamboo, and Firestarter are currently carrying her computer equipment upstairs. Friendleader bursts in searching for Hacker Plus. He ordered some sort of military axe from a website that she said would be discrete, but the package arrived very much in axe shape with a very large "Caution: Weapon" sticker. His parents have questions. Hacker Plus plays coy, but Friendleader only gets angrier when she won't apologize. Spiro looks absolutely drained with the non-stop bickering at this point, to which she begs for War Soul to stop the fight. Featherblade and Icarus show up next dragging their gigantic suitcases across Spiromaniac's kitchen. Fisherwoman sends her regrets that she can't make it, but a nearby oil rig is leaking oil and they need to be punished. That was the word she used: punished. Globe comes in last, leering at Missile but saying nothing. Oh, and Fearboy. We didn't invite Fearboy. We rarely invite Fearboy.

Before the meeting, each of the Child Soldiers takes a turn cautiously approaching Kid Metroplexer to say a few nice things about Lady Metroplexer. All true, too. There wasn't a nasty bone in Lady Metroplexer's body. That woman is who we should all strive to be. Strived to be. Grant thanks everyone, but refuses to express anything more. He just wants to find the rest of the nukes, he says.

After everyone's fed and the arguing is at its minimum, we begin the meeting. Spiro tells me to start.

"When I got home this morning, Freedom was waiting for me. He told me he has cancer and he's dying."

That's all I get out before the room erupts. Cheers and

excited chatter. Skepticism. Demands of proof or verification. As Spiro quiets everyone down, Kid Metroplexer mumbles that it won't be the cancer that kills him. I tell them everything he told me. That he'll be at a hospital today. That we need to defeat Mephista. About the Liberate. A plan starts to form.

Five of us will hit Mephista – we don't want to risk too many of us in case of an ambush. Another group will be stationed near each of the seven major hospitals in Burlington in hopes of spotting Freedom. The other superheroes will do whatever Mentalmind and Hacker Plus tell them to do. The chances of us catching Freedom this way are nil to none, as he'll almost certainly use a hospital outside of town or have tech-savvy supervillains block any signals, but it'd be foolish not to try.

Because Freedom specifically came to me, Spiro places me on the assault team. We know he'll have someone somewhere observe us and he'll almost certainly want to see me there. Since everyone would rather fight demonic goo lizards than sit on a rooftop or be bossed around by the two brainiacs for the next several hours, the rest of the room becomes quiet as Spiro thinks through the remaining members for the mission.

"I'm thinking our best shot would be—"

"I'm going. I'm the most powerful of all of us," Kid Metroplexer interrupts. "We don't know what Mephista can do and you'll need my versatility for—"

"Me too. I'm the only one of us who can use magical energy or contact the forces of nature, and I'm certain Mephista's power uses one of those two," Globe interrupts Kid Metroplexer.

"Sure," Spiro sighs. "But only because I chose you both for the team. Not because you bullied your way in. For the remaining members—"

Missile interrupts.

"Belial and I are going, too. We can help. We're on Team Demon."

"Will anyone let me finish a damn sentence?" Spiro yells.

"No. Not you two. Not you or Belial."

"You don't know what our powers are, do you? Do any of you know what we can do? We've been on the team for nine months and no one knows what we can do?"

No one guesses. Belial explains.

"Our fathers beat us when we were kids. That's how we became friends, with the two of us living next door and comparing our bruises. Long story short, we made a pact with some demon – we Googled how to summon him – to kill our dads, but we didn't want to give up our souls and such. We keep our souls in exchange for spilling two gallons of human blood a week. You've seen our knives, yeah? These were given to us during the demon pact."

If you grab any stranger off the street and ask them to sketch the knife Satan himself would use, Missile and Belial just pulled out two. Black as a moonless night with a surprisingly well-adorned handle, the blades alone must be eight or nine inches long. They slide the knives back into their sheaths.

They grin, expecting compliments on their weaponry, but only Mentalmind speaks up.

"Two gallons a week? The human body only has a gallon and a half of blood. Like, total."

The girls nod. They ask if anyone else has any questions. Friendleader raises his hand.

"Then why are you called Missile?"

She shoots him an offended look.

"What? Missiles are cool."

Firestarter raises her hand.

"How did you join the team if no one knew all this?"

Missile shrugs. Mentalmind speaks up again.

"I remember. War Soul, Kid Metroplexer, and Bamboo convinced everyone to let Missile join because they said it would make the group 'hotter' and 'more attractive' – Missile was only voted in because they wanted to sleep with her, and Missile wouldn't join without Belial. That's why."

The accused immediately deny such allegations. Missile accuses Mentalmind of jealousy, but with way more obscenities. Hacker Plus threatens to post nude photos stolen from Missile's phone if she touches Mentalmind. Belial pulls out her knife, offering to meet her weekly blood quota right now. Spiro, slouched with her head buried deep in her palms, declares the meeting over and decides to force herself onto my team. She mumbles something about better safe than sorry.

Eventually, the Mephista team heads out, while Hacker Plus – making sure Missile and Belial can hear as we exit – loudly suggests that maybe we should take a re-vote on their membership when we return.

―――――

I receive a text from an unknown number as we exit the apartment. We're headed to Alfred Pyle Park – named after our first mayor. The park has been gaining popularity lately for the fancy food trucks that hang out in the park on weekends. Kid Metroplexer opts to fly there and survey the scene before we arrive with Globe driving the rest of us in her mom's jeep.

During the drive, I can see Globe getting antsy.

"Missile. Belial. What demon did you contact?"

"I don't know. Cindy, do you remember?"

"I think so," Belial replies. "He told us his name was Craig. Hey, Globe, can you turn on some music. Let's get the adrenaline pumping!"

Globe shakes her head.

"Your demon was named Craig? You sure this was a real demon and you didn't get kidnapped and doused with drugs?"

"Yeah, I remember. Definitely Craig. Nice demon. He sometimes sends us cards on our birthdays."

To further avoid baiting the crazy that sits in Globe's backseat, she turns on the radio. I spot Spiro typing a note in her phone, reminding herself to convince the two girls to go see a psychologist, figuring they may be suppressing some unpleasant memories. See if someone can get more information about this man. Because whoever this Craig is, he killed these girls' dads and gave them ornate military-grade knives.

By the time we get to the park, news vans and police cars litter the perimeter. We'll have to battle in public, by far the worst kind of battle. Thankfully, before we left the apartment, Spiromaniac insisted we look the part – costumes and everything. Spiro's facemask and a spiral emblazoned on her t-shirt. My hoodie with the atomic symbol on the chest and back. Globe wears a long, olive robe. Bracelets cover all six of her forearms, a flowery and ornate headdress across her forehead. She doesn't need any of the accessories, but she always says people believe magic-based superheroes sooner if they look the part. Missile and Belial wear identical combat boots, black leather jackets, and masks adjusted for large, unbalanced rubber horns on top of their heads. All of us terrible dressers, yes, but when Kid Metroplexer and Captain Hanson see us embark from the jeep and wave us over, the crowd parts to let us through. Kid Metroplexer wears his bright unitard to make sure everyone around can see the outline of every bulging muscle.

"A civilian called the police fifteen minutes ago after he spotted Mephista sitting on a bench surrounded by tigers made out of some sort of sludge," Captain Hanson briefs us. "Kid Metroplexer got all the civilians out of the park, but—"

"But when I went for Mephista, she summoned some sort of sludge shield that I couldn't pass through. I hit her hard too. It must be something supernatural."

"I'll apologize to the police commissioner later for using superheroes against his edict," Captain Hanson continues. "I'll take whatever punishment he gives out. I contacted the BSO, but I never received a return call. I've tried for the past couple days to contact them. That's strange and that never happens. Do you know where they are?"

We don't. Another problem to solve. He shakes his head.

"So, it's up to you all. Please, be careful. For everyone."

Spiromaniac kindly thanks him before turning to command the rest of us. Kid Metroplexer will keep a watch on the perimeter to make sure no one else interferes – vigilantes or police or henchmen or other bad guys. If any of these summoned monsters try to escape the park, Kid Metroplexer will lure them back. Globe, already ahead of Spiro, sits cross-legged on the concrete attempting to figure out the source of Mephista's power, and hopefully, cut off that source. Spiromaniac and I will attack Mephista directly, distracting her so our self-proclaimed demon girls can destroy the monsters created by the supervillain. Missile and Belial assure us their knives can pierce Mephista's shield.

Spiro, Missile, and Belial begin their march into the park when Captain Hanson pulls me aside.

"Liza, it's good to see you. As a superhero, I mean."

"Thank you. It's good to see you too. Will we be arrested after we defeat the bad guy?"

"If you win," he pulls me close and whispers. "Run quickly. Now go show the city what you can do."

"That's a lot of pressure," I whisper back. "By the way, thank you for what you said at the jail."

"I meant all of it."

"Yeah, thanks. I appreciate it."

I pull away and catch up to the others.

The five of us barely touch the grass when the first ooze monster approaches. The tiger-like figure grows. Ten feet tall. Then twenty. Thirty.

"Freedom sent children? He didn't even have the decency to come himself?"

Mephista follows behind her monster, her robe and staff glistening in that disgusting demon juice.

"I'll show Freedom. I'll show you! I'm a servant of Lord Mephistopheles! I'll show you what my master gave me!"

Forty feet. Fifty. The monster's hand grabs onto Mephista and separates its torso, allowing Mephista to climb inside as the ooze wraps itself around her. Sixty feet.

And then the creature shrieks, dropping to a knee.

"This is the best I can do," Globe screams. "It won't get bigger, but we can't stop it unless we pull Mephista out! Do it!"

The monster, recovered from Globe's magical severing, picks itself back up. Mephista's laugh erupts from within. A wet, confident laugh. Belial points to Missile.

"Mephi-whoever can go screw himself! He's got nothing on Craig!"

Remember how back in the car I said we should find and arrest this man Craig for the trauma he inflicted on these girls? I was wrong. Craig is not a man.

Bones crack and contort in Missile and Belial's backs. Two sticky, sulphuric rods sprout from their shoulder blades, piercing their leather jackets. The rods spread, revealing steel-like appendages. Wings. They grew wings. They weren't lying – they made a deal with a demon named Craig.

"Leave the monster to us, Spiro. You and Miss Nucleus stay away. We're going to rip Mephista out and poop in her eyeholes."

"C'mon, watch what you say!" Spiromaniac retorts. "We're on live TV! We have an image to maintain."

Missile and Belial flip her their middle fingers before flying toward their sixty foot opponent.

"Never become leader of anything, Liza," she mutters to me.

With no other choice, Spiro and I switch to support duty, opting to head back toward the perimeter.

Missile and Belial, surprisingly agile, circle the creature, slashing where they can. When a giant oozing arm smashes into Belial, she shrugs it off, immune to demon goo. As the monster maneuvers itself to attack Belial again, Kid Metroplexer zooms ahead to remove any nearby bushes, trees, statues, and benches that could cause the monster to trip and fall on the crowd. Spiro discreetly heals the injured pedestrians when the paramedics' attention is focused elsewhere. I stand guard next to Globe, who seems to gone into some sort of trance. Whatever Globe is doing, she's doing well: each cut made by the demon knives leaves permanent scars on the monsters. Mephista's stuck with what she already summoned.

A few tense minutes later, neither side appears to be gaining any ground. The demon girls can't do much other than superficial damage and the monster doesn't seem to be getting tired or slower. Suddenly, Mephista wises up, using the monster's giant arm to grab a tree and slam it into Belial. Missile, distracted by what just happened to her best friend, is blindsided by a follow-up swing and hurtles toward the grass. Kid Metroplexer's reflexes kick in as he catches them both before they hit the ground, dashing the two girls to the side of the battlefield.

Unsure of what to do now, Kid Metroplexer speeds toward the center of Mephista's monster. A man-sized battering ram moving at the speed of sound. The superhero hits hard, unexpectedly bouncing off, and knocking him into a nearby building. He smashes through the fragile glass windows, landing in a 5th floor office. Okay. Now things have gotten out of control. The creature moves closer to Globe and me, Mephista's laugh resounding from within. A few more steps and she'll reach the spectators. Spiro doesn't have the superpower to fight this thing, Globe can't break concentration, and the other three are useless.

Well, it's up to me.

"Spiro, help the girls!" I bark at her. "Kid! Kid! Over here!"

I sprint to Missile and Belial's location, snatching each of their knives. Much lighter weapons than I expected. Kid Metroplexer lands next to me, awaiting my command. I won't lie; I like being in charge.

"Grant, fly me to the top of that ooze pile and drop me off."

Without hesitation, he does. No snarky comments or suggestions, just teamwork. I hit the monster's head a bit too fast, frantically piercing the monster with the knives to keep me from falling off. And as if the secret to my eternal happiness lies at the monster's heart, I stab and dig. Stab and dig. I'm soon fully immersed in this demonic Jell-O mold. I can't be hurt. I can't drown. I don't need to breathe. So I pray that my coworkers keep the monster from flailing in the wrong direction as I slowly make my way toward Mephista. The acidic demon magic quickly burns most of my clothes off. That's why I never wear my good shoes when I go out superhero-ing.

Mephista comes into view. Parts of her, anyway. Her cackling suddenly comes to a halt when she sees me, the two of us floating together inside the giant, leaking monster. I approach her upside down, my face inches from hers.

"Hey, no more of this, okay?"

"Miss Nucleus! This will not be a repeat of last time! I will make you wish you were dead!"

"You and me both, Mephista."

I thrust both knives into her torso. That shouldn't kill her. The monster rumbles and I tumble around.

Immediately, I realize my mistake.

Globe specifically said to pull her out.

But I didn't pull her out. I stabbed. And now the creature's breaking apart as Mephista can no longer control it. The sulfuric, fiery, demonic goo turns into sulfuric, fiery, demonic liquid. A wave that'll kill everyone surrounding it. I fall to the ground hard, a good thirty-foot drop. Mephista lies unconscious next to me. I hear the screams of the civilians and the police. I can smell the burning flesh. I dare not look around. Mephista's robe covers my naked body.

––––––

Dozens of people suffered third-degree burns. No one died, but only because Spiromaniac got to the more serious cases before they were carted off by the paramedics. To keep her healing lie intact, Spiro declared that with Globe's magical interference, she was able to briefly reverse her hurting power into a healing power. The police and the reporters were too busy to ask for further clarification. In the confusion, the six of us hurriedly took off before anyone could arrest us.

None of us talk on the drive back. Missile and Belial are sleeping, Globe is exhausted, and Spiromaniac furiously texts Hacker Plus with updates on the hospital stakeouts to find Freedom. At least we beat Mephista, right? A Pyrrhic victory is still a victory, Kid Metroplexer optimistically tells us.

Globe drops me off in front of my apartment to get new clothes. The debriefing will be in an hour at Spiro and War Soul's condo and I need to be there. I tell her not to wait for me – I need to take a shower. I'll take the bus back to the condo. I enthusiastically declare that I'll see them in an hour.

Mercifully, there are no supervillains watching TV or cooking breakfast in my apartment. But a small box sits on top of my kitchen table. I open the note beside it.

"Thanks for the help! I figured you all might try to use the Liberate on me, so early this morning I disposed of the remaining pills and the scientists working on the project. But I made a deal with you and I'm honoring my promise. I hereby release you from your hamster cage. Goodbye, my furry friend. Love forever, Freedom."

I open the box and remove the tissue paper inside. One Liberate pill. Freedom gave me one pill. I close the box and shove it into a kitchen drawer.

Great. Good job, Liza. All I want to do is sleep. Upon entering my bedroom, I receive a text from Kid Metroplexer.

"Don't worry about what happened. I think you did great. But if you're upset, do you want me to come over tonight so we can talk about it?"

Yeah, talk. That's what he wants to do.

I text him back, "My new rule is to only sleep with those who are also mediocre at sex. Sorry."

He doesn't respond. After two glasses of whiskey, I take a nap.

———

"I heard about what happened today with Mephista. Thirty people were admitted to the hospital because of you. I don't think you're a bad person, and I consider you a friend, but I think it'd be best if you quit for good this time."

I shoot up in bed. What the hell? What's going on? Who said that? There. On the side of my bed sits War Soul in full combat gear.

"What the hell are you doing in my apartment? Why is everyone breaking into my apartment?"

He stands up, holding my Miss Nucleus hoodies. He's been rummaging through my clothes drawers. Of course he did.

"I'm taking these with me. Once the Freedom problem is taken care of, I'll let you go about your life again. It's too risky to have you around right now."

I jump out of bed. I'm in my underwear, but I don't care.

"How dare you!" I yell. "I get it. We're teenage superheroes and we're all insane and we're all getting worse at hiding how crazy we are!"

"Where is the Liberate, Liza?" he yells back. "You never made it to the debriefing! While you were here wallowing in self-pity, we were trying to figure out how stop Freedom! We need the Liberate to stop him!"

"You want the Liberate? I shoved it up my ass, so come and get it!"

He doesn't take the bait.

"I'm going to wait for you in your living room. Put on some clothes, pack an overnight bag, and then you're coming with me. You'll stay at a motel on the edge of town and you won't leave until Freedom is dealt with. On the way, you're going to tell me where you stashed the Liberate."

The door slams behind him. I glance at my phone. Seven missed texts and five missed phone calls. Too bad. I throw on clothes and open my bedroom door, immediately breaking into a sprint and tackling War Soul.

We barely begin to wrestle before he pins me on the carpet.

"I gave you a second chance, Liza!"

A knock at my door. A louder knock.

"Where is the Liberate, Liza? We can't defeat Freedom unless we use it on him!"

The front door breaks open and Spiromaniac rushes in.

"Nick! I told you not to do this!"

"She knows where the Liberate is!"

"I told you I shoved it up my ass! Go ahead, grab it!"

"Liza, stop that! War Soul! Get off her!"

"Enough, Stella! All you do is defend her, but I'm not going to have your charity case running around freely anymore! She didn't show up to the meeting, she smells like booze, and every shred of evidence has her working for Freedom!"

Spiromaniac charges toward us, kicking War Soul off me.

"Liza never showed up to the meeting because she doesn't have any coping skills. She smells like booze because she's an alcoholic. And you know damn well that she'd never betray us, much less let a whole town go up in a nuclear explosion."

War Soul stands up, demanding proof. Spiromaniac shoves him into my wall.

"No, you listen to me. I am your leader. I'm in charge of the Child Soldiers! Let me make myself crystal clear. You *will* stand down. This is an order. Stand down, soldier!"

The two stare at each other, waiting for the other to back off. If War Soul was going to try to take down the boss, he doesn't get the chance when Kid Metroplexer lands on my patio.

"I'm not an alcoholic," I clarify. "I'm not."

After the tense situation defuses, I tell the three of them what happened. Freedom destroyed the Liberate and anyone who had the knowledge to make it. We know the last of it was pumped into Metroplexer several days ago. Because Freedom isn't stupid and he knew we'd want to use it on him. I don't mention the single pill hidden in my kitchen drawer.

War Soul explains that even after attempting to track down the BSO, utilizing every available form of contact – some very much illegal – no one in the BSO can be found. We can assume Freedom had something to do with their disappearance. But we have no more leads and only a day and a half at most before we hit the deadline Freedom gave us. And seven nukes are still missing. And an hour ago, the police commissioner, under pressure from the growing angry masses of citizens demanding his resignation after the Alfred Pyle Park incident, doubled down on his promise to arrest superheroes on sight.

So the question that keeps popping up, is what now?

"If we can't find Freedom or the suitcase nukes, we should at least look for the BSO," Spiro suggests. "We'll need them anyway if we're going to battle Freedom."

"We'll need Metroplexer," War Soul corrects her.

The two scowl at each other, the tension still very much there. Kid Metroplexer rolls his eyes. I decide to interrupt the death glares.

"Where do we start?"

"We?"

"Go to hell, Nick."

"No, *we* aren't doing—"

He takes a step in my direction. Spiro jumps in front of him to block his path.

Stella switches her tone – changing her tactic – speaking calmly to the enraged superhero, who definitely looks about to hit her.

"Listen to me. I'm the general of our superhero army, but we have an election in January. Run against me. Until then, Liza is still one of us and will go wherever we go. That's my call. You are free to search by yourself, Nick. Make your own decision."

His eyes glance up and down, almost certainly sizing up Spiromaniac. I hope they don't fight, if just to prevent any further damage to my living room. Televisions are expensive. But when War Soul's eyes shift to Kid Metroplexer, who looks quite annoyed, he backs up and leans against the wall. Crisis averted – like how one stops a potential knife fight when someone else walks up with a vest full of grenades.

"Okay, general. Where are we all going?" War Soul asks sarcastically.

"I don't know," she responds. "Does anyone know where the BSO headquarters are? If all the members of the BSO are missing, there must be some clue there to help us. But they also didn't tell anybody where they built the new building after Freedom bombed their old one."

War Soul scoffs.

"The BSO still don't trust us, and if they had been more open with us these past couple weeks then we might have taken down Freedom already. But nope. They're old men and women. I know I could take Screwdriver and Mankiller in a fight. If I get the jump on Mermaid, then her too."

Spiromaniac, who's both still angry at War Soul and always ready to defend fellow superheroes from criticism, responds.

"Please. They're only in their forties. Don't talk crap about them; we're the future members of the BSO, after all."

"Mankiller has a beer belly."

"So what? She can still kick your—"

The floor shakes violently. Kid Metroplexer lifts up his foot.

"Don't make me do that again! Enough out of both of you! I know where the BSO headquarters are. My dad runs the damn team. If you continue to argue, I'll bring this ceiling down on top of us."

I pray no one calls his bluff, if only because I'd like to one day get the security deposit back on my apartment. But Spiro and War Soul drop their disagreement, like schoolchildren frightened after being scolded by the school's scariest teacher. Kid Metroplexer motions for them to head to the front door, and we head out on our mission.

As I lock the door behind us, Nick turns to me.

"I still think you're lying about the Liberate."

I jog ahead of him to keep pace with the others.

"Who knows? Life is full of mysteries."

11

The Burlington Safety Organization was established twelve years ago when Metroplexer discovered he wasn't alone in his superhero crusade. He figured he'd try out teamwork, so he rounded up the five other superheroes in the city – no one refuses an invitation from Metroplexer – and created the United States' first public superhero team. They held a press conference outside their new headquarters, inviting every news outlet and politician they could manage. Even the governor showed up.

The people ate the spectacle up. Finally all of our city's heroes standing together. Metroplexer! Screwdriver! Tenacity! Mankiller! Warthog! Major Fryshock!

Maybe fifteen or so superheroes have cycled in and out of the BSO throughout the years. I think four of the members died. I know a bunch retired. Metroplexer told me that Jupiter and Putrid got married, leaving soon after Putrid became pregnant with twins. Globe's father, Worldview, departed when he was offered a million-dollar yearly contract to protect an environmentally-disastrous oil rig from Fisherwoman's constant attacks. Now the two fight each other every few months as arch-nemeses. A few others moved away or vanished or whatever else happened. The current roster, the smallest it has ever been, leaves the Burlington Safety Organization with only Metroplexer, Screwdriver, Mankiller, and Mermaid.

War Soul's narcissism makes it impossible for him to compliment others who are not War Soul, but I agree with Spiro about the BSO. They're just like us, only with a decade more experience and hopefully far less severe mistakes to haunt them at night. I've heard a few stories about the team members.

Screwdriver can make any nearby machines sentient for a few minutes. His proud arrival on the superhero scene came when a large group of robbers burst into a store while the Screwdriver was shopping. The store being a Best Buy. He annihilated them. I heard an Xbox controller almost strangled a guy.

Mankiller has infinite blood. That's her superpower. Whenever she bleeds, her body triggers a reaction that replaces lost red blood cells faster than she can lose them. So the lady's absolutely terrifying. Criminals report seeing a machete-wielding woman running toward them, drenched in blood pouring out of every orifice of her body. The police like to use her for their trickier suspect interrogations. In her civilian life, Mankiller teaches kindergarten.

Mermaid's singing voice hypnotizes anyone who hears it. Realizing her incredible luck, she spent years as an opera singer bilking money and jewelry from wealthy patrons until the truth about her powers was discovered. Metroplexer negotiated a deal with the prosecutor that instead of a ten-year jail sentence, she would join the BSO for ten years. Mermaid belts a few bars and the bank robbers drop their weapons and surrender. The BSO couldn't pass that up. I don't know if her parents are half-fish or not.

And so when we arrive at the docks on the far side of the city, in front of a small, decrepit houseboat, we have some questions for Kid Metroplexer.

"All of you stop talking. Yes, this boat. This is the Burlington Safety Organization's headquarters. You're looking at it."

Rust covers most of the bottom. The paint has chipped off everywhere else. Broken slabs of wood lie on the deck, I assume to eventually mend the broken wood attached to the boat. Tarps lay over the roof's few holes.

The houseboat sits in a long line of houseboats, but the others look at least livable. What the hell is going on? Has Kid

Metroplexer gone insane and this is where he murders us? Well, murders the other two, I mean.

"Screwdriver lives here," Grant explains. "He got divorced recently and his law business has dried up and you get the idea."

"Doesn't your dad make two hundred grand a year?" War Soul asks. "He won't help out his friend?"

"He makes more than that, but Screwdriver is too proud to accept money. I don't know. Maybe. My dad rarely tells me anything damning about other superheroes. But this is where they're currently headquartered. No one would ever think to look for the BSO here. After Freedom blew up their first base and all those civilians died, I guess..."

He trails off, climbing onboard the boat. We follow, and we all quickly notice the same thing.

"Oh my God, something stinks," Spiro announces.

"You said Screwdriver lives here?" I ask.

War Soul pushes past us.

"I recognize that smell. Stay here."

He opens the door and the stench intensifies, forcing the rest of us to clamor off the boat and back onto the dock. I clamp my hand over my mouth in case I vomit. Spiro gags. We're happy to let War Soul investigate alone. Poor Kid Metroplexer, who brought us here in the first place, attempts to distract us.

"Who in the BSO do you hate the most? Past or present?"

"Who cares?" Spiromaniac yells at him before heading as far away as she can.

"If we don't think about the smell and we're waiting for War Soul anyway—"

"Shut up!" she screams.

We move back far enough for most of the odor to dissipate. The scent does seem familiar though.

"Warthog," I say. "He's the one I hated the most."

"Really? He was always nice to me."

Our voices are muffled by our hands covering our mouths

200

and noses. Spiro barfs in the distance.

"I met Warthog soon after I started superhero-ing," I begin. "He told me he saw my potential and wanted to train me. Hell yeah, right? Got myself a mentor – an original member of the BSO. I met up with him alone one night at a gym. We trained for a couple of hours. And then the next night. And the next. The night after that, he tried to kiss me. I was thirteen."

"Oh. I didn't know that."

"I don't think you were his type. Someone else eventually ratted on him and that's why he went to prison. Not that bull excuse of extortion or whatever he agreed to on the plea deal. Who do you hate the most? You brought up the topic to talk about yours, right?"

Stella walks back over to us, wiping her mouth off with her sleeve. We don't look at her and I expect she wants it that way.

"Well, no," Grant lies. "I wanted to hear yours, but for my choice, totally Major Fryshock. Once he—"

War Soul reappears and excitedly calls to us, interrupting a disappointed Kid Metroplexer.

"You all will want to see this! You'll get used to the smell."

The reason for the stench becomes evident as soon as we step inside the houseboat. Suddenly the stink is the last thing on our minds.

Three dead bodies. Screwdriver. Mankiller. Mermaid.

Spiromaniac gasps in shock, immediately burying her head in my shoulder. Kid Metroplexer opens his mouth, but nothing comes out. War Soul, with a smirk, spreads his arms wide, like everything he badmouthed about the BSO is suddenly justified. We're done for. It's over. They were our role models. Our inspirations. Our safety nets.

War Soul begins his report.

"They must have died sometime yesterday. I'm not completely certain when, but they all have a single large wound on their chests, like something burst through them."

I take a guess.

"Freedom and his fists?"

"Maybe. Hard to tell. I'm going to throw the bodies into the water. None of us can concentrate with this smell."

"Could we wrap them in something? Something more than just pushing them off the boat?" Spiro asks.

"Who cares? They're dead," War Soul replies.

"They were superheroes! What's wrong with you? They deserve our respect!" Spiro shouts back.

"Go grab a bedsheet then! Go say a prayer! Go be a good Catholic so you can feel better about yourself! The rest of you don't move. I need to investigate the crime scene and I don't want any of you messing it up."

Kid Metroplexer, regaining composure, ignores him and begins opening drawers. Spiromaniac helps War Soul – who is visibly irritated – wrap and dispose (respectfully) of the dead superheroes.

But we can't find single clue. Not one. Trash bags and empty bottles litter the boat, but nothing remotely revelatory. Did Freedom clean this place out? I mean, did he clean the place out of useful information? He definitely didn't clean.

I give up after touching something orange and sticky.

"A bust," I announce. "This place is a bust. Waste of time. We learned nothing except to never believe in our heroes. Are you sure that Screwdriver lived here?"

"I'm sorry," Kid Metroplexer concedes. "I should have told you all sooner. I visited a very drunken Screwdriver a few weeks ago, and he revealed way more than he should have to me. He's wanted on fraud and tax evasion charges. He came here to avoid arrest. Mankiller was recently fired from her teaching job after hitting one of her students. Mermaid has continued to commit petty theft during her time in the BSO. My dad—"

War Soul interrupts Grant with a hard shove.

"What else, huh? The Child Soldiers have been infested with terrible people for years too! We keep accepting people who have no business being superheroes!"

That not-so-subtle last sentence was almost certainly aimed at me. It hurts a little. Nick's anger, his disgust, his frustration – whatever boiled over in his mind after so many disillusioned developments – can no longer be contained.

"And now I learn that the BSO operates in a crappy boat inhabited by crappy people? By people who should have been imprisoned alongside the very same people they arrested? We're superheroes, dammit! We're supposed to be the good guys! Half the Child Soldiers are bigger criminals than the supervillains and now you admit everyone in the BSO is too?"

"No! Not Metroplexer! Not my sister! We—"

"Stop making excuses!"

War Soul slugs Kid Metroplexer in the nose. All four of us pause as Nick steps back in a defensive stance, though it's not like that would do him any good if Grant were to retaliate. Stella butts in.

"Nick, both you and I became superheroes for selfless reasons. We wanted to make Burlington a better place, not a better place for ourselves. None of us are perfect, but you know damn well that someone doesn't have to be a good person to fight a bad person. Part of our job description has always been to take these morally ambiguous people and push them in the right direction."

War Soul turns toward her; I swear he's about to cry.

"And Liza? And Grant? What about the two of you? Why are you two superheroes?"

Grant and I look at each other. War Soul yells for us to answer. So we do. Truthfully.

"I could lift cars by the time I was a toddler. I didn't have a choice."

"I wanted strangers to love me."

War Soul plops himself down on a torn couch, the same one where Mermaid's corpse was leaning against when we walked in. He stares out a window. Kid Metroplexer sits next to him and speaks quietly.

"Many of the former BSO members were good, moral people. But my dad has always been drawn to certain types of people.

The ones who are on the cusp of supervillainy. The ones who still stand a chance of become good people. The ones who can turn their lives around and give themselves a chance of redemption. War Soul, I think you've learned over the years just how many people fail to live up to your expectations. Those who take these opportunities and squander them. But my dad keeps trying. He won't give up."

War Soul doesn't move or speak. Kid Metroplexer continues.

"Sixteen years ago, my dad accidentally killed his six-year old niece. My dad never told me what happened, and I never asked – my guess is they were roughhousing and he underestimated the extent of his powers. I don't know. While he admits it was an accident, redemption forced him into the superhero world and it's driven him ever since."

Spiro furrows her brow.

"But I thought it was Freedom that forced this life on him?"

Kid Metroplexer nods.

And everything clicks for me.

"No wonder Metroplexer won't talk about his costumed or personal life," I say. "No wonder he won't divulge any details about himself or tell any stories regarding his past or take on any protégés. Because Metroplexer created Freedom, didn't he? Because Dr. Mel Johnson blames himself for being the cause of every awful thing Freedom has done, am I correct?"

All three glance over at me.

"Grant, when Freedom was forcing me to listen to him drag on and on about himself, he blamed all his villainous actions on his selfish business expertise. But that's not entirely true, is it? Because why does he have this insane obsession with Metroplexer? Freedom has plenty of enemies, so why does he only care about Metroplexer?"

"I don't think—"

"No, let me finish. I'm thinking out loud. Freedom told me in my kitchen how much I looked like his dead daughter. None of us knew he had a family. But— If what you just said— Grant, what's Freedom's real name?"

"I'm not—"

"Tell me!"

His gaze drops to the floor.

"His real name is Ethan Johnson."

"Your Uncle Ethan. Metroplexer accidently killed Freedom's daughter, didn't he? Revenge is what led the distraught Freedom into supervillainy and forced Metroplexer, the only person who had the power to stop Freedom, into superheroism. Am I right?"

"Most of it, yes."

The lingering smell of death, the dangerous décor, and the misery and aggravation of my teammates fades into a lengthy, hesitant silence.

War Soul stands up. His voice cracks slightly.

"Well, I've heard plenty. I've hit my breaking point. I learned that every ideal I've fought for is a big, fat lie. Grant, you irresponsible, deceitful piece of crap. How could you keep this from us when we sacrificing everything to save Burlington? I'll make this right, and you can't stop me. I'm going to the police. I will tell them everything I know. I am going to tell them why Freedom hates Metroplexer so much. I am going to tell them why he wants to destroy Burlington. I will tell them the true identities of Kid Metroplexer and his father. Then, I am going to come back for you, Liza. I will find out where you hid the rest of the Liberate and then I will throw you into a volcano where others will be safe from you for the rest of your treacherous and useless life. And Stella, if I ever see you again – you, who presides over and defends so many of these Child Soldier monsters – I'm going to kill you. Right where you stand. You have enabled these kids for far too long, and I'm going to clean house after all this is over. Now, if you'll excuse me, I'm on my way to the police station, and then I'm going to evacuate as many people from this doomed city as I can."

He marches off, slamming the boat's door behind him. Spiromaniac jumps up as soon as the door closes. Her voice never wavers, only a frigid conviction that resonates with each word.

"Grant. Liza. There still might be something left in this houseboat to help us find Metroplexer and Freedom. Please keep looking. I apologize that I can't help, but there's something I need to take care of. Something I should have done a long time ago."

She speaks her next words not as a suggestion, but an unbreakable, authoritative mandate.

"Don't interfere. No matter what."

She runs out the door. From the window, I see her tackle War Soul on the pier. The two superheroes begin to battle that both of them desperately need to see to the end.

I hear Kid Metroplexer mutter to himself.

"He won't make it to the police station. No one talks to me that way. I'm a Metroplexer, and I will have my respect."

What is going on? Is everyone as messed up as I am? Is everyone else just better at hiding it? Is anyone who decides to wear a costume and punch bad guys a giant bag of crazy?

"Grant?"

I have to know.

"What?"

"Do you remember Quotientia? Was she a good person? She never had a scandal?"

"From what I could tell."

I breathe a sigh of relief, my idolatry thankfully well-placed.

I leave Kid Metroplexer to search the houseboat. I go outside to watch my best friend fight the man who hates me the most.

The two combatants move from the pier to the grass. When Spiromaniac jabs, War Soul ducks. She kicks, he sidesteps. They grapple, he throws her to the ground. Occasionally, he punches her in the chest or punts her in the ribs — nowhere that the inevitably reflected blow would incapacitate him. Each time she gets knocked down, she stands back up. Each time, she charges back toward him. But each time, she fails to defeat him.

He's a better fighter than her, and they both know it.

Spiromaniac looks frantically around the battlefield. She

won't be able to beat him without a weapon. War Soul takes the opportunity to strike her in the jaw, and as Spiro reflects it back, both superheroes take a brief breather to recover.

Kid Metroplexer shouts from inside the boat.

"Hey, Liza, I found a folder hidden inside the wall."

I ignore him.

Spiro looks exhausted. Her chest rises deeply up and down with each breath. She wipes sweat off her forehead. Her stance has stooped. War Soul stands ready, seemingly unfazed. No weapons nearby. No tactics he can't see coming.

She knows she can't win. Yet, she doesn't stop.

Stella swings a sloppy haymaker that War Soul dodges. She lunges at him, but he lunges back further. Snatching her by the hair, he picks her up and tosses her back onto the pier. She tumbles over the debris, smashing her head hard on the edge of the boat.

Don't interfere, Liza. She said don't interfere no matter what. But if I don't do something…

Spiromaniac pulls herself up, and we lock eyes. I see her determination. No, not determination. Acceptance.

"Okay," she says, returning to face War Soul. A large cut drips blood down her left eyebrow. She leans against the boat, grabbing onto one of the broken fragments of wood. A sharp one.

War Soul rolls his eyes.

"Give up, Stella. That won't penetrate my armor."

"I hate that word," she replies.

Spiromaniac holds the piece of wood in front of her, and angles it toward her chest. She grins.

"Though the Child Soldiers are far from perfect, don't you understand how important it is to have allies? Friends? They're why I can do this."

What is she doing? What the hell is she doing?

"Oh, and Nick, I think this is a good time to tell you I've decided to move out of our apartment."

Stella stabs the wood deep into the middle of her torso, just below her ribs. She pushes the shard downwards, slicing herself open to the navel. I've never heard her scream like this before. War Soul has no idea what to do – and then, she points at him. His own stomach rips open and the two fall to the ground together.

Kid Metroplexer looks up from his folder. I yell at him to get out here as I sprint toward Spiro.

"Stella! What the hell was that?"

"Proof that War Soul could never beat me," she says. Blood soaks through her shirt. "I win."

She attempts to laugh, but doesn't get far before she spits up more blood.

"Can you ask Grant to take me and Nick to the hospital now?"

We're screwed.

No plans, no clues, no hope. My best friend disemboweled herself. The city of Burlington creeps closer to its doomsday.

———

Kid Metroplexer and I stand over Spiromaniac's hospital bed in a clinic somewhere in a not so nice section of town. But the doctors – and I use that term loosely – don't talk to the police, so hopefully nothing can get traced back to us. It's the best we can do.

Kid Metroplexer returned to the houseboat after dropping off Spiro and War Soul to pick me up and bring me here. My pants are stained by the grass, but I refused to sit anywhere near that stinky, rotten headquarters of the greatest superhero team in the country. The team that no longer exists. I still smell a whiff of rotting flesh in my hair.

The doctor tends to War Soul, telling us that he'll pull through. I mean, he'll be out of commission for a while, but he'll be okay. And sporting a nasty, unattractive scar, I bet. Spiro took a nap before I arrived, giving her body time to heal. At the minimum, her stomach wound looks to have closed up.

"Stella, you're the bravest woman I've ever met."

"And the dumbest," Kid Metroplexer adds.

She grabs both our hands.

"I agree with both of your statements."

Kid Metroplexer mentions a few phone calls he made prior to picking me up. The Child Soldiers are in disarray, scattered throughout the city looking for any last minute miracle clues, but no one's optimistic.

We grasp at straws.

"Could we negotiate with Freedom? Is there anything he wants in exchange for Metroplexer and the nukes?"

"He's dying," Kid Metroplexer counters. "What does he care? He says this is his endgame. There's nothing he wants."

But, nothing? Nothing he wants? Everyone wants something. Even Freedom. Inspiration strikes me.

"We might have something he wants. Something he'd exchange for Metroplexer and the nukes. Stella, does Grant know about your healing power?"

"Now he does, I guess. Way to be subtle."

"Do you think you could cure cancer?"

She thinks for a moment before she answers.

"I doubt it." A pause. "But there's only one way to find out."

I grab my phone from my pocket, ignoring the disapproving silence from Kid Metroplexer of what could disastrously be the worst idea I've ever concocted – making a deal with the man who killed his sister and kidnapped his father. I scroll to the last text Freedom sent me and I reply.

"Freedom, we'd really like our superhero and nukes back. We have a proposition for you that you should take us up on."

The three of us stare at the phone, waiting for the reply vibration. A minute. Two. Three. No one talks, refusing to miss the notification. At minute four, my phone buzzes. I click on the message – just three words.

"Tell me more."

This is our proposition. If Spiromaniac can cure the cancer in Freedom's body, he'll release the captured Metroplexer and give us the locations of the remaining nukes. No detonations. It's a win-win. We save the city and he can ride off into the sunset to be evil for decades to come.

Freedom declines.

He explains that the best healers in the world have already failed, a biopsy to see if Spiromaniac has healed him would take several days that he doesn't have, and he's already put in too much money and work to not go through with his plan of killing everyone in the city of Burlington.

And before he stops responding, he writes a final taunt: Freedom gives us the address where he's currently staying at, along with a selfie of him and a bruised, unconscious Metroplexer bound to a chair. The caption reads, "Grant, come join dad and me for a family reunion!" The corner of the suitcase nuke is spotted in the background.

A furious Kid Metroplexer paces, but he doesn't leave. He speaks to us through clenched teeth.

"Stop looking at me like that! I'm not stupid! If my sister and I together couldn't stop Freedom, what makes you think I can do it alone? He knows this. He wouldn't give us his address unless he knows for certain that he's already won."

"Why?" Spiromaniac cautiously asks.

"Grace and I are twins and the superpowers passed down genetically is split between us. We are each half as powerful as our dad. Were half as powerful. Our dad can survive a nuclear explosion. He actually did about a decade ago. But my dad and Freedom were on that same camping trip. Just the two of them swimming in a lake together when they came across an abandoned, ruined facility. They were exposed to or injected or maybe even swallowed something inside there that gave them their powers."

Grant starts to choke up, but he refuses to give in out of what I can only assume is pride.

"I don't have a choice, do I? I have to go to that address. An address that he will almost certainly detonate a nuclear bomb at if I show up. Or if I don't show up. Freedom has accepted his end and nothing is going to scare him or convince him otherwise."

Kid Metroplexer and I share the same somber expression in agreement: we're not strong enough to defeat Freedom. We talked about this on the way to the hospital to avoid having to discuss it vocally with Stella.

Neither of us can think of a plan that won't cost civilian lives, and neither of us wants to admit we'd be willing to forfeit a few lives if the plan takes down Freedom. The two of us announce we don't have a plan to avoid the shame of having to say out loud, "What if only a few hundred people die?"

Until finally, she speaks up. Spiromaniac, that shining beacon of goodness not weighed down by cynicism or violent thrills or the joy of power or any other terrible reason those around us became superheroes. Because she wouldn't be okay with acceptable losses.

"Stop looking so sad. I might have a plan, but it's an awful, risky plan. I think it has a very high chance of killing Kid Metroplexer if anything goes wrong or our timing is off."

Grant immediately chimes in.

"Doesn't matter. I'm in."

"Just a quick question, Grant. When your dad was caught in that nuclear explosion a decade ago, did it hurt him?"

"Badly. He needed a few weeks to recover, but he survived it. But it was only the force of the blast that hurt him; we're immune to radiation."

"Okay. Good. I have a plan then. Let me set up a quick conference call with some of the Child Soldiers. But if everything goes as planned, then the last part will rely on Liza. There's no other choice. The fate of the city and the people in it will be in your hands. Are you willing to accept that responsibility, Liza? I'm sorry. Not Liza. Miss Nucleus."

Spiromaniac might as well have proposed marriage to me during a large, open, and very public major event. What else am I supposed to say?

"Yes. Of course."

We're going to need to talk in private after this. The fate of the city should never be in my hands.

———

Kid Metroplexer and I walk from the bus stop toward the Shelfield company headquarters – the address Freedom texted us. Walking sucks, but if Grant flew us there – even in our street clothes – we'd be recognized instantly by any policemen who happened to glance upwards. Or civilians who would call the police. Or anyone connected to law enforcement who saw us land near the Shelfield building. Since we're still very much banned from the city, walking allows us maneuverability and access to more escape routes, but honestly, walking sucks. It's slow and I'm out of shape and I have to spend way more time talking to Kid Metroplexer than I care to.

"After Stella finished coordinating with the Child Soldiers," I tell Grant to break up the awkward silence. "I told her I wasn't okay with the plan relying on me to defeat Freedom and save the day."

"What'd she say?"

"That she wouldn't have thought of this plan if she didn't think I could do it and I should save my objections for after I defeated Freedom and saved the day. Then she told me to hurry and leave."

He shrugs.

"Well, good luck to you."

I know Freedom didn't invite me to tag along to the Metroplexer family reunion, but we need all the time we can get and Freedom tends to talk a lot more when I'm around. Plus, he did text my phone, so it's not as if I'm not invited, right?

Spiromaniac's plan involves three parts, all equally risky. First, the Child Soldiers need to get ahold of another nuke. Hacker Plus found the four bombs we already secured and given to authorities (one by Spiro and me, the other three by Kid Metroplexer) placed inside the military base on the outskirts of town – making theft almost impossible. But it's still a better option than miraculously finding one of the other seven hidden suitcase nukes despite having no leads or any ideas where one of the remaining nukes is being stashed. Next, the Child Soldiers need to drive that nuke miles outside of town without Freedom or his goons knowing we stole one or have it in our possession. That leaves the most difficult task to Grant and me. We need to stall and distract Freedom long enough for that to happen. We have no idea how to do that. I pray that Freedom is in a mood to go see a movie.

Kid Metroplexer and I enter Shelfield corporate office, situated in the middle of downtown Burlington. The very middle. If Freedom wants to detonate a nuke, this would be the spot. A life-sized portrait of Freedom hangs in the lobby, the first thing any person sees as they walk in. He stands proudly on railroad tracks, clad in a perfectly tailored business suit. If I didn't know him personally, I'd say he almost looks respectful.

"For a supervillain who hides so little, how is Freedom not always under some sort of criminal investigation? How does he get away with so much?"

Kid Metroplexer sighs.

"A bunch of pseudonyms, money laundering, a long record of missing or dead government employees who pry too much, tens of millions of dollars in bribes, and my dad tells me that a quarter of every dollar Freedom earns goes into a retainer fund that pays for his lawyers. The city and the country rely on Metroplexer to punch him into a prison cell because they certainly can't rely on the courts."

"But he either escapes or gets the charges dropped."

"Yeah."

"Is that why he calls himself Freedom?"

"No. Has he given you his Prohibition speech yet?"

"Yes."

"Then you should know why. He doesn't care about laws or consequences. Thus, he has the freedom of doing whatever he wants whenever he wants to do it. No one can stop him whether out of fear, frustration, or inability. But you know how it goes; no one's first attempt at naming themselves is particularly great, and if the news outlets latch onto your terrible name when you become famous or infamous, you're stuck with it. Correct, Miss Nucleus?"

"Correct, nineteen year-old legal adult Kid Metroplexer."

The Shelfield headquarters harbors a different vibe than Harold Industries. The people dress the same but there's a definite hurry in their step and hushed tones when they speak. Everyone is nicely groomed or cleanly shaved. The receptionists frantically stare toward the entrance every time the main doors open. They know Freedom owns their company. They know he's upstairs. They know their mistakes could bring consequences far more severe than just losing their jobs. Kid Metroplexer and I approach the main receptionist, who looks appropriately nervous.

"I'm Grant Johnson and this is Liza Lewis. We're here to see Michael Conello."

She just stares.

"Michael Conello. The man who owns the company? The man on the giant painting behind you? Look, just call his secretary Amber Brown and tell her Grant Johnson is here. She'll know me."

She reluctantly picks up the phone and dials, not breaking eye contact for an uncomfortably long period of time. After a whispered phone conversation, she hands us visitor passes. Smartly, she says nothing beyond what floor to find Michael Conello's office. Because only certain types of people visit Mr. Conello. Bad people.

We step into the elevator.

"Are you nervous?" I ask.

"Nope." He fiddles with his phone before putting it away. "Everything will work out. We're superheroes. This is what we do."

As the elevator doors open to Freedom's office – an office that occupies an entire floor and dwarfs my entire apartment several times over – his bodyguards welcome us with guns drawn. Kid Metroplexer explains that he's Kid Metroplexer and I'm Miss Nucleus and bullets don't work on us, but you know henchmen – stupid and stubborn and difficult to convince. We're at an impasse.

Freedom's secretary, fearing Freedom's reaction if he hears unnecessary gunfire, escorts us past his guards and into the main room.

Windows take up a whole side of the room, giving us a gorgeous view of the city. More life size portraits of Freedom hang on the opposite wall. One of him sensually lying down next to a train. One of him casually leaning against the train's engine. One of him lecturing a large group of excited train conductors. Actual portraits someone had to paint and Freedom commissioned.

The supervillain sits at a large, round glass table in conversation with a few men and women. No casual wear this time – Freedom's suit and tie tailored perfectly to fit his imposing frame. And there's Metroplexer. He sits in the corner drugged (or beaten) to unconsciousness, gagged and bound to the chair. There's a nuke placed on the bookshelf behind him. I pray Kid Metroplexer doesn't make any rash moves.

Upon seeing us, Freedom dismisses his guests and asks if we'd like to sit at the table. Then, seeing us freeze, he repeats his words without the asking apart.

"Miss Nucleus and Grant. I'm glad to see both of you, although Miss Nucleus wasn't invited."

"Well, it'd been eight hours since I last saw you and I missed you."

"I release you from your cage and the first thing you do is come scurrying back to my loving arms? The game is over, Miss Nucleus. No more joking between us. No more curves to throw your way."

He grabs a large bottle of brown liquor from his cabinet. He pours three glasses.

"Scotch. Drink. I'd impress you with the age and make, but I've seen the liquor in Miss Nucleus' apartment and I don't imagine she knows anything about liquor that costs over, what? Ten dollars?"

"The bottle under my sink cost $12.50."

I see Kid Metroplexer tense up. We don't know the extent of

his father's injuries, but we have to play this slow. Really, really slow. The Child Soldiers need all the time they can get to prepare for our plan. Freedom points at Kid Metroplexer.

"Relax, Grant. Drink. I won't tell anyone about you drinking under-aged. Your daddy is alive. I'm not going to detonate the nuke for another couple of hours. I promised my guards and secretary that I'd give them a head start before I detonate the bomb. That's what good bosses do. Talk to me, Grant. Don't sit there frowning like that. We're family, after all."

The Scotch is quite good. Smooth. Smoky. I finish off my glass to calm my nerves, but seeing the other two barely managed a sip – their judgmental glances cause me to slink back into my seat. Kid Metroplexer takes a deep breath.

"We're not family, Freedom. Not any longer. Dad wanted a normal life. He didn't want to be a superhero and you know that."

"I wanted to watch daughter grow up, but we don't always get what we want."

Kid Metroplexer ignores his response.

"But because of your actions, my dad has had to devote his life to stopping you. And it's cost him my mom and my sister. So I'm quite happy you're dying and I'm even happier that dying from cancer is slow and painful. That's all."

"What do you mean that's all?"

"Because as I told Miss Nucleus and Spiromaniac, I'm not stupid!"

Grant stands up. The guards put their hands on their weapons, but a wave from Freedom changes their minds.

"You murdered the BSO!" Grant persists. "You have cameras everywhere in this city! You have spies and computer techs and informants by the thousands! My dad has beaten you with his fists a dozen times, but how many times has he – have any of us – beaten you by deception? I'm not stupid! Give Miss Nucleus and me an update on our secret plan to defeat you. Go. What's our plan?"

Freedom finishes off his Scotch, and smiles – the most

arrogant, superior grin I have ever witnessed.

"For starters, your friends Featherblade and Icarus have infiltrated the army base – the same army base their parents live on – and are making their way toward the stored nuclear weapons there. I have snipers ready for when they arrive at the nuke's location. I promised the soldiers $100,000 for each superhero they kill."

"See?" Kid Metroplexer throws his hands up. "Our plan was never going to work. I knew it from the moment we agreed to Spiromaniac's plan."

"Then why agree to go through with the plan at all? Why come to my office to see me?" Freedom asks.

"Because I know that my dad is far more important to this city than I am. Because I know you better than the Child Soldiers do. I have a different plan. A plan I only told Hacker Plus. And only because she's the only one who would agree to a plan this evil."

Freedom rises from his seat, towering over his nephew. But Kid Metroplexer isn't intimidated. I have a horrible knot in my stomach. Grant keeps talking.

"You missed a folder in Screwdriver's houseboat. Do you know about all the incidents it listed? Five years ago, a supervillain attacked Moscow. She exhibited the same powers as you and my dad. Three years ago, a similar man brought Nigeria to a standstill. Two years ago, Thailand superheroes fought an equally powerful supervillain. Just last month, police in the Australian Outback were all wiped out by just one flying, invulnerable teenager. What if these men and women come to the USA? How many of them already have? I only have half my dad's power. Half your power. I can't stop them. But my dad can. My dad is the only one who can protect this city and this country. Not me."

Grant turns to me.

"Spiromaniac was right about one part of the plan though: everything will rely on you, Miss Nucleus. You'll still have to save this city, okay? No other choice."

Realizing something is about to happen, Freedom jumps

across the table and grabs Kid Metroplexer by the shirt, pulling him up close.

"Whatever you think you're going to do, I'd recommend you reconsider. You'll fail, and I'm going to make sure I kill every damned soul in this city. Are we clear?"

Kid Metroplexer cackles.

"I found another of your nukes yesterday, Freedom, but you were there at the time and I couldn't remove it. I wanted to go back later, but then Miss Nucleus got herself arrested and I didn't have time. Then Spiromaniac asks us to find a nuke, and how lucky! I know where one is! But if I dared grab it, even flying at my top speed – tell me! You would know, wouldn't you? You would know instantly! And you'd detonate it. And I wouldn't be able to stop you. I'm not strong enough, so I'm making a choice! A choice that my dad or Spiromaniac or Miss Nucleus would never make! Because you're going to detonate all seven remaining nukes and the city will be ash! Millions will die and we won't be able to stop you! How soon? This evening? Tonight? Too late!"

Freedom smashes his fist into Kid Metroplexer's face. And again. And again.

"It's too late!" Kid Metroplexer screams. "I sent the text to Hacker Plus when we were in the elevator! My phone just buzzed. She activated the timer! C'mon! You and me! We're going to experience this together!"

He grabs Freedom by the waist – to Freedom's surprise – and crashes the two of them through the glass window, soaring across the city far too fast for me to follow.

The northwest section of Burlington, home to thousands of people and their businesses and hopes and dreams and families and everything they could ever be, ignites.

The nuclear explosion kills them all.

That moron. Oh my God. That moron.

Kid Metroplexer is dead, and deep within the epicenter of the blast will be Freedom.

12

The chaos. The city simultaneously reacts with a confused silence and a fearful panic.

Everyone within a half mile of the explosion is already dead from the force of the explosion. The blast itself would collapse most of the infrastructure a mile each way, killing far more people. Easily fifty thousand dead.

I'm resigned to my fate. I know what I'm supposed to do, regardless of how little I want to do it. Freedom's guards rightfully bolted as soon as the nuke went off, leaving me to help Metroplexer across the office and into the elevator by myself. When we reach the lobby, I send out a frantic group text.

"Freedom is in the explosion. Kid Metroplexer is dead. I have Metroplexer. I need a ride to the blast site. I'm at the Shelfield building. We can get the nuke at Shelfield later."

Globe texts back first, announcing she's at the hospital with Spiro and they're both on their way. Sirens loudly wail through the streets as police cars and ambulances speed toward the blast site. People stare and run and huddle together. No one knows what to do.

But I do. And it's going to suck.

I'm going to stop Freedom – a crispy, crippled Freedom. If he manages to escape, he'll return with a vengeance. If I don't stop him here, Burlington will cease to be. So, yes, there's a lot of pressure. Pressure I'm not used to.

I watch superheroes like Spiromaniac and War Soul and the

Metroplexers fight crime with a purpose – a mission. Burlington has real superheroes who fight because, while their methods and superpowers vary tremendously, they just want to help people. Need to help people. Have a responsibility to help people. I've never felt that way. I can't even help myself. I drank another glass of Scotch before I dragged Metroplexer onto the elevator. I know, I need to stand strong – tell you and tell myself that after everything that's happened over the past few weeks, I've matured and grown into the superhero I always knew I could be, and my final test will be Freedom. But I don't think I have. All I can think about is that single Liberate pill tucked in my kitchen drawer.

No time to hate myself though. I'm the only superhero who can walk into that nuclear mess, and I'm the only one who can haul Freedom out to spend his remaining months in the prison he so much deserves. To die slowly from cancer in a nine-by-five-foot cell.

Globe pulls up in her jeep and Spiro ushers me to the backseat. Stella's pale and sweaty complexion can't hide her abdominal pain, but Globe would never have been able to tell her not to come. My Miss Nucleus hoodie and a backpack lie next to me. We buckle the still woozy Metroplexer into the seat next to me.

"I'm sorry we couldn't bring you more weapons. We jumped in the car as soon as you texted us."

I open the backpack and Spiro explains each item inside.

"Friendleader's axe. The military one he ordered online. It's beautiful, isn't it? A canister of bear pepper spray from Featherblade. Two Tasers from Mentalmind. A pistol with eight bullets. I don't know where Forestchild found the pistol and I have some question for him later. That's all that was available."

"It'll have to be enough," I say as I pull my hoodie on over my shirt.

A block from the police barricade, Globe drops me off. They'll bring Metroplexer back to the hospital with them to get looked at.

As long as I get past the barricade, then I'll be in the clear.

No one's going to chase me inside the explosion aftermath.

"I'm really nervous. Any last words, Stella? What about you, Globe?"

Globe speaks up first.

"When we win, after the funerals and everything dies down, we're going to have the most amazing party, okay? Think about that if you get scared."

Spiromaniac shushes her. She painfully steps out of the car and grabs me in a long, tight embrace. I can hear her voice tremble as she talks.

"Liza, thousands of people are dead because of this man, and he needs to be brought to justice. You don't represent Miss Nucleus or the Child Soldiers. You represent Burlington itself. So go, fight like hell and end this once and for all. For Grant and Grace. I love you."

She lets go and heads back to the car.

I love you too.

"Stop!" I tell her.

She turns around.

"I forgot to tell you. Kid Metroplexer didn't set off the nuke. Hacker Plus remotely detonated it. The two of them planned this in advance."

A darkness flashes across her face. Her pursed lips and arched brow give away her shock and anger.

"I understand. Leave her to me. Go save the city."

Globe and Spiro peel away, not willing to risk capture by the police. Now, it's just me. Miss Nucleus. I easily slip past the police line as they struggle to contain the crowd, and I begin my march toward the epicenter of the blast. Just me and my bag of weapons. I'm glad I'm not sober.

Walking through the aftermath of a nuclear explosion, I'm fully convinced that I'm witnessing Hell incarnate. The horrific screams of pain and mutilated bodies. People holding people who are holding people who are already dead. This is Hell. I'm walking through Hell. Everyone searches for a way to escape. Shouts of help go unanswered. Cries of sorrow are abandoned. I'm going to spit on Kid Metroplexer's grave. I wouldn't wish this on anyone.

I ignore those around me. I ignore those who need me. By saving their lives, by dragging them to safety, Freedom will make his escape. So I walk past the dying and the dead. Lots of dead. The guilt will haunt me for the rest of my life. I should probably up my therapy to twice a week after this.

I think back to Stella chiding War Soul a few hours ago. She called him "soldier," and that stopped him long enough for Kid Metroplexer to arrive. And as I march through the ruins of the only decent spot in Burlington for Indian food, I understand why he hesitated. We call ourselves the Child Soldiers, but we *are* soldiers, aren't we? Unorganized, insubordinate, and hormonal – but soldiers nevertheless. And how much I'm not. When I quit six months ago, I briefly considered joining the military. I mean, very briefly, like for a few minutes, but why not? I had no idea what to do with my life, I'm indestructible, and it would give me something to keep my mind occupied beyond maintaining a constant buzz. But I started researching the military and why people join. Some, like me, join because of their indecision about their future. But most, I found, carry very specific reasons to be a soldier, like patriotism or honor or pride. None of those noble reasons fit me.

Because of course War Soul was furious at me. He grew up on an army base and spent years and years training his body and learning military strategy. His only superpower is that crazy innate drive to spend his entire life preparing for combat. Most of the Child Soldiers have. Spiro started learning martial arts at age six. Featherblade and Icarus spend hours in the army base's library studying and examining weapons and technology. Even Hacker Plus still devotes some time every night to researching the newest computer databases and systems. But not me. I lucked into my superpowers, and I figured that would be the fastest way for people to like me. I seek the adoration of the bank tellers when I stop the bank robbery, not the satisfaction of protecting the city's citizens. But now? Knowing no love will come out of this? Knowing that the city will blame the superheroes for this? That the police will arrest me even if I'm dragging Freedom's unconscious body behind me? I'm painfully aware that I was chosen for this mission not because I'm the most qualified to fight Freedom, but because I'm the only one who can venture through this disaster unharmed. It's okay. I'm okay with this. I'll protect Burlington. I don't recommend it, but who knows? Maybe potentially saving millions of people from the worst megalomaniac in the entire country would be good for me. Emotionally. Knock me down from six to five beers a day.

Eventually, I reach the epicenter. Freedom isn't hard to find. I spot a gigantic man with major third degree burns crawling away from the inferno originated by the blast. No hair. Barely any skin. Definitely no clothes. But I know. This is Freedom. This is the only person I've seen alive within a quarter mile. I call out to him.

"Hey! Freedom! Over here!"

He turns to face me, propping himself up against one of the few structures barely standing.

"You came!" He coughs, then laughs – a hacking, gravelly laugh. "I'll tell you, Miss Nucleus. That hurt. That damn child. My brother may be the smartest man I know, but his children are so incredibly dumb."

I grab his arm, pulling him toward me.

"Let's go. You have a lot to answer for."

"No."

He flings his free arm at me, his elbow connecting with my jaw. I fly back. A lot. The wreckage of a car stops my momentum.

"I'm going to escape, Miss Nucleus. You can't stop me. You can't—" His words are interrupted by a series of coughs. But true to his word, he pushes himself off the wall, limping in the opposite direction toward the edge of town.

I run at him, digging through my backpack. My first Taser nails him in the shoulder and he cries out. The second Taser sticks into his right arm. But he doesn't stop. The pain hardly slows him down. He turns and leaps at me before I can react. And he pummels me, one blow after another. The ground cracks open beneath us. His breathing slows as agonizing sounds pour from his mouth, but he doesn't let up. A final punch knocks me across the street.

"What else, Miss Nucleus? What else do you have? Show me what other toys you brought."

I stand myself up and pull out the bear pepper spray. He dodges the spray entirely, his super speed stopping himself within striking distance of me. He grabs my neck and lifts me into the air. I don't know what to do. How could he still be so strong? His speech is slow and steady as his burnt vocal chords try to keep up.

"Don't you realize why I kept contacting you? Talking to you?"

"Because I look like your dead daughter?"

"Because I understand you! When I saw your file at the hospital, I knew. Our circumstances are different, but we share the same destiny. Permanent despair. Unhappiness. Anguish. Since that day I cradled my daughter's lifeless body. Since that day my brother killed her. Answer me! Am I wrong? Are you not the same as me? Will you ever be happy?"

I struggle in vain.

"Let me go, you asshole! Did you forget the first rule of depression? Just because you're not happy doesn't mean you get to ruin others' happiness!"

He roars as intensely as his melting body can muster.

"Speak to me that way again and I'll spend my last days hunting down your family! Answer me! Will you ever be happy?"

And I answer him.

"No, I don't think so. I don't think there's a person or pill or therapy that can make me happy. I'll always be miserable. Just as you'll always be a terrible, awful person."

He throws me as far as his remaining strength can muster and I land in a mess of broken concrete. Ignoring me, I see him begin to levitate in the air, gradually gaining height and speed. No no no no! I grab the pistol from my backpack and I immediately regret that I never learned how to shoot or aim a gun. But having no choice as I watch him float away from me, I raise my arm, aim, and fire.

Miss. Miss again. The third shot finally connects, hitting one of his ankles. He reaches down in surprise and loses his equilibrium. As he attempts to regain his balance, I have time to run closer, and my fourth and fifth shots strike the scorched meat of his back. He drops to the street.

I pull out the axe, shoving the gun in my pocket. My first swing connects with his shoulder as he begins to rise once more.

"I am Freedom, child! Freedom! I have devoted decades to becoming the man I am today and I won't be stopped by a lazy, alcoholic teenager! Come on, let's fly together."

With no other choice, I wrap my legs around his torso, one arm around his neck and the other gripping the axe handle. We soar over the buildings and through the clouds. Thank God I'm me. The force of the acceleration alone would probably flatten anyone else. He pauses as we float in the last bastions of the earth's atmosphere. Maybe. Science isn't my specialty.

"Where are we? Outer space?"

"Did you go to school, Miss Nucleus? We're barely in the stratosphere. Hmm. So you can still talk? I know you won't freeze, but I didn't know your invulnerability won't allow you to suffocate."

His hand grabs my hoodie as he pries me off him, and I flail harmlessly at the extent of Freedom's gigantic arm.

"I liked you from the moment we met outside that warehouse, Miss Nucleus. Unlike so many other superheroes, you've always believed your own insignificance."

"Please, no more speeches," I beg.

"Metroplexer and I fought at this altitude once, looking out in the vastness of this miserable planet. He refused to admit the minutiae of the human existence. Can't you see how tiny and meaningless we are? Kid Metroplexer sacrificed how many lives? Fifty thousand for the chance to kill me? But what does it matter?

Over three hundred thousand people are born every day. Over a hundred and fifty thousand people die every day. Why would anyone fight to save these people? Any people? I killed twelve scientists yesterday. Within three seconds, twelve more people were born in this world."

Freedom shudders and we drop a stomach-churning distance before he steadies himself. He groans and shivers.

"I'm apparently hurt worse than I thought. It's about time we finish our conversation and I let you go. I still need to detonate the remaining nukes. But tell me, Miss Nucleus. Why do you care about these people? You know the misery of life far better than so many others, so why are you doing this? Why do you care?"

"I don't know. I don't understand why people cling so much to life either. So be it. But no one is going to die because of you. Not one more."

I claw my fingers into the seared flesh of Freedom's biceps, releasing myself from his grip. I twirl my body until both hands are on the axe handle, and taking advantage of Freedom's immediate jolt of pain, I take out the pistol, aim at the back of his head, and fire the final bullets. My weight yanks the axe out of his shoulder, and the two of us plummet to Earth.

We fall for an eternity, and it's most serene I've ever been. The most at peace I'll ever be. Goodbye, Freedom. Cheers to the fall.

My thoughts turn again toward the Liberate pill stashed in my kitchen drawer. At least one of us will get the victory we want.

———

The government sent in every member of the National Guard they could call to search for the remaining nukes, and by the sixth day after the explosion, all had been secured. Freedom's body was found in the rubble a few days later by the hazmat teams. Everyone assumes he died in the explosion, and I'm not about to tell them otherwise.

I walk around the wounded city each afternoon. No one cares or recognizes me. Everyone has bigger worries to be concerned with.

Yet the people I see don't seem scared, but aimless. Confused. Unsure of what to do and where to go and who to look toward. How does anyone move on? Fifty thousand people died and a hundred thousand more were injured – in a city of only a couple million, that means everyone knows someone affected by the nuclear explosion. A whole city dealing with personal trauma all at once. A trauma that won't recede. Yet—

I saved millions of people's lives. That's an actual, objective fact. But how come I don't feel better about myself? My thoughts keep returning to those killed – there must have been something I could have done to save them. There's always something I could have done or something I didn't do. I remember Kid Metroplexer and me discussing the idea of acceptable losses on our way to Stella and the hospital – that we were both okay with losing a few people to save a much larger number. Our consciences could handle it. But now? Hell no. If Freedom was the worst supervillain in the history of our city, Kid Metroplexer comes in a close second.

I can't stop reliving my walk through the blast zone, everything permanently etched in my brain. The horrific screams of pain and mutilated bodies. People holding people who are holding people who are already dead. Everyone searches for a way to escape. Shouts of help go unanswered. Cries of sorrow are abandoned. And so I drink, then I cry, then I drink to stop crying. I've smelled like a brewery or distillery for a week straight.

News reporters say that if current trends continue within the next two or three months, a third of the citizens of Burlington are going to move away. Fear from the nuclear aftermath, fear of another nuclear explosion, general anxiety, and just bad vibes all around. No doubt the city's economy will soon crash and crime will rapidly increase, but the police's new no-superheroes-ever-no-matter-what rule became actual city law within days of the explosion. Even my parents, with their lifetime guaranteed jobs, are thinking about packing it up and retiring early. So Freedom might not have completely lost. So I haven't been doing great.

In a useless attempt to make the citizens feel safer, the police commissioner resigned after the suitcase nuke went off. People sleep better when they're pointing fingers – figuring out who's at fault prevents this disaster from being spooky, random chaos. If only the police had done this or done that, nothing would have happened! And while the police commissioner wasn't at fault, neither were those caught in the explosion. Captain Hanson took over the job and hopefully that means an eventual loosening of the anti-superhero laws. I sent a card to the police station addressed to Captain Hanson – a picture of a puppy on front and inside it said, "Congratulations on your job, I hope it won't be too ruff." I think that might be the only nice thing I've ever done for him. God, did I treat that great man like crap.

As Grace deserved – not so much her brother – Kid and Lady Metroplexer's funerals were beautiful. Metroplexer went all out for his children, spending tens of thousands of dollars on flowers, a full choir, and hand-carved gravestones. And Dr. Mel Johnson, better and stronger than the rest of us, continues his daily life uninterrupted – from therapy to superhero-ing to rebuilding the city. Stella guesses that Metroplexer is throwing himself into work so he doesn't have time to think about his kids.

After the funeral, the Child Soldiers tried to have that celebratory party Globe promised me. My God, did they try, but no one really felt like celebrating. Though that didn't stop any of them from drinking. I didn't attend the party.

Tonight, on the two-week anniversary of the explosion, Burlington holds a candlelight vigil in front of the capital building for the victims. Most of the city watches the event on TV, gratefully distracted from uncomfortably trying to resume their lives after a life-altering tragedy.

I have something else planned for tonight. The only good decision I've made in weeks. The only way after all these tragedies that I'll get my win. Taking my chance, I break open the roof of the Goldstein Star Hotel, the one closest to my apartment.

Twenty floors up, the chilly night breeze feels good against my skin. I sit down on the edge of the building, my legs dangling over the side. I finish my beer and open another.

I'm not writing a letter. People will know why I jumped. I'm sorry, though. I always hoped that this whole Freedom ordeal would have sparked an epiphany. A reason to keep going. And maybe it's my fault that I hoped to solve my depression by an act of God – a lightning bolt that triggers a deus ex machina where I'm rewarded with the hidden secret to happiness for defeating Freedom. But that's not going to happen, is it? I looked for the strength to continue on and only found more weakness. More guilt and pain and shame. The only way not to be miserable is to slowly work on my personal life through years of doctor's visits, therapy, positive life choices, dropping the booze, finding a purpose, pursuing my passions, and many other things that I don't plan to do. Because even if I do all that? It's still only a maybe that I'll be able to manage the misery – and that's the best-case scenario: manage. Not a cure. Impossible to cure. If I don't do this now, I'll never get another chance.

I stand up, peering over the edge onto the street below. No one's below. Good. My parents won't ever forgive me for jumping, but they'll eventually forgive me for not saying goodbye. I hope. God, I hope.

I take a deep breath. On the count of three. One. Two.

My phone rings. Stella. I pause and decide to answer. It'd be nice to talk to her one last time. That'll be a nice last memory.

"Hey, Liza, where are you?"

I sit back down on the edge.

"Goldstein Star Hotel. The roof."

"Oh. That's weird. Okay, I'm on my way. I want to ask you something, and I think it's better in person. Do you want me to bring anything to drink?"

"I have enough beer for both of us."

"Okay, great. I'll see you in fifteen minutes."

Fine, then. I'll jump after we talk.

She arrives, and after she realizes how close I'm sitting to a twenty floor drop, she sucks up her fear and sits next to me. I open two beers for us.

"Hey, Liza. Nice Hoobastank shirt. Is it new?"

"Yes."

"Cool. I haven't heard from you since the funeral. Why are you up here? This is scary."

"Just taking in the view," I lie.

"Oh, well, the city looks gorgeous tonight, doesn't it? Anyway, big news: I stepped down as leader of the Child Soldiers and I quit the group. I think I need to take a long break from being a superhero."

"Why? That's not like you."

"Well, the mess of the past few weeks, for one. But Hacker Plus? I did nothing. Not one thing. I knew that turning her into the police was the right thing to do and that we could definitely gather enough information to prove she detonated the nuke – for instance, recordings from Freedom's Shelfield office if she hadn't thought to delete them yet – but I can't do it."

"Because you care about her? Hope she'll redeem herself?"

"What? No way. She's unpleasant to be around and her moral compass shattered into tiny, unfixable pieces long ago. Only Metroplexer's optimism is that unbreakable. I just, I knew she'd retaliate. She'd release all the personal information and any records she could find about me and my family. Information that could destroy everything my family struggled so hard for to succeed in this country. I left her alone, not because it was the right thing to do, but because I'm selfish. I willingly let a mass murderer go free. That's when I knew I couldn't lead the Child Soldiers anymore. War Soul will take over and he'll do fine. Or whatever he morphs the team into."

She places her arm around me, gripping my tightly.

I finish my beer and open another one. Spiro doesn't judge

my drunkenness. Not tonight.

"Liza, I want to ask you something. I'm falling apart and I tried this week to keep myself upbeat and hopeful for the Child Soldiers, but the disguise is fading fast. After Grant and Grace died, I realized how short a superhero's lifespan is. Seriously, they were almost invincible. Yet I constantly throw myself in harm's way; a single bullet in the wrong place and I'm done. I'm thinking of looking toward my future. Maybe I can go to college or vocational school and get myself a career like Metroplexer. Maybe as a social worker, wouldn't that be nice? I can help troubled kids before they become supervillains. But before all that, I've thought about this, and I think I need to start over. Move to a new city – I've heard Chicago is lovely – and get away from the insanity of Burlington. But I'm uneasy going by myself, so I came here to ask you: would you like to come with me to Chicago? I have plenty of money saved up, so we can get an apartment together. And you're my best friend. And I have a feeling that it'd be good for you to start over too. What do you think?"

I don't answer. Stella continues.

"Liza, don't you lie to me. I saw that scratch on your hand as soon as I sat down. There's only one way that's possible, and I don't know how you got hold of a Liberate."

She removes her arms from around my waist and takes a moment to collect her thoughts.

"I can put the pieces together of why you're up here. Look, I don't know if you'll ever beat this depression. I'm not going to promise you that you will. But I can promise that you'll never be alone. We'll fight this together. It'll be our depression, okay?"

Stella stares into the night sky.

"But if you don't think you'll ever be happy, and that your life will be another seventy years of despair and pain and suffering, then jump. Do it, because I know this is your last chance. I'll understand. I won't like it, but I'll understand. I won't stop you."

As Spiromaniac speaks, I can hear the fragility in her words. The same feebleness I hear in my own thoughts – that desperate desire to overcome, but not knowing how. Not knowing if it's ever possible.

I feel Stella's breath against my neck as she lays her head on my shoulder.

"I love you, Liza."

We listen to the traffic below. The honks and the shouts and the music playing from the nearby windows. Twenty floors below, a couple argues about cab fare, a truck screeches to a halt to avoid hitting the car in front, and a group of drunks laugh and scream as they leave the bar. The world will go on with or without me, unabated.

The breeze picks up, and I welcome the heat of Stella's body. I still agree with Freedom – our lives are ultimately insignificant and meaningless.

But not to those who care about us.

I wrap my arms around Stella, squeezing as tight as my arms will allow.

"Okay," I announce. "Let's move to Chicago."

———

Audio Transcript for October 11th, 11:00 AM

Licensed Therapist: Dr. Mel Johnson

Patient: Liza Lewis

JOHNSON: It's been a long time since our last session. How are you feeling after what I can imagine was a difficult series of weeks.

LEWIS: How are *you*? You had it rougher than I did.

JOHNSON: I'll be okay. It won't be easy, but I'll be okay. I have always been aware of the costs that come with this life, and I am slowly coming to terms with my judgment errors.

LEWIS: You truly feel that way?

JOHNSON: Some days, yes. But we're talking about you today. How are you feeling?

LEWIS: Are you actually doing okay?

JOHNSON: I am keeping myself occupied. Regardless of my own personal feelings or not, I'm needed in this city. But how are you feeling?

LEWIS: I haven't improved since our last session, or really, any of our sessions. I'm not saying that what you do isn't working, but I don't see a lot of growth. You're not a bad therapist or anything. I think it's me.

JOHNSON: Therapy doesn't provide miracles. You can't expect breakthroughs or healing to come quickly or often. Sometimes until that time comes, the best therapy can do for you is provide you a place that lets you speak honestly and openly without anyone judging. I'm more than glad to be that place for you.

LEWIS: Then bad news. I'm moving away.

JOHNSON: I did not know that. Why are you moving?

LEWIS: Stella and I are getting an apartment in Chicago. I need to get far away from any superhero-ing for a while, and I don't know if I can do that in Burlington. We have superheroes and supervillains everywhere.

JOHNSON: We do seem to have a lot, don't we? I've been in talks with the city council to lift the superhero ban, but even with Commissioner Hanson's support, I think we're in for a long, uphill battle. He and I will keep at it, though. I've turned many losing fights into wins. What about you? Do you think you'll ever return to being a superhero?

LEWIS: Maybe. I know my luck, and sooner rather than later I'll be in the wrong spot at the wrong time and forced to interrupt a mugger or stop a robbery or whatever crime always seems to happen in front of me. I'm not going to stop helping, but I don't know yet if I'm going to seek out crime fighting either. You understand, right?

JOHNSON: I do. Crime never goes away, and it'll be waiting for you if you decide to return. Or wherever you go. Our fight never ends.

LEWIS: You say you get it, but Grant said that you never wanted to be a superhero.

JOHNSON: That's true.

LEWIS: Then why do you continue to be one? Freedom only showed up publicly to cause trouble twice or three times a year, but you still went on patrol and responded to police emergencies daily.

JOHNSON: Just because I didn't enjoy being a superhero at first doesn't mean I didn't grow to love it. I am very proud of and greatly enjoy being Metroplexer. Helping people, fighting supervillains, and solving crimes has become immensely satisfying.

LEWIS: I never felt that way, and I'm five years in. I feel guilty. Don't you feel guilty that you were given these amazing powers and you didn't use them selflessly until you were thirty-two years old?

JOHNSON: Sometimes. You feel guilty if you don't use your powers?

LEWIS: I can grab people from burning buildings without putting firemen in danger. Etcetera. I don't need a bunch of examples, do I? Are people going to die if I live my life as a normal citizen? I know I was never perfect, but I saved more people than I got killed if that is any consolation.

JOHNSON: You've had many great successes. Besides saving the city, didn't you save that cruise ship a few years ago?

LEWIS: Oh. No. I made that up. I discovered people felt more at ease if I tell them I did something huge like that instead of, say, once stopping a thief from siphoning gas at a gas station. Which I also did.

JOHNSON: To answer your question, when I started patrolling every night, you should know that crime didn't decrease. With each new superhero that shows up, so do new supervillains. Nature seems to balance the scales when one is dipped in a certain direction.

LEWIS: So I'm under no obligation to be a superhero?

JOHNSON: Liza, you've been coming to me for months. What am I going to say next?

LEWIS: That I need to do what's best for me, whether that's being Liza Lewis or Miss Nucleus.

JOHNSON: Exactly. Congratulations on your therapeutic progress.

LEWIS: But I don't know what's best for me. I should probably work on curbing my self-destructiveness. But it's going to be baby steps. For everything. Then, no doubt, a few baby steps back. And I don't see myself kicking booze for a long time.

JOHNSON: You'll always be heading in the right direction when you take more steps forward than you do back. Patience has never been your strong suit, Liza.

LEWIS: Nope.

JOHNSON: Tell me, what do you think of your future?

LEWIS: I'm not optimistic, but I'm not pessimistic either, and that's the best answer I've ever been able to give you.

JOHNSON: You're an amazing woman and I'm proud of you.

LEWIS: I hope so. I'm paying you a fortune for this.

JOHNSON: Do you think you'll be okay?

LEWIS: Who knows? I'll have to find out the hard way, I guess.

JOHNSON: Liza, there's never been any other way.